HONOR LOVE

SAINTS PROTECTION & INVESTIGATIONS

MARYANN JORDAN

DEDICATION

When an author first writes a book, they hope someone will read it and when that actually happens, it is a wonderful feeling! Then, to have readers become fans...even more amazing! I am so fortunate to have many loyal readers who eagerly await the next book and beg for stories to be told about their favorite characters. Readers were introduced to Monty in my book, Gabe from the Alvarez Security Series. He was a secondary character and I never planned on writing his story but persistent readers begged for his story to be told. So here it is!

This book is dedicated to my readers...the ones who stumble across me and begin to fall in love with my stories. And the ones who were with me from the beginning and have eagerly awaited each book. Thank you...and here's to lots more stories to tell and characters to fall in love with!

PROLOGUE

Arriving at his destination, Monty Lytton parked his large, black SUV on the tree-lined street, due to the large number of cars in the driveway. He sat for a moment, looking at the comfortable homes in the neighborhood. Most were two-story colonials with few distinguishing differences. A few bicycles and swing sets littered across the lawns, in between snow-covered flowerbeds and trees.

His gaze landed on the house outside of his vehicle and his lips curved upward thinking of the family living there. A wisp of envy floated through him, while not desiring this exact scenario, he wondered what else might be out there for him. Smiling, he remembered the easy camaraderie and the fun times he enjoyed with the family residing inside.

Checking his appearance in the sun-visor mirror, he ran his hand through his dark hair, making sure it was neat. Not a fastidious man, he nonetheless maintained a professional appearance—perhaps from his time as an undercover FBI agent working in the State Capitol. Satisfied, he stepped down from his SUV, before twisting around to take out the brightly colored package. Walking toward the front door, he heard the sounds of screaming children and barely made it to the porch before the door flung open.

"Uncle Monty!" yelled the little girl dressed in a pink ballerina costume.

"Hey, baby girl," he called, bending to scoop her up in his arms after quickly moving in from the cold and managing to set the package on the dining room table without dropping it. "How's my favorite four-year-old niece?"

"No, no, not four anymore!" she squealed. "Today I'm five!"

A quick assessment of the dining room revealed an explosion of pink, purple, and teal. Streamers hung from the light fixture over the table to the edges of the ceiling. The colorful circus tent effect overwhelmed the senses. Princess placemats were set on the table along with plastic crowns at each chair.

He wondered if he had ever heard his niece speak softly, but laughed all the same. "No," he pretended not to believe her. "You can't be five!"

As he lowered her wiggling body back to the floor she saw the huge present, her eyes widening with glee.

"Is that for me?" she beamed.

"Are you the birthday girl?"

"Yes!" she screeched. "Then it must be for me! Thank you!" She scooted down the hall toward the den, her little arms waving above her head, still screaming, "Five, five, I'm five today."

Looking up, he saw a lovely woman walk from the kitchen toward him. Her dark hair mirrored his own, but her smile was much easier. She did not stop until she walked completely into his arms, wrapping hers around him, squeezing as though she had not seen him in ages.

"How you holding up, Sis?" he asked, hugging her back.

She leaned back and looked into his blue eyes. "I'm fine." She cocked her head toward the back of the house where the noise of the party blared. "I've got eight little five-year-old princesses back there with Bob and dad entertaining them. Mom's in the kitchen trying to figure out how to get the ice cream into the packed freezer. I've got a pouty seven-year-old upstairs because he got fussed at for attempting to sneak a cupcake."

"Wow," he replied, honestly awed at his sister's ability to handle such chaos. Growing up, their parents, often working on furthering their degrees, required Monty and Felicity to stay as quiet as they could. Since they were expected to follow in their parent's academic footsteps, staying quiet had not been difficult as both spent a great deal of time reading. *So how the hell does she keeps her cool with all of this racket?*

Before he could walk down the hall to enter the madness, she stopped him with her hand on his arm. "Guess I should tell you now since I won't have a quiet moment later."

He glanced at her, immediately noting her hand resting lightly on her stomach. His gaze jumped back to hers. "You're…"

"Yes indeed," she grinned. "Bob and I are expecting again."

"Congratulations, Sis," he replied sincerely, pulling her back in for another hug. Chuckling as they released each other, he said, "Well, you're certainly living up to your name."

"Oh, thanks! Felicity, the Patron Saint of expectant mothers strikes again!" Smiling, she added, "At least one of us is!"

"Don't remind me," he said, shaking his head. His

3

parents groomed him for a political career but much to their chagrin, he entered the FBI Academy after obtaining his law degree.

"But you were always meant to be a lawyer," his mother reminded him when he told them of his choice.

"Son, you were named Montgomery after my father, a magnificent lawyer and politician, and your mother's grandfather, the town's mayor for over thirty years. You could excel at a brilliant career if you would just listen to your mother and me."

Yep—that's how I got stuck with the name Montgomery Honor Lytton. He hung his head for a second, thinking of his great-grandfather, the Honorable Honor Seaton. *I can't believe he didn't hate that name too!*

Giving himself a mental shake, he hugged Felicity a little tighter. It seemed both of them disappointed their parents when it came to their choices.

Finally separating, they were about to walk down the hall when their mother came in from the kitchen. Lois Lytton, a tall, elegantly dressed woman appeared distressed as she held her hands out with a gallon of ice cream beginning to drip. "Felicity, I can't get the ice cream in. I don't know why you have to have it so full of junk."

"Mom, frozen meat is hardly junk."

"Humph," their mother grumbled. "How do you know what you've got in there?"

"Bob's friend went deer hunting and gave us a bunch of venison. It's all labeled, mom," Felicity answered, rolling her eyes.

Before their mother could retort with her opinion of venison that did not come from an exclusive butcher shop, she laid eyes on Monty. "Montgomery! I didn't know you were here."

Felicity giggled as she moved past her brother, heading toward the back of the house after taking the ice cream from their mother's hands.

He walked over, his arms embracing his mom. *I've gone by Monty my whole life and she has to be the only one who insists on calling me, Montgomery. I guess I should be glad she doesn't call me Honor just to stick it to me that I'm not a judge.* Sucking in a deep breath, he asked, "How are you, mom?"

"Oh, the same. Your father should be up for the Dean of the Law School once Lionel retires next month. I'm on the board but, of course, can't vote for Russell, although I think he would be the best. I am thinking of cutting back on my classes now that I'm Dean of the Law School Admissions, but who knows if that will happen."

Wanting his mother to finish her dissertation so he could make it to the party, he smiled politely while nodding at the appropriate times. "Well, it sounds like you and dad are staying busy."

A questioning expression crossed her lovely face. "What I don't understand, Montgomery, is why you threw away a perfectly good law degree to become a policeman?"

Feeling the familiar rush of irritation when in his mother's presence for more than thirty seconds, he stated, "I worked for the FBI, mom, not the local police department. Although, if I had worked as a policeman, I would have considered it a worthy career. I was perfectly happy there and am now even more happy as an investigator for a private firm."

She turned and started to move back to the kitchen, but fired a parting shot, as usual, over her shoulder, "Why you want to run around playing private eye is beyond me. Such a waste of an excellent education!"

Felicity walked out of the kitchen at that moment declaring, "Mom, I got the ice cream in."

Monty watched as his sister stepped up, linked her arm through his, and said, "Come on, cowboy. Let's go play with the princesses!" She leaned in and whispered, "At least dad has mellowed a bit with age!"

Laughing, the two made their way to the den.

An hour later, Monty and his dad stood back as Felicity and her husband, Bob, circled around the table serving the drinks and ice cream and generally handling the pandemonium. The eight little girls giggled and squealed at the decorations. The older brother, no longer pouting, made his way to the table, anxious for the treats.

"How is your...uh...work?" his father asked.

Still on color-explosion-overload, Monty turned his head toward his father and replied, "It's fine, dad. And before you ask, I still work for Saints Protection & Investigations."

"Um hmm," his dad murmured.

"And yes, I still love my job and find it quite rewarding."

"I didn't say anything, Monty," his dad admonished, drawing himself up.

"You didn't have to, dad. You and mom have made it abundantly clear that my career choices are lacking in your eyes."

Before his father could refute the claim, his mother walked over to them. "I tried to get Felicity to have the party at one of the lovely clubhouses and be catered," she said, shaking her head in frustration. "How they stand this noise, I'll never understand."

Monty said nothing, knowing no reply was expected. Before he was forced to endure more comments from his loving, but clueless parents, Felicity walked in from the kitchen carrying a massive platter of the most ornate cupcakes he had ever seen.

Each one was piled high with swirls of white, pink, purple, and teal colored frosting and flowers.

"Angels!" the little girls screamed in delight.

"Oh, my, now that is impressive," Lois said, unusually awed. "She got them ACH."

"What's ACH?" Russell asked.

"Only the best bakery in the whole area. Angel's Cupcake Heaven. It's said that the owner has orders from all over the state and she even sends some to a few events in D.C. If she had any business sense, she would expand as quickly as possible and not just keep her little shop here in Charlestown."

"Uncle Monty!" screamed the birthday girl. "You have to eat one."

He stared dubiously at the pink, purple, and teal lips of every girl at the party and wondered how he could excuse himself from the confectionary explosion. His eyes searched his sister's gaze for assistance but found none.

"Come on, little brother," she called. "You only get to party with the birthday girl once a year."

Sighing, he nodded as he walked over to the table, hoping his clothes would be able to escape any icing disasters. He was not sure his white dress shirt would weather a pink or purple stain.

"Go big or go home," his no-longer pouting nephew pronounced. Cocking his eyebrow at him, he shook his head. *What the hell,* he thought as he tried to get his mouth around the enormous cupcake. Unsuccessful at maintaining his dignity, he gave up and began to shove in as much in as he could to the raucous laughter of the partygoers.

7

Felicity came to the rescue before he choked. "Here, you can spit some out if you need."

As the sweet, creamy deliciousness melted on his tongue, he shook his head, continuing to chew. The moist cake paired perfectly with the light confection on top. As he finished, he looked triumphantly at the crowd as Bob snapped his picture. The children giggled as he walked past his parents to the hall powder room and gazed in the mirror. Pink, purple, and teal. All over his lips. All over his tongue. Even smeared on his right cheek.

Washing it off good-naturedly, he headed back to the party. *Definitely color-overload. Won't be sorry if I never see those three colors again!*

The evening skyline was striking as Monty stood staring out of his floor to ceiling windows. His condo resided in a large downtown warehouse that had been revitalized along with the area. The open space was minimally decorated. For him, a home was just a place to eat, sleep, and be alone. Leery of too many mementos lying around seemed to be an occupational hazard from his investigating days as an FBI agent. He had pored through homes filled with knick-knacks, photographs, old furniture, and closets stuffed with childhood memories. Coming home to his immaculate condo gave him a sense of order.

Walking from the windows to the kitchen, he pulled down a tumbler and poured a few fingers of whiskey. He heated a slice of last night's pizza, left over from a party of his co-workers. Plating his slice, he took the drink and plate over to the kitchen bar and settled on a stool.

Digging into the hot, melted cheese combined with spicy pepperoni, his mind wandered back to the previous evening. Jack Bryant, his boss, hosted an engagement party for one of their co-workers. Bart, a reformed player, was now planning his wedding to a woman who had helped them on their last case. Faith, a psychologist and artist, was also a seer with the ability to sometimes help solve crimes. The petite beauty had managed to tame the notorious Bart and witnessing the two of them together gave Monty hope that, one day, he might find his match.

Chuck's Bar and Grille hosted the party and he smiled as he thought how the group had grown. Jack was now married to Bethany; Cam married his rescue mission, a sweet nurse named Miriam; Jude was engaged to Sabrina, Bart's cousin; and now Bart and Faith were engaged.

Running his hand over his face as he finished the pizza, he took his drink to the sofa and sat down after kicking off his shoes. Sipping his drink, he remembered six months ago, as Jack moved into his new compound for the Saints, the eight original men wondered if a woman would ever fit into their lives.

Jack's business, Saints Protection & Investigations, was exactly what they had all been looking for. A former Special Forces soldier, Jack had brought together a team of men from various backgrounds, including DEA, SEAL, CIA, FBI, weapons and explosive experts, using their combined specialties for a security business that flew under the radar. Private and government contracts provided lucrative enticements, but every one of the men who were Jack's elite would have done their jobs for a lot less money. The chance to investigate crimes and protect, without the bureaucratic bullshit that hampered each of them in the past. Monty's lips curved up at the thought.

Polishing off his drink, he moved to the bedroom. Another room sparsely furnished. Utilitarian...but male. Stalking through to the bathroom, he caught a glimpse of himself in the mirror. Leaning closer, he noticed a slight streak of pink on the edge of his jaw. Chuckling to himself, as he washed it off, the thought of the colorful morsel from his niece's party had him licking his lips once more. The sweet confection no longer remained on his face...but stayed in his memory.

2

A week later, Monty and his date were escorted to a reserved table in one of the elegant restaurants in Charlestown. The lights were low in Revelations. The upscale restaurant was one of his usual date places. Easily at home in Chuck's Bar and Grille chowing down on wings, he knew his date preferred the chic restaurant.

Sitting across from the beautifully polished woman, Monty observed his dinner date. Rich brunette hair pulled sleekly into a chignon at the base of her long, slender neck. Her navy silk, pin-striped suit was set off to perfection with a light blue, lacy blouse and a strand of pearls. Her make-up was subtle, expertly applied.

She sat, carefully cutting her salad into small bites, ignoring the steak on his plate. Her conversation revolved around the cases she was currently working on since becoming a partner in the law firm her father owned.

Claire was the perfect date for Monty. He tended to date elegant, intelligent, cultured women. He was never envious of Bart and Blaise in the old days as they left Chuck's Bar with at least one woman on each arm. One-night pickups were never his thing. He grinned thinking of Bart's player days put to rest now that he had found Faith. Of course, that still left the other single Saints to close down the bar.

"Monty, are you listening?" Claire asked, her mouth forming a slight pout as she carefully laid her fork down.

"I'm sorry," he admitted. "What were you saying?"

"I was telling you about the new office that is mine now that I'm a partner. The oldest partner is going to retire and instead of everyone rotating offices, I'll move into his former space. It's on the corner. Can you believe that I'll already have a corner office? Of course, his décor is ancient, so I think I'll hire a new interior designer. I've heard of Sabrina Taggart."

At that, Monty's concentration focused back on her. "She's the fiancé of one of my co-workers. In fact, she's also the cousin of another colleague." He caught Claire's expression of interest as she sipped her wine.

"Hmmm, that's nice," she responded. "Well, if she's as good as they say, then I'll have her redecorate. What style do you think would be appropriate?"

Monty, usually in tune with his dates, found his mind wandering once more. A group of women walked into the restaurant and made their way to the bar. He glanced over, their laughter making it hard to focus on what Claire was saying.

The five women were attractive, dressed for a night out, and appeared to be celebrating some occasion. Hearing one ask for a table, he was glad that they were moving on, not wanting to have his quiet dinner interrupted continually with loud conversation.

"Oh, here comes our straggler," one of the women called to the bartender.

"Hey everyone," a woman called out and as Monty

looked toward the bar, his fork halted on its path to his mouth.

The sultry voice belonged to a stunning woman, also dressed for a night out on the town. The riot of color assaulted his senses, as well as captured his attention. She had just pulled off a bright purple coat, draping it across her arm. Her emerald green wrap dress showed off her considerable cleavage and small waist, before flaring out at hips that would make most men drop to their knees and weep. Black fuck-me heels completed her outfit. Her face was carefully made up, showcasing ocean blue eyes and shiny pink lips the color of bubblegum. But her hair held Monty's full attention.

The silky blonde tresses were streaked with hot pink, purple, and teal colors. One colorful stripe of each color filtered through the yellow blonde length. *Jesus, she looks like a cupcake!*

He watched as she made her way to the group of women, greeting each one with a hug. Slapping her hand down on the polished bar she ordered a Lemon Drop. *She looks like candy so what else would she drink?* Mesmerized, he tried not to gawk as she leaned her hip against the bar waiting for her drink and continued to talk to her friends.

He turned his attention back to Claire, never the type of man to be with one woman but looking at others. Claire was still describing what her office should look like when the Cupcake laughed at something one of the others said. His head turned involuntarily as he watched her. She lifted her chin in laughter, causing the cascade of colors to fall down her back, rippling as she shook. Her voice was rich and his cock twitched.

The women, drinks in hand, turned to move to the back where a waiter showed them to their table. Bending down to fix the strap on her shoes, Cupcake caught

Monty's stare as she stood. For an instant, their gazes held, before she winked, smiled, and headed to the back with her friends.

Monty forced his cock to behave. *What the fuck is wrong with me? She's not even my type.* Thinking about his type, he turned his full attention back to Claire. By now she had finished her salad with grilled chicken strips and still sipped on her first glass of wine.

"I agree with your mother that you should have gone into law," she continued.

"I did," he answered, noting the shrewd look in her eyes.

She cocked her head in question.

"Law enforcement."

Waving away the waiter as he brought the dessert tray, she laughed before saying, "You're being pointedly obtuse, Monty. Law enforcement is not the same and you know it."

Her laugh sounded forced, not joyful. Her words, pointed, not encouraging. His gaze drifted over her shoulder to the table where Cupcake sat with her friends, thoroughly enjoying herself.

Looking back at Claire, he suddenly realized that she represented everything he thought he wanted in a woman. And was utterly boring. *When was the last time I actually enjoyed a date?* When he could not come up with an answer to his own question, he gave up, determined to escort Claire to her car after the dinner, no longer desiring to have it lead to anything else.

He stood and walked around to assist Claire from her seat when his eye caught Cupcake again. This time, she held his gaze with a small smile before he saw her shift her gaze to Claire and then quickly turn away.

She thinks I'm some slime who's with one woman while scoping out others. As soon as the thought popped into his head, he realized that she would be right...at least this one time. Disgusted with himself, he helped Claire into her black woolen coat and walked to the front of the restaurant, determined to put an end to what turned out to be a very dissatisfying date.

Angel Cartwright had walked into the restaurant late, eagerly looking forward to meeting with some of her old sorority sisters. Hustling in from the cold, she draped her coat over her arm before moving toward the bar.

"Theresa! Betty!" she greeted the first two women she came to. Hugging the others as well, she turned and winked at the bartender, catching his eye. She ordered her drink, wanting to catch up with her friends, hoping he would not take long with the crowded bar. The wink worked and her cocktail was soon delivered.

"Thanks, Tommy," she called out, blowing him a kiss.

"Anything for you, doll face," the bartender answered back, his eyes dipping to her cleavage before his wolfish grin returned to her eyes.

Laughing, she took a sip of her Lemon Drop. The sweet-tangy drink leaving a slight burn on her throat was just what she wanted.

As her gaze moved across the restaurant, it landed on a couple at a nearby table. The woman, a carbon copy of any successful woman working in the area. Her clothes were immaculate, not much different from the outfits worn by a few of her friends. But it was the man that halted her perusing.

Dark hair, with a neatly trimmed beard. *Hmmm, not many men in this establishment have facial hair, but damn, that's hot!* He had taken off his suit coat, leaving only his shirt to attempt to contain the muscles visible below. Not the type of woman to gawk after another woman's date, she struggled to shift her gaze away. *Why are all the interesting ones taken? And by a beautiful woman. Just my luck.* Allowing her eyes to drop from the man to his date's plate, she rolled her eyes. *Yep, a beautiful woman eating just a salad in this place that serves the best cooked-to-perfection steaks and twice-baked potatoes that are to die for! Bet she skips the dessert tray also!*

Jolted from her musings as her friends called for her to follow them to their table, she bent down to fix the loose strap on her killer heels, when she caught the handsome stranger's eyes on her as well. Standing, she expected his gaze to move away, but it stayed on her.

Mesmerized, they stared, neither willing to drop the gaze. Laughing, she winked at him flirtatiously before walking to the table with her friends. *What the hell did I just do? I never do that...well, never when a man is with another woman.* Glancing down at her almost empty drink, she shook her head. *Must be the exhaustion and the alcohol.*

Determined to forget the man who had set her girlie parts tingling, she settled in with her sorority sisters for their monthly dinner.

"So, who's seeing who? Who's pregnant? And who's getting a new job?"

"Wow, Theresa. Way to jump to the gossip!" Angel laughed.

"I'm nosy, so sue me," Theresa retorted.

Betty, tossing her red curls, answered, "Well, I know the reason Cynthia isn't here tonight is that she's only two weeks away from delivering her second baby and her husband didn't want her traveling."

"Who can blame him after the trouble she had with her

first," Theresa replied. "I also know that Anne is looking for a new job. She hates her boss."

"She should move to Charlestown or Richmond," Angel said. "I bet she could easily get a new job here."

"How's being your own boss, Marcia?" Betty asked.

"It's not bad, but I still have to report to the corporate head," she replied. Marcia's father was Senator Creston and he had used his influence to land his daughter a job with a prestigious investment firm.

"Betty, you dating anyone special?"

"I just don't feel like I have time right now. With my new brother in my life, I'm not looking too hard for a relationship until I figure out my own family." Seeing the curious expressions from the other women, she added, "My brother always seems to need money and I'm not comfortable giving him more. He's always hinting that he could use a loan."

"What do your parents think?" Angel asked, digging into the steak on her plate.

"They know I'd loan him money if he needed it, but Bill always wants more than he can earn. He's a pharmaceutical technician in a good pharmacy, so I can't image he's hurting for money."

"Oh, God, this roast is to die for," Marcia gushed. "Anyone want some?" Several forks immediately appeared as the women eagerly tried each other's dishes.

Angel gazed around at her friends fondly. College graduation had been five years ago, but this core group of her sorority sisters remained close and met every month for dinner to catch up on their lives.

She purposefully sat with her back to the man who caught her eye when she was at the bar, but she was unable to resist a peek over her shoulder. He was looking at his date with what appeared to be a bored expression, but her overactive imagination was probably working overtime.

"Sally, is there anything new with Brian?" Caroline asked, tucking a flyaway blonde wisp of hair back behind her ear.

Sally's face scrunched in anger. "Nope. He's a dick. End of conversation about him. I won't allow our dinner to be marred with his dickiness!"

"Dickiness? Is that a word?"

"If not, it is now!" The women laughed once more, knowing their friend was able to handle her angry ex-boyfriend.

"So, Cupcake Queen, how's business?"

Turning back to her friends, Angel smiled widely. "It's great. I'm thinking about expanding but, honestly, the idea of the business aspect of doing that scares the crap out of me."

Marcia looked at her in speculation. "We need to talk," she said, tapping her long fingernail on the table. "I can help you with that."

"You're already helping me with investments. What else is there?"

"Oh, honey, you concentrate on the delicious goodies you create and let me worry about the rest!"

Lifting their drinks, they toasted to new ventures and old friends.

Several minutes later as the women moaned over their desserts, causing the men nearby to stare at the orgasmic sounds emanating from their table, Angel turned her head once more. The handsome mystery man stood at his date's chair, assisting her into her coat. Unable to tear her eyes away, she saw how tall he was. His date was leggy and willowy, but he still towered over her.

Licking her lips unconsciously, she perused him from

head to toe, not finding a blemish anywhere. He certainly was not the only attractive man in the restaurant, and there were a few that gave off just as suave a vibe as this man. As her eyes moved back to his face, she startled as she saw him staring at her as well. *Animal magnetism. That's what it is!* Like a panther stalking its prey, she felt his eyes boring straight into hers.

A small smile escaped before she glanced at his date. *Jesus, what a slut I am—staring at a man who's with another woman!* She turned away once more, but cold slid over her as she missed his hot gaze.

Taking one more glance, she saw him escort his date out the door and into the night. *Well, that lucky girl is probably going to get some good luvin' tonight.* Why that thought bothered her, she had no idea. But it did. The desire to be the one in his arms—if only for a night—was overwhelming.

Monty escorted Claire to her car, stopping at the door. He saw her eyes light up speculatively but, before she could ask, he saved her the embarrassment of a rejection. "It's been lovely as always, Claire, but I'll need to say goodnight now. I've got a long day ahead tomorrow and I'll need to prepare for it by reading over case files," he lied smoothly.

"Oh, I see," she replied, irritation marring her features. "Perhaps next time."

Kissing her cheek, he gave a non-committal response, "I hope so," knowing he probably would not call her again. *Why the fuck not? She's my type. Isn't she?* Finding no easy answer to that question had him thinking of the colorful woman inside the restaurant.

After watching her drive away safely, he climbed into

his SUV but sat in the parking lot. He did not wait long before the group of women left the restaurant. They giggled and hugged before breaking apart. He watched them all to the safety of their cars but knew he was lying to himself if he thought he was only doing his gentleman's diligence.

His eyes stayed on the woman whose purple coat now hid the green dress and the delectable hips underneath. The parking lot lights illuminated the pink, purple, and teal stripes in her glistening blonde hair. Seeing her unlock and get into a hot pink VW bug, he shook his head. *Totally not my type of woman. Is she?*

Irritated that his night had been such a bust he headed home, but was unable to erase the vision of the enchanting Cupcake from his mind.

3

ONE MONTH LATER

Walking into the bar, Marcia Creston slid onto the padded barstool, her confidence shining as she took a long, purposeful gaze around. Unabashedly checking out the single men, she turned back to the bartender. Not recognizing him from her previous visits to Eclipse, she ordered her drink.

Her phone buzzed and, glancing at her messages, she saw Angel was not going to be able to make it for drinks. Giving an inward shrug, she texted a regretful acknowledgment. It did not take long for a shadow to pass on her left side, a man's arm setting his drink onto the bar next to hers. She waited the requisite minute, to make him wonder, and then twisted her head to see if she were interested. *Hmmm, not bad.*

Her phone buzzed again and she texted Angel to let her know that she was being replaced by the gentleman who now sparked her interest. With a grin, she dropped her phone into her purse and turned her attention to the man who was now leaning toward her.

This could be a very interesting night.

———

Monty pulled up to Chad's house and watched as his large, dark-haired friend and co-worker jogged down the front steps before hopping into Monty's SUV.

"Thanks for the ride, man," Chad greeted. "I thought my truck would pass inspection but it needed brake work."

"No problem," Monty laughed. "But when are you going to replace that hunk-a-junk?"

"I'll keep it as long as I can," Chad replied easily. "I know it's an eyesore next to all y'alls fancy trucks, but it's got sentimental value."

Monty sobered, knowing the old jalopy of Chad's had belonged to one of his former ATF Bomb Squad buddies who died. His mother had not wanted the old truck and gave it gladly to Chad. "Well, as long as someone can keep it running, you might as well drive it," Monty agreed.

The two men talked about current cases the Saints were working on as they drove to the compound, located securely underneath Jack's massive house on twenty acres nestled next to the Blue Ridge Mountains. The back of the property butted against part of the parkway and a winery with acres of grapevines. The other side faced Mountville Cabin Rental and Wedding Venue, owned by Bethany, Jack's wife.

Driving through the gate after entering the security code, the men headed to the house that Jack, and now Bethany, lived in. The large log structure resembled a luxury rental cabin, but underneath housed the Saints' compound. Rooms full of equipment needed for their security business, plus the huge conference room filled with computers that assisted them with their investigations.

The Saints all lived nearby, although they did not meet

at the compound daily. They generally held meetings there twice a week, unless an active case required them to gather more often. It seemed lately, as busy as they were, they met more frequently. Pulling to the front of the house, they saw the vehicles of most of the Saints already there.

"Sorry if I made us late," Chad said.

"We're good on time," Monty replied, glancing down at his dashboard clock.

"Yeah, but we don't want to be stuck with the crumbs."

Bethany baked muffins or massive cobblers when she knew the men were called for special meetings. Her reputation among the Saints meant that none of them wanted to be late.

Hustling up the broad front steps and into the foyer, they were not disappointed to see her just pulling out the apple-peach coffeecake from the oven. The other Saints piled around, plates at the ready. The greetings made the rounds as she served the hot cake.

"Damn, I thought you two would be late and I'd get your piece," Bart, a large, former SEAL declared, trying to elbow Chad out of the way.

"I made up the time it took to pick Chad up," Monty confessed, winking at Bethany. "Wasn't going to miss this."

The Saints headed down to the conference room to grab coffee along with their treat. Luke, a former CIA analyst, bypassed the Keurig and made his own, super-charged coffee. Seeing the bemused looks of the others, he shook his head and continued toward his computer station.

"Fuck, it must be a doozy of a meeting if Luke's getting his caffeine fix so early," said Blaise, a Nordic blond, sitting down to shovel the tasty morsel into his mouth. A veterinarian, whose government career had been with DEA, was also their medic.

Marc, sitting next to Blaise, looked over remarking, "I swear you've got black fur on your sleeve. I didn't think you had a black pet."

Blaise glanced down, shrugging. "I adopted a little black cat and she likes to sleep on my pile of clothes from the dryer."

"So all your clean clothes get covered in cat fur?" Marc asked. The former CIA pilot loved his dogs, but had never been a cat person.

Blaise's fork stopped halfway to his mouth as he turned and looked over at his friend. "Yeah. What's wrong with that?"

Shaking his head, Marc laughed. "Not a damn thing, man."

Monty, always meticulous with his clothes, caught Marc's gaze and shook his head as well, grinning. *Blaise had better find an animal lover girlfriend or his bachelor days will continue.*

The last two Saints came down the stairs. Cam, a former undercover police detective, plopped down in his chair, dark circles underneath his eyes. Seeing the curious gazes from his co-workers, he answered with one word. "Miriam."

The others nodded, knowing that his pregnant wife spent most mornings from about four a.m. until seven a.m. throwing up.

"Is she doing okay?" Jude asked. The newest Saint had readily slid into the camaraderie of the group.

"Yep. If she can make it to about seven or eight o'clock, then she's good the rest of the day."

Jack stepped into the room, eyeing the empty plates of his men. A no-nonsense, former Special Forces soldier, he sat at the table. The others immediately pushed their plates to the side and grabbed their tablets. Luke was already loading them with the information Jack had supplied him.

"I've been contacted by the governor and Senator Creston," Jack began. "His daughter, Marcia Creston, was declared missing yesterday morning when she did not show up at her office."

Every pair of eyes stayed riveted to their screens as Jack continued. "It hasn't hit the news because the Senator wants to keep it quiet. The FBI knows we've been contacted and we're moving this to top priority. Agent Mitch Evans will coordinate with Monty again in this case."

"What have we got so far?" Chad inquired.

Luke added more information to their tablets. "Here's her picture. It was taken two months ago for her business cards."

Monty startled as he eyed the dark-haired, beautiful woman. "I've seen her." The others looked at him and he continued, "About a month ago, she was with a group of women at a restaurant that I was at." A flash of Cupcake flew through his mind—not the first time since that night.

"You notice anything unusual at the time?" Jack demanded.

Shaking his head, Monty said, "No. There were about six women having a gathering. From their greetings, it looked like they all knew each other for a while."

"She runs a small investment firm, although she is under a corporate headquarters."

"Daddy's influence probably helped with her career since she is a local president at her age," Blaise surmised.

"I'm looking into the financial aspect of her company," Luke said, "but first I've been trying to get the initial police and FBI reports."

"Give me a second and let me see if I can get Mitch."

Monty stepped away from the table to call his FBI contact, Mitch Evans, who had worked with the Saints on another case.

"Mitch? It's Monty Lytton. You know Jack's been tasked for the Senator's daughter? Yeah, can I patch you in?" Monty looked at Luke and nodded. Luke made the connection and in a few seconds, Mitch's face appeared on their tablets.

"Good to be working with you all again," Mitch greeted. "Just wish to hell it wasn't for something like this."

"What can you tell us?" Jack asked.

"Marcia Creston did not show up at work yesterday. Her assistant called several times and then finally went to Marcia's condo. She had a key, given to her by her boss for when Ms. Creston was out of town and the assistant would water plants and pick up her mail. She went inside and found nothing unusual, but it appeared as though Marcia had not been home the night before."

"Did it ever occur to daddy that maybe his grown daughter was just out all night partying or with someone?" Bart asked. He leaned forward, his forearms resting on the table, his expression full of concern. "I don't mean any disrespect, but most parents have no idea how their adult children spend some of their...um...recreational time."

"According to the Senator, and the assistant corroborated, Marcia was a consummate professional. She had a Tuesday morning meeting and would never have missed it. Given the prominence of the Senator, the police did not wait for the usual amount of time for a missing person's report to be filed. He went straight to the head of the FBI."

Luke sent the FBI initial report to the tablets showing her apartment. Before the Saints could ask questions, Mitch continued.

"Initial investigation from this morning showed no fingerprints on the doorknobs."

"They were wiped?" Monty queried.

"Yeah, someone was thorough with their fingerprints."

"What do you need from us, besides the usual?" Jack asked.

"Right now, just check her background, business, and finances," Mitch answered.

"Was she in a sorority?" Monty wondered aloud.

Mitch shrugged, replying, "Don't know. Why?"

"I saw her a month ago with a group of women and I thought I heard one of them talking about their sorority days."

"I'll let you check that out. We're short staffed here right now and, with a heightened terrorist possibility in D.C., I don't see me getting new agents, even with the profile of our victim."

"We'll let you know what we find," Jack promised. Disconnecting with Mitch, he turned to his group. Eyeing Monty, he said, "You're on point with this case. I'd suggest you start with finding who her friends are."

Monty nodded, glad for the vote of confidence from his boss. He wanted to tell himself that checking for Cupcake would just be another part of the job, but he knew he would be lying. *She hasn't been far from my mind in weeks.* Refusing to think of her as anything other than a possible interviewee, he could not stop the pounding of his heart.

A few hours later, back on video-conference with Mitch, the Saints pulled together again to review their initial investigation findings.

Monty began, "We know she was recently promoted to

president of the investment company over several others and while no one would speak directly about the situation, from the initial FBI report, I'll bet there were hard feelings amongst a few of her co-workers."

"I've got nothing yet on her finances, either personal or the business. From outward appearances, there's nothing unusual standing out, but I've only begun to dig," Luke added.

"The FBI interviewed the assistant and, with another walk through the apartment, she still says that she sees nothing out of place other than Marcia's laptop is missing. But she also cannot swear that it was taken home that day," Jude said.

Monty interrupted. "My initial digging came up with a number of social acquaintances, an active social media presence, some close friends. We're going to start interviewing them today."

Jack nodded his agreement. "Monty, I want you to stay close, so you investigate the ones here. Blaise and Chad, you take her friends in D.C. Bart, you and Cam go back and check out her apartment and office. Monty, when you go to interview the Senator, take Jude with you. Luke'll be digging into the finances and Marc, I want all the background info you can get for us."

Bart and Cam fist bumped each other, knowing their assignment came from their skills with breaking and entering undetected. Bart's from his years as a SEAL and Cam's from his early delinquent youth.

Mitch, still on video chat, rolled his eyes. "Don't even want to guess what the fuck you two will do, but you find anything, let me know so we can get the evidence legally." He then asked, "Monty? You wondered if she was in a sorority. She was and I'll send you the info that came in from her college records on that."

Signing off, the Saints then turned to the table to continue their meeting. "I've confirmed that you'll meet with the Senator and his wife this afternoon at two p.m.," Jack said to Monty. "You can interview the friends later in the afternoon."

As the men moved to their workstations, each with their tasks, Monty fired up his secure laptop. Quickly going through the university information sent to him, he focused on the sorority. An old yearbook photograph showed a group of women posed perfectly for the camera. A small group of only twenty women, he searched the faces. He knew he should be looking for Marcia Creston first, but his gaze landed on a beautiful blonde with a wide smile, seemingly without a care in the world...his Cupcake. There were no colorful streaks in her hair, but the same vivaciousness he had witnessed in the restaurant was present in the photograph from six years prior.

Angel Cartwright. Angel. Fuck, if that name doesn't just fit. A quick internet search brought up Angel's Cupcake Heaven. *Damn, she's the creator of the delicious swirls of color that had been all over my mouth at my niece's party.* He continued to peruse her website, learning that she was indeed the owner of the premier cupcake bakery and designer in the area. Her website sported an up-close photograph, the same winning smile aimed at the camera. The pink, purple, and teal colors in her hair flowed across the screen. Quickly noting her location, he realized he would be able to interview her after meeting with the Senator.

"Got anything interesting?" Jude asked, looking over Monty's shoulder.

Quickly covering, Monty replied, "Just checking to see if any of Marcia's old sorority sisters were at the restaurant where I saw her a couple of months ago."

"See anyone familiar?"

"Yeah, several of them," he said noncommittally. "I'll interview one on my way back from the Senator." Looking up at Jude, he asked, "You ready?"

"Yeah, but I'll need to stop by my apartment to grab my suit first." Glancing down at his jeans, he said, "Sorry, boss. Wasn't expecting to meet the Senator today."

Jack nodded as Monty and Jude headed up the stairs, saying goodbye to Bethany on their way out.

Monty sat in his SUV waiting for Jude to change clothes staring at his tablet again. The picture of Angel Cartwright staring back at him, her smile lighting up the screen. *What would it be like to have that aimed at me? Just once, have that kind of light aimed at me.* He hoped that afternoon, he would have that chance.

4

An hour later, Monty and Jude were met at the door of the Virginia Senator's estate on the eastern side of Charlestown. The large, stately home was surrounded by white fences encompassing fields where horses roamed, nibbling on the grass. A housekeeper showed them to the private family room, bypassing the other, more formal living, and dining area.

The room could have appeared light and airy with the pale colored walls on three sides and the dark wood floor to ceiling bookcases surrounding a fireplace on the back wall. Windows were plentiful, but most of the drapes were closed, casting a gloomy darkness over the occupants.

Senator Creston sat on the sofa, his arm around his wife. Monty noticed her pained expression as one delicate hand rubbed her temples as though to massage away a headache. *Probably the reason she has the drapes closed.* Several other men and two women wandered around the room as well forming a protective circle around the distraught parents.

The Senator's gaze lifted as Monty and Jude moved into

the warm, comfortably furnished room. A gas-lit fire glowed in the fireplace and Monty's eyes immediately noted the abundance of family pictures on the mantle.

As he walked over, the Senator stood with his hand outstretched. "Mr. Lytton? Mr. Stedson? I'm Senator Creston. Donald Creston." He shook hands with both Monty and Jude before turning to introduce the devastated woman sitting on the sofa. "May I present my wife, Audrey."

The men bent to take her limp hand in theirs before being shown to two chairs facing the sofa. The Senator sat back down, wrapping his arm around his wife's shoulders.

"Senator, let me first say how very sorry we are for having to meet you under such distressful circumstances," Monty stated. "I understand you have been interviewed by the FBI, but we'd like to ask some questions of our own."

"Anything we can do to help. And please, call me Donald. At this time, the title of Senator feels cumbersome."

"All right, Donald. Instead of me asking specific questions at this time, I'd like you to talk about your daughter. Her life. What you thought of her business. Anything you can think of. Oftentimes, people can think of things freely when not barraged with a lot of questions."

Nodding, Marcia's father glanced at his wife before beginning. "She was a model student all through school. Smart, pretty, popular. She went to college here in Charlestown and majored in business. I wanted to set her up in a firm that I worked with, but she wanted to do things on her own. She got a job with Colonial Financial Group and has done amazingly well there. She was recently promoted to president." Catching the eye of Monty, he admitted, "I'm aware some think she was very young for that promotion and it was all my doing but, I assure you, she got it on her own."

A slight snort emitted from one of the other men in the room and Monty forced his eyes to stay on the Senator, but made a note to talk to the man later.

"She was on the board of several committees and charities. Very popular, not only in college, but since graduation as well. There's nothing about her life that would have made her disappear. That's why we think foul play must be the cause," her father's voice shook with emotion.

"It must have been a robbery," Audrey commented, tears forming in her red-rimmed eyes. "She must have surprised someone in the middle of a random robbery and they took her. Or maybe she was out somewhere—"

"Shh now," Donald comforted.

Monty and Jude listened for a few more minutes as the parents extolled their daughter's virtues. While their responses were typical, no new information was forthcoming. Donald finally stood, assisting his wife. "Gentlemen, I'm going to ensure my wife takes a sleeping pill to see if she can get any rest. She hasn't slept in over twenty-four hours." Looking over to the other men in the room, he said, "Carlton, will you assist the investigators?"

"Absolutely, Uncle Donald."

Two of the females in the room followed the Senator as he and his wife walked toward the staircase. The two men who had been standing near the fireplace moved over to introduced themselves.

"I'm Carlton, Marcia's cousin, and this is Scott, a friend of mine who works with Marcia."

"Without sounding blunt," Monty began, "I got the feeling you were not in complete agreement with your uncle's assessment of his daughter."

Carlton blushed deeply and apologized. "I'm sorry, that was inexcusable of me."

"But honest?" Jude prompted.

Carlton and Scott shared a glance then Carlton admitted, "Marcia's a wonderful woman, just like her father said. But she wasn't perfect. No one is."

"And to be honest, painting her only in a favorable light won't exactly help you find her, will it?" Scott added.

"You're right," Monty said. "So why don't you enlighten us." Monty stared intently at the two, lifting his eyebrow quizzically.

"Marcia was smart. And driven. Sometimes it felt as though getting to the top was her only mission in life," Scott said.

"Did she step on anyone to get there?" Monty asked.

"Oh yeah. Our office wasn't large, but there's almost no one there without the heel marks of her stomping over them!" He hesitated for a moment then added, "Except for Cindy. She's Marcia's assistant. The two of them got along perfectly." Shaking his head, he said. "Cindy is smart as well. College educated. I couldn't figure why she took an assistant job when she could have used her degree to get paid a lot more somewhere else."

The silence stretched out in the room, the two being interviewed glancing down at their hands, adding a nervous quality to the atmosphere. Scott fidgeted while Carlton attempted to meet Monty's cool stare but failed.

"But hey, Marcia being driven in the workplace isn't a crime and I've got no doubt it's harder for a woman," Scott added.

Carlton rolled his eyes. "Oh, she made sure to take advantage of being a woman every chance she got." Holding the gazes of Monty and Jude, he continued, "She's not quite the virtuous woman that her parents assumed.

Just because she didn't bring men to Sunday dinners didn't mean they weren't in her life. She partied and, at times, would party hard."

"Drugs?" Monty queried.

Scott frowned. "Not that I ever saw, but she rarely left a bar or party alone, if you know what I mean. And before you ask, I'll tell you that she could be a barracuda." Rubbing his hand over his face, he sighed heavily. "Yeah, I was one of them. I was her boss at one time, but she made quick work of taking over some of my clients and moving ahead of me within the first two years." Suddenly looking up, he said, "Does this make me a suspect?"

"Right now, we're collecting information and the investigation is in the early stages. But, since you brought it up, were you with her the night she went missing?"

"Good God, no! I haven't seen her outside of work in over six months. After she took over my position, we met up at a bar once. I was drinking alone and she came over and began drinking with me. She made it abundantly clear she wanted sex and we went back to her place. She was... well, she was..." he stopped and looked at Carlton.

"Jesus, man, just say it. I know she slept with anyone and everyone. You're not going to tarnish my image of her."

"Okay, she was really into it. Wanted it hard. Fast. Wanted me to slap her ass almost violently. She was totally in control and honestly...it wasn't very good for me. We finished and I got the hell out of there."

"Do you have the names of others who have been with her?" Monty asked.

"If you're talking about at work, no. Her reputation was discussed, but no one admitted to having slept with her."

Carlton added, "Marcia worked hard, no doubt about it. But she also played hard. If you want to get more information, I'd suggest you check with some of the bartenders at the nicer bars in town. She frequented them and, from what I hear, generally did not leave alone."

Monty nodded, his mind considering the information. *She may have left a bar with the wrong person this time.* His suspicious thoughts realized that perhaps she was not missing...*she may be dead.*

The interview continued for several more minutes until the sound of the Senator's footsteps were heard coming down the hall.

Carlton quickly said in a hushed voice, "Mr. Lytton, I know it seems like I've been ragging on Marcia. The honest to God truth is we were fairly close and I can't believe she's missing." His voice broke as he continued, "But thinking she was some kind of angel won't help you find her."

"You're right," Monty conceded. *I know the Angel and it's not Marcia Creston.*

The four men stood as the Senator came back into the room. Monty walked over, shaking his hand once again.

"Donald, we're finished here for the moment. We'll be assisting the FBI and interviewing her friends and co-workers."

"I appreciate it. If there's anything I can provide, please contact me."

Monty assured, "We'll keep you apprised of our investigation."

"So what do you think?" Jude asked as soon as they were driving down the Senator's long driveway.

"Not sure," Monty answered honestly. "It's not unusual

for parents to extoll the virtues of their child, especially when their fear is so raw."

"And the cousin and the co-worker?"

"Yeah, that bears more investigation. I'd like to know how close the cousins are. It seems as though Carlton had an axe to grind and wanted us to know the more sordid details of Marcia's life."

"You want me to check on him and Scott?"

"Absolutely," Monty affirmed. "I'd like to know how Scott fits in with her at work and with the cousin."

"If you drop me off at my apartment, I'll start seeing what I can dig up. I'll call Luke and work with him. I can also check in with Bart and Cam to obtain their intel on Marcia's workplace."

Within a few minutes, Monty dropped Jude off and, with a wave goodbye, he drove across town to the bakery. Parking, he walked toward the door, finding it locked. Peeking in through the front glass it was hard to see the interior, but it appeared no one was inside.

"Who you looking for?" asked an elderly man with an apron tied around his rotund middle and a broom in his hands. Monty's gaze moved to the sign above the store-front. **Vito's Pizzeria.** The man's eyes squinted from the late winter sun as he held one hand over his forehead to shade them as he peered at Monty.

"I was looking for the owner of the bakery," Monty said.

"They're closed," came the reply.

Monty looked at the dark, locked door with the **Closed** sign on the front. "Um, yeah, I figured that out."

"Heard one of the employees say that the owner closed for the day. Some personal crisis."

"You Vito?"

The man grinned as he nodded. "Best damn pizza in Virginia. You should try it sometime."

Monty returned his grin, saying, "I might take you up on your offer."

Continuing to nod, Vito turned back to his sweeping. "You do that, young man. You do that." Then, glancing toward the bakery, he added, "And bring the pretty owner with you when you come."

Thanking the man, Monty drove away, his mind meticulously turning over the few known facts of the case as he tried to tamper down his disappointment in not seeing Cupcake again. *I've got to stop calling her that. Angel Cartwright.* He could not decide which name fit her best...*Angel or Cupcake.*

That afternoon, the Saints met again at the compound. Bart and Cam had managed to get into Marcia's apartment...after the FBI team had left.

"Her place was nice. Really neat," Bart said. "Without knowing her, I'd say she was a control freak."

Cam agreed, "She had the cans in her kitchen cabinets stacked perfectly and facing the same way." This comment elicited a few raised eyebrows before he continued. "In the bathroom, her makeup drawer was organized. I don't know about you, but I grew up sharing a bathroom with two sisters and am now married to a fairly neat woman and I've never seen a bathroom drawer full of makeup that was organized."

"The place certainly had decorations and pictures around and nothing looked out of place."

Jack added, "I heard from Mitch. It appears her place was wiped down. The few fingerprints found belonged to Marcia or her assistant."

"That could indicate someone had looked for something and wanted to get rid of fingerprints, but that theory sucks," Marc said. "If an intruder was thorough enough to be looking all around the apartment for something, then they would have worn gloves."

"Cleaning service?" Monty asked.

"Or maybe the assistant was trying to hide something. If she knew her boss was used to having men around, she wanted to get rid of the evidence?" Bart surmised.

"Check both," Monty ordered. "This evening I'm following up on a lead about some of the bars she was known to frequent. Marc, we'll split them up. Bart, you and I will plan on going back to her office this afternoon for interviews. I want to know what the assistant has to say about everything. I don't care if the FBI put her through the ringer yesterday, turn on your charm."

"Hey, I'm a happily engaged man," Bart protested, shock on his face.

"You've still got that Taggart charm," Monty argued, teasing his co-worker. He grinned, adding, "Don't sleep with her, just question her."

The men chuckled as Bart agreed, leaning back in his chair, a twinkle in his eyes. "You got it. She won't know what hit her!"

"Cam, find out what you can about who cleans her apartment and when. Interview whatever maid service she used."

Luke, downing a gulp of hot coffee, reported, "So far nothing suspicious is showing in her personal accounts. Her checking account is stable, although it shows she had a penchant for expensive shoes, boots, and purses. Other than that, it's pretty normal. Her savings show that she definitely diversified. She had two saving accounts, one IRA, and several investment accounts. Only one is through her own company, so that's interesting. I'm taking a deeper look later today to see what I can find."

Each with their assignments, the men went upstairs finding Bethany, Miriam, Sabrina, and Faith waiting on them. Bethany's face beamed as soon as her eyes landed on Jack. The taciturn boss' face broke into a smile as he walked over to embrace his wife. Kissing the top of her head, he noticed the food out on the long dining table. "You guys didn't have to do this, babe," he said. Her smile was his only answer as she snuggled into his arms for a quick hug.

Monty watched the exchange, wondering if he would ever find that kind of relationship. His mind wandered over his typical date, trying to imagine them in this group. *Nope, can't do it,* he thought ruefully. For an instant, he thought of Claire and knew she would never be able to be one of the Saint's women. As he gazed at the other couples, he found himself longing for something more than his solitary existence.

Miriam, wearing blue, maternity nursing scrubs, waddled over to Cam. She was dwarfed by her massive husband as he picked her up gently, placing a chaste kiss on her lips. He whispered in her ear and she giggled, nervously looking around the group. Swatting his shoulder, she continued to blush as he set her down.

Sabrina winked at her cousin before greeting her fiancé, Jude. "What have you ladies been up to?" he asked, tucking a wayward strand of hair behind her ear.

"Wedding planning," Sabrina replied. Bethany's wedding venue business next door to Jack's secure property had been the perfect place for their upcoming nuptials. "I know we want simple, but Nonnie's gonna want her hand in things if I don't take charge."

Nodding his agreement that Sabrina and Bart's grandmother was a force to be reckoned with, he said, "It's our wedding. Babe, you do whatever you want."

The group headed to the table to load their plates before moving back into the large living room. The room's floor to ceiling windows illuminated the Blue Ridge Mountains in the vista while allowing the light to pour over the group. The oversized furniture surrounding the two-story stone fireplace easily held the gathering.

Bart saw the concerned expression on Faith's face and moved over to embrace her as well. "What's up, princess?"

Faith's long dark hair was pulled back into a ponytail that hung low behind her as she lifted her head to search his face. "I know you're working on something important. I was wondering…well, if you needed me to try to help?"

Bart's gaze met Jack's over the top of Faith's head, silently communicating his feelings. Jack shook his head firmly and Bart turned his attention back to his girlfriend. The men had already discussed—and rejected—the idea of Faith assisting them on cases. Her extraordinary ability of sight had almost gotten her killed on their last major case and the men did not want a repeat performance.

"Princess, Jack and the rest of us agree that you're not on Saint's payroll. Right now, we're investigating a missing person but, I promise, if you get any insights, then tell me and I'll handle it."

Smiling, her arms tightened around his trim waist as she placed her cheek against his heartbeat. "Come on, let's eat," she said.

The group quickly ate, the topics of discussion remaining firmly off the case as they enjoyed the easy banter and camaraderie. As soon as the meal was over, they dispersed. Monty and Bart headed out, determined to find out what Colonial Financial employees had to say about their boss.

Angel walked to the back door of her bakery having let out the last of her employees. The front door was already closed and locked. "Sorry guys, I'll put the rest of the cupcakes in the freezer and we should be back in business tomorrow."

"You sure you're all right?" asked Helen, one of her most loyal employees.

She smiled although it did not reach her eyes as she answered, "Yeah, I just have something I need to do tonight. You know, a night to forget all my troubles."

"Sure thing," her cashier grinned. "I hope you get a little horizontal action while you're forgetting."

Rolling her eyes, she locked the door. Pulling out her cell phone, she moved her thumb over the keys and stared at the text that came up. Heaving a sigh, she walked out of the back, locking the door to the alley before heading to her car. *Time to get ready for the evening.*

5

The afternoon proved difficult. While Bart attempted to charm information from the indomitable assistant, Monty interviewed several of the members of the office. Scott was present and introduced him to the other employees.

"We're a small office, but I can set you up in the conference room, if you'd like," Scott offered.

Nodding his agreement, Monty quickly moved through the employees. On the surface, everyone expressed concern about Marcia's absence. He got the impression that while they assumed something was wrong, since they all reported that missing work or an important meeting was unheard of for their boss, he could also tell that she was not a popular boss.

She's driven and expects everyone else to be just as driven...as long as they don't try to take over her position, Monty recalled one employee stating. He pondered what he had learned so far while waiting for the next interviewee.

An elderly gentleman walked in, shaking his hand, nervously glancing at Monty, who immediately got down to business. He had no time or inclination for pleasantries when a person was missing.

"She came on time and worked until the day was over. Can't say she ever slacked when on the job. She was an excellent broker and good with clients. Smart, sharp, intuitive with the business. But..." Marcia's co-worker's voice drifted off as he squirmed in his seat.

"But?" Monty prompted.

Shaking his head, the older man colored slightly. "Mr. Lytton, I know I'm old school and getting near retirement. I know these younger folks have a different way of seeing things. I understand that, but it's still hard to fight against your way of thinking when you're my age."

"What are you referring to, Mr. Johnston?"

The man looked down at his hands clenched together on the table, struggling in an inner battle.

"The truth of the matter is that Marcia is about my daughter's age. So I'm familiar with the modern woman, but I guess I'm still stuck in the dark ages. She had a reputation." He hesitated for a moment before continuing. His face blushing, he admitted, "In my day, we'd have called her a slut." Rushing on, he hastily corrected, "I'm embarrassed to say that because, in my day, a man could sow his wild oats and we thought nothing of it. So I know it's a double standard, but honestly...well...I was uncomfortable with what I'd hear at the office."

"Others talk from facts or just rumors?" Monty asked.

"Hard to tell, but a lot of the young folks around here will frequent bars after hours. It gives them a chance to unwind and be with their friends. Hell, they even make business deals there the way we did at the golf courses back in my day." He chuckled nervously before sobering as he shook his head. "I thought of trying to work another year before retiring, Mr. Lytton. But I'll be honest, her missing is turning into a sordid deal around here. The scuttlebutt is that she went off with some lover. The whole thing makes me just...sad."

"I appreciate your candor," Monty replied honestly.

The gentleman stood, leaning over to shake Monty's hand. "It's been really difficult around here. Marcia was not a popular boss, only because she was driven and didn't mind stepping on a few people to get to the top. But to harm her? I don't see anyone in this office doing that." He walked to the door slowly, patted the doorframe for a second and added, "Yes, indeed. I think it's time to retire."

Monty found the rest of the employees saying essentially the same thing that Mr. Johnston had alluded to. He met with Bart outside and they walked to his SUV.

"You get anything out of the assistant, Ms. Bartley?"

"Nope. She locked down everything as tightly as she could. As an assistant, she's perfect. No one will get past her to get to the boss. According to her, Marcia was a saint and the others in the office were just jealous."

"Did she have any ideas as to where Marcia might be?"

"No. She's the one who called the Senator to alert him that Marcia did not come to work. And she's plenty pissed that the others seem to be more interested in smearing the boss' reputation."

After dropping Bart off at his house, Monty drove home. Fixing a bite to eat, he stood at his bank of windows for a moment. He wanted nothing more than to find the elusive Cupcake but knew that would have to wait until tomorrow. *Time to hit the bars.* Sighing as he grabbed his keys from the table next to the door, he headed back out into the night.

The evening had proven to be informative, if not eventful. Monty had made the rounds to several of the higher-class bars and restaurants with bars, showing a picture of Marcia to the bartenders. Most recognized her and admitted that she frequented them once a month or so. She tipped well and, if she met with men, they noticed but did not care.

"Look, mister, there's nothing wrong with a woman picking up a man at a bar. Men've been doing it forever," was the response from most.

Before walking into Eclipse, the last one of the night, he called Marc and discovered that his experience had been the same.

"Seems like she was known to be a woman on the take," Marc commented, "But no one spoke ill of her."

"Yeah, it appears that tipping very well helped seal the eyes, ears, and lips of many a bartender," Monty added. "You head on home, I've got one more place I want to check out, and truthfully, plan on sitting for a while and actually enjoying a drink. I'll see you tomorrow."

Disconnecting, he walked through the thick, amber glass door of the last bar, entering the upscale establishment. He had been a customer here before and admitted to himself this was why he chose it last. A quiet interior with soft music playing in the background provided a nice contrast to a few of the noisier bars with live bands that he had been to. Making his way over the plush carpet toward the dark wooden, highly polished bar he selected a stool near the end. It sat in the shadows and allowed him a chance to rest his back against the wall. Eyeing a table nearby, he was determined to ask his questions and then settle in a seat to enjoy his drink.

He caught the eye of the bartender and, pulling out the picture of Marcia, he slid it forward as he ordered his drink. The bartender's eyes flashed recognition and he lifted his gaze up to Monty.

"Be right back with your drink," he said, walking away from Monty. "I'm John, by the way."

In a minute he came back, setting the drink on a napkin in front of Monty and leaned on the bar. "I guess you want to know if I've seen the woman in that picture. I gotta tell you, she's a regular customer, never causes problems, and tips like nobody's business. So mister, you'd better have some kind of badge to get me to talk about her."

Deciding this bartender was worth the risk, Monty decided to be upfront. "She's missing."

John reared back, his eyes wide in surprise. "Missing? Like missing for good?"

"Didn't know there's another kind of missing."

"Well, sure there is. Some people just want to disappear for a while. You know? Get away from it all."

"You think that's what she did?" Monty asked.

John chewed on his lip for a moment, then shook his head. "Naw. She loved life. She'd come in, drink...but not too much. She'd usually have men buying her drinks eagerly, but she always tipped the bartenders like she was the one buying."

"You ever see her with anyone in particular?"

"No, no. And to be honest, I don't remember her picking up too many local men. When I was working, I generally didn't recognize anyone she would leave with."

"Were you working two nights ago? Was she here?"

"I couldn't say. I wasn't working." He caught Monty's gaze and quickly added, "And I was at a family gathering so I've got lots of witnesses!"

"Alright," Monty chuckled. "Just do me a favor and check with your co-workers to see who might have seen her that night." Sliding his business card over along with a fifty-dollar bill, he added, "And for now, I'm off the clock and going to enjoy my drink."

"Yes, sir," John grinned, taking the money and heading back down the bar.

Monty moved over to the table in the shadows and leaned his head against the paneled wall. Closing his eyes for a while, he allowed the soft tones of the music to settle deep inside.

Suddenly, the sound of deep-throated, gentle laughter met his ears and he jerked his eyes open. It only took a millisecond for his gaze to land on the beautiful woman now sitting at the opposite end of the bar. Her blonde hair shone in the soft lights as the pink, purple, and teal stripes created a symphony of color. Her clear complexion glowed, her blue eyes sparkled. But her luscious cotton-candy pink lips held his gaze. Her smile lit her face as her eyes focused on the man sitting next to her. *Cupcake. Lucky bastard. I wonder if that's her boyfriend.*

He tortured himself a few more minutes before realizing, by snatches of her conversation, she was meeting the man for the first time. *No boyfriend? She's looking for a pickup? Is she into the same thing her friend was?*

Watching carefully, he noticed her slightly slurred speech and disappearing drink. *How much has she had?* Feeling like a voyeur, he could not take his eyes off her. He watched as the man leaned forward to whisper something to her and knew the man's eyes were on her abundant cleavage.

Monty's fingers tightened around his glass then relaxed before it shattered. *It doesn't matter to me what her game is.* But he knew he was lying to himself.

As her drink was refilled, her giggling increased. Monty wanted to be repulsed by her behavior, but found himself as enthralled as every other man in the room. Glancing around the dim interior, he saw the looks sent her way. *Yep, that man at the bar must think he's won the lottery. I would too if she shot that smile at me.*

Monty looked down at his empty glass and almost ordered another one. *I'd really like to go home and sleep.* Even as that thought went through his mind, he knew he would stay. The desire to see what Angel was going to do was too strong to resist. He dragged his eyes away from her and focused his gaze on the man she flirted with.

Tall. Blond. Mustache. Dressed in a dark suit. Not expensive, but not shabby. The man reached his hand back to scratch his neck and the movement of his hair was almost imperceptible. Monty blinked before looking harder. *A wig. He's wearing a wig.* Instinct along with protection kicked in as he watched the man's mannerisms with renewed interest. Admitting to himself that a man wearing a wig was not a crime nor did it imply the man had anything to hide...*but something's off.*

As he watched, the man's behaviors became more pronounced. Leaning in to whisper in Angel's ear, dragging his fingers along her arm, sliding his other arm around her waist. Monty felt a slow burn as jealousy coursed through his body. *Jealousy? What the fuck am I thinking? We've never even met.* But as much as he tried to convince himself it was only his investigative duty, he knew it was more.

Thirty minutes later, Angel appeared to slide off of the barstool, the mystery man reaching out to hold her against him. Giggling again, she held her arms out as he slipped her coat onto her body. Monty watched as they turned and moved out the doors.

Warring with himself for only a few seconds, Monty threw more bills onto the table and followed the couple out. The bar was next to one of the nicer hotels in the city and he was not surprised to see the man lead her into the lobby.

Hesitating for a second, he followed them discreetly. The elegant lobby, with gleaming tile floors, echoed the clicks of Angel's heels as she continued to lean drunkenly on the man. Seeing them enter the elevator, he watched as the lighted floor button stopped on two. *Thank God.* He knew he could run upstairs quickly, but preferred to not have to go more than a flight up. Jogging, he cautiously stepped into the hall on the second floor, seeing them approach a room. The man held Angel tightly against him as he used his keycard to unlock the door before they stumbled in and the door shut with a resounding click.

Monty padded across the carpeted hall, stopping at the door. *What the fuck am I doing? Just because she's drunk doesn't mean she can't pick up a guy. Jesus, she can screw anyone she wants.* Battling the sexist attitude of a double standard, he could not fight the wish that she was not inside with the man from the bar.

Hesitating, he turned to walk away when he heard raised voices. Instantly on alert, he backed up and placed his ear on the door.

"What the fuck are you talking about?" a man's voice growled in anger.

"Have you seen her? Were you with her?" Angel asked, her voice strident.

"Look, I don't know what your game is, but you can get the hell out right now, lady. No fuck is worth this."

"Stop, stop!" her voice cried out.

Suddenly the sounds of a struggle were heard and Monty knocked loudly on the door. "Hotel management!" he shouted. "Let me in!"

The noises in the room did not abate and instinctively Monty stepped back and kicked the door. It took three kicks but the light wood splintered by the lock and flew open. Inside, he saw the two occupants in a standoff. To his surprise, Angel was holding a gun to the man, whose wig sat askew on his head.

Drawing his weapon from its holster, Monty growled, "Put it down."

"You? What are you doing here?" she asked, her eyes wide.

To Monty's surprise, Angel's words were clear…as were her eyes…which had just registered recognition. *She's not drunk. Fuck, what the hell is she doing?*

The man took advantage of Angel and Monty's stand-off and grabbed her gun arm at the elbow. Pulling her in front of him, he backed to the bathroom door. Keeping his head low, he slung her fiercely away from him as he ducked into the bathroom, slamming and locking the door. Angel's body launched several feet before she fell, hitting her head on the dresser. Hearing glass breaking in the bathroom, Monty started toward the door but halted as Angel's body lay still on the floor, blood running from the front of her head.

6

The harsh lights above had her squinting in pain as Angel attempted to open her eyes. Her head throbbed and when she lifted a shaky hand, her fingers touched a large bandage. Attempting to sit up, she fell back on the bed with a groan, swallowing several times in an effort to keep the nausea at bay. Licking her lips, she breathed deeply. *In. Out. In. Out.* When the stars stopped dancing behind her eyes, she noticed the bright light was blocked. Opening her eyes once more, she saw a familiar face between her and the light.

"Who are you?" she asked, her brow crinkling in confusion, causing another bolt of pain through her head. "Augggh," she groaned.

Monty leaned down, his face a mixture of concern and anger. "I'm the man who's going to get some answers and paddle your ass if I don't like them! Hell, I may just paddle you for the situation you put yourself in!"

Attempting to sit up again, she found her shoulders gently pushed back.

"Stay still," he ordered softly, lowering his voice.

"My head?" she asked.

"A couple of stitches and a concussion."

"Oh," she moaned.

Just then the light in the room became even dimmer as the small space filled with men. Large men. *What the hell? I must be concussed or died and gone to hunk-heaven.* She let out an unladylike snort at that thought, then giggled.

Monty looked down, his fury over what had happened still blazing, he nonetheless found himself chuckling at the woman lying on the bed, giggling and snorting.

"You know anything from her yet?" Jack asked.

Angel observed a bearded man, with a dour expression, questioning her rescuer.

"No, not yet. But I will."

The three men stepped outside of the examining room. Jack said, "Bart's over at the hotel right now with the police. The suspect slipped out of the bathroom window, onto a ledge and then down the fire escape. When Bart talked to the man working the reception desk, he said the suspect comes in a couple of times a month. Always trying to hook up with different woman. He'd noticed that the man wore disguises and figured he was married, looking for a little fun."

"Did the receptionist recognize a picture of Marcia?" Monty asked.

"Said he didn't," Marc added, "but admitted that he only works three nights a week, so Bart'll check with the other receptionists tomorrow."

Jack nodded toward he ER bay. "What about her?"

"I'll take care of her," Monty pronounced. Jack raised his eyebrow and Monty swore, "Fuck, don't read more into this than what it is. She's not even my type."

Throwing his head back in laughter, Jack clapped him on the shoulder saying, "It hits at the damnedest time, bro."

54

He and a chuckling Marc stayed outside the room, leaving Monty to walk back to Angel.

Before she could ask what they were laughing about, the doctor walked in. "Ah, Ms. Cartwright, your x-rays look fine. You received four stitches on your forehead but the scarring should be minimal. You do, however, have a concussion. You will need to have someone watch over you for the next twenty-four hours. I'll send the nurse with your discharge instructions."

The harried doctor popped back out as quickly as he had come, leaving Angel staring dumbly in his wake.

"Do you have someone who can come stay with you?"

"What?" Her confused face looked up into the handsome face of the man who had rescued her...and had seen a month ago at the restaurant. His neatly trimmed beard now sported stubble on his cheeks, making him appear even more dashing.

"Do you have someone who can come stay with you tonight?" he asked, emphasizing each word.

Pulling herself out of her musing, she blinked. Twice. Finally finding her voice, she replied, "No, but I'll—"

"I've got her," Monty said, turning to Jack and Marc, who upon hearing her response, stepped back into the crowded room.

They nodded and turned to leave. Jack stopped at the door and glanced over his shoulder, "Meeting tomorrow morning. Bring her."

"Yes, sir," Monty replied, nodding at his boss before turning back to the woman lying on the bed, her expression morphing from confusion to anger.

"Look, mister, I don't know what you're doing, but—"

"Monty. Monty Lytton. I'm with Saints Protection and Investigations." He pulled out his identification, but could tell her eyes were barely able to focus on the card. "And as of right now, Cupcake, you're under my protection. And once I get you home, we're gonna have a little chat about what the hell you were doing tonight."

She opened and closed her mouth several times, but nothing came out. Unsure if she were more concerned about going home with the hot man...or explaining holding a gun on a man in a hotel, she laid back on the bed.

An hour later, after checking out of the hospital, Monty pulled up to the bakery's storefront, behind her pink VW bug. He looked over at his quiet passenger and quipped, "You live in your store?"

She turned her head toward him, her eyes shooting daggers his way. "I live above the bakery," she replied. "I would have thought a good investigator would have known that."

"Sorry, I've been too busy chasing leads on your missing friend to find out everything about you," he bit back. Leaning closer, he added, "But that stops now. I intend to discover exactly who and what you are."

"Look, I know you seem to be trying to help, but I don't know you," she declared, watching him warily.

Pulling out his wallet again, he produced his identification once more. "I get that you're nervous and you'd be right to do so, but you saw the detective at the hospital talking to us. We're a legitimate security service."

Nodding, she agreed. *Oh, hell, the way my head hurts right now, he could murder me in my sleep and I'd probably appreciate it!*

Getting out of his SUV, he walked around the front to her door.

She noticed that he handled her with care as he lifted

her out. He set her feet on the ground, carefully holding her arms until she was steady. Not trusting that she would not topple over, he kept one hand on her arm as he guided her toward the door next to the bakery entrance. Her hands fumbled with the key until he took them from her, unlocking the outside door leading to a staircase. Propping her on the wall, he made sure to bolt the door before turning to look back at her.

Her face was bruised, her eyes glassy, and her smile... lopsided. *And fuckin' gorgeous.* Knowing she could not safely navigate the steep stairs, he gathered her into his strong embrace as she flung her arms loosely around his neck. He took the stairs quickly but, carefully, not wanting to hit her head on the wall and cause more damage than the already disastrous evening had done.

Grinning, Angel felt as though she was flying as her rescuer swooped her up the stairs. *Oh, I hope I don't hurt him. I'm kinda heavy.*

"Babe, you're not heavy," Monty said, reaching the top of the stairs and stopping at the door to her apartment.

"How'd you know what I was thinking?" she said, her brow in a delectable furrow.

Trying not to chuckle, he said, "You said it out loud. Now you got your keys or do we have to spend the night in the stairwell?"

Digging in her purse, she grinned triumphantly as she pulled her house key out. Giving a celebratory wiggle in his arms, she hoped he would not drop her as he unlocked the door. Setting her down, she moved into the apartment, still unsteady on her feet.

Monty rooted in place in shock as she flipped on the overhead light, seeing the room illuminated. Color bounced from every direction. It was almost over-whelming compared to his sterile living quarters. A dark blue sofa with green and red pillows seemed strangely inviting. An antique chaise lounge was covered in a purple material and, with the pile of books on a small table next to it, the chair appeared to be well used.

Red curtains hung on the sides of the tall windows. To the right he could see into a large kitchen, stainless steel appliances stark against the soft yellow tiled back-splash. Distressed white cabinets were hung on the wall and underneath the counters.

To the left was an open door and he was able to see an unmade bed, the teal comforter crumpled at the edge. Not seeing another door, he assumed the bathroom was through the bedroom. He was almost afraid to see what colors it was decorated with.

At the far end of the living space was a long table, mismatched chairs around, waiting for a gathering of friends. It was not hard for Monty to imagine a group of Angel's friends doing just that. And the scent of sugared vanilla hung about the room, exuding a feeling of home.

Pulling his mind back to the matter at hand, he took her gently by the arm, leading her into the bedroom.

Angel glanced at her messy room and mumbled an apology. "I'm sorry. I'm really not a slob but, I confess I've had other things on my mind this week."

He sat her down on the edge of the bed and leaned down, peering into her eyes. They appeared clear, although she had dark circles underneath and bruising showing from the edges of her bandaged forehead.

"I know we need to talk, but right now you need your rest more than anything. I'll let you get comfortable and I'll wake you each hour to make sure you're still okay."

She returned his perusal. "Monty, I don't even know you. Why are you here?"

He sighed as he squatted in front of her. "I understand, Cupcake, but—"

"And why do you call me Cupcake?" she huffed, then quickly grimaced as the action caused a twinge in her head.

"It's a long story and can be saved for tomorrow," he said, watching her yawn. "Right now, you sleep. I'll watch over you and we'll talk in the morning." He looked at his watch showing two a.m. "Or rather, we'll talk later today."

Too tired to argue, Angel nodded and made her way into the bathroom. Once inside, she stared at herself in the mirror. *Holy moly!* Stunned, she gaped at the dried blood in her hair, it's rust color mixed in with her other signature colors. Her large blue eyes stared back, noting the dark circles underneath. Purple bruises were peeking from the edges of the bandage on her forehead.

She hung her head for a moment, overwhelmed with everything that had happened. *Oh, Marcia. What have you gotten yourself into? And what the hell am I trying to do to help? Jesus, I must be crazy.*

Turning on the water in the shower, she quickly stripped. Just as she was about to step into the water, she heard a knock on the door.

"Cupcake?" Monty shouted. "Don't get your stitches wet."

Her hand moved back to her forehead. "Gotcha!" she called back. Stepping into the shower, she let the water hit the back of her head, sluicing down her back. She gently washed her hair, desperate to clean the blood from her body. A quick scrub and she stepped out, toweling off.

The warm shower felt incredible, but she was exhausted from the effort. Pulling on clean panties and polka-dotted, flannel pajama bottoms, she carefully slid a large t-shirt over her head.

Walking out of the bathroom, she found Monty sitting

on the edge of her bed. Dark brown hair, trimmed neatly. Black dress pants creased at one time...now slightly wrinkled. A grey button-down dress shirt fitted to his apparently toned chest, blood stains marring the material. The top button was undone and she vaguely remembered that he had been wearing a now discarded tie. He was leaning forward with his elbows resting on his thighs, his head hanging down. It was the first time she had a careful look at him since he first burst through the motel door. His head lifted slowly and her eyes locked onto his blue-grey ones. A mixture of emotions poured off of him, not the least was anger. *Oh, what a colossal fuck up I've made!*

Stepping hesitantly into the room, nervously fingering the bottom of her pink t-shirt, she forced herself to move closer to him. "I...I need to apologize," she said, at first haltingly and then with more determination.

She wanted him to say something. Anything. Nothing came from his stone expression so she continued, "I was hoping to find...well, you see I have this friend and...I thought that I could find...it...um...I—"

"You think maybe you could finish one sentence before starting the next?" he asked, lifting his eyebrow, his grey-blue eyes piercing directly into her blue ones.

She pressed her lips together tightly, glaring daggers his way. "I was trying to apologize! And I thought we were going to talk tomorrow."

The silence pounded her head almost as much as the concussion. Her fingers lifted to the bandage on her forehead and she watched as he hung his head once more.

Suddenly he stood and walked over to her, looking down from his height. Her blonde hair was darker now that it was wet, but the purple, pink, and teal stripes could still be seen easily. His eyes moved from where her fingers touched the bandage, down her face and body, before lifting back to her eyes. "You need to rest. There's nothing we can do about Marcia right now and, after you sleep, we'll talk."

Tears hit the back of her eyes and she blinked several times rapidly to keep them at bay, but he noticed. He slid his hand to the back of her neck, giving a little squeeze before pulling her head toward his. Kissing the top of her head, he held her tightly for a second.

Reacting to the warmth of his nearness after the harrowing disaster of the evening, she leaned into his front. He slid his other arm around her waist, pulling her in closely. Her cheek rested against his chest and she shuddered. With chill or adrenaline crashing she had no idea.

Recognizing the after-effects of shock, Monty gave her the warmth of his body while making little comforting noises against her head. *When was the last time I comforted someone?*

His calm finally sunk in and Angel lifted her tearful face to his. Glancing down, she noticed the wet spots on the front of his silk shirt. "I'm sorry," she said, pushing back from his embrace.

He never looked down as he said, "Don't worry about it. Let's get you in bed."

For a second she wondered what it would be like for him to say those words to her and not mean sleep. Being comforted in his embrace, she felt his virile body...the ribbed muscles of his abdomen, the hard chest that felt perfect against her cheek, the muscular arms wrapped around her.

Blushing, she pushed the rest of the way back and simply nodded. Stepping toward the bed, she turned and asked, "Where will you sleep?"

His eyes shot to the bed behind her, for a second wishing the answer would be "with you", but he jerked his head toward her living area. "I'll be fine. Remember, I'll be waking you up every couple of hours."

Nodding again, she turned and climbed under the covers, pulling the messy sheets up over her. He leaned down, snagging the blanket and comforter, draping them over her as well. Unable to resist, he kissed the top of her head once more.

He waited for a few minutes until he saw her breathing even out and deepen. *What the hell was she doing tonight? And what the hell am I doing with her?*

He left the bedroom door partially open, then began to walk around the apartment. A desk in the corner yielded items concerning the bakery below but nothing pertinent to the case. At first glance upon walking into the room, the placement of furniture and the riot of color gave the appearance of a crowded space but, as he carefully walked around, he realized that she used the arrangement of items in the room to her advantage.

The apartment no longer seemed overstimulating; instead, he felt its warmth. As though the colors wrapped around him, chasing out the darkness of the night. Finding nothing significant, he lay down on the sofa after setting his watch alarm.

For a few minutes, he allowed his mind to rove over the events of the last several hours. Seeing her at the bar and wishing those eyes and that smile had been directed at him. Feeling jealous when he had never officially met her. The foolishness of following her to a hotel. The fear when he heard a struggle and the rage when he saw the man fighting with her. And seeing her unconscious on the floor...*Jesus, I've gone through more emotions in one night than I have in weeks. Maybe months. What the hell is it with this woman? She's turning me upside down.*

Before he knew it, his alarm went off and he moved

into the bedroom to wake her. He stood for a moment, staring at her face peacefully sleeping. Long lashes lay on her cheeks. Porcelain complexion glowed in the moonlight, except for the bruising on her forehead. Her long hair beckoned to his fingers, but he refused to give in to the urge. Finally, he gently shook her shoulder. She grumbled, but her eyes were clear and he managed to get her to drink some water. She grabbed his arm as he began to pull away.

"I'm cold," she mumbled. "Please stay with me."

Feeling her hand shiver on his arm, he slipped off his pants and shirt, leaving on his t-shirt and boxers, before sliding into the bed behind her. Pulling her in closely, he wrapped his arm around her waist as she laid her head on his shoulder.

"You're safe now," he whispered into her silky hair, sweetly scented with her floral shampoo. Assuming he would never sleep he forced his body to relax, hoping to create a comforting embrace for Angel. Before he knew it, he followed her into slumber.

7

The morning sun peeked through the blue sheers on the bedroom window, casting the room and its occupants in a calm glow. Opening his eyes, Monty was surprised to see a pair of crystal blue eyes peering directly into his. Embarrassed to have slept so soundly, he struggled to find something coherent to say.

Giggling, Angel put her finger on his lips. "You don't have to try to explain why you're in bed with me. I remember begging you to stay." Her expression sobered. "I was cold...and to be truthful, frightened...and you gave me comfort even though I know you were angry with me." Moving her finger ever so slightly across his lips with a feather-light touch, she whispered, "Thank you."

Before he responded, she moved out of the bed, grabbed some clothes from her closet and headed into the bathroom, closing the door behind her with a soft click. Her touch sent his blood rushing from his head to his dick, but he willed it to behave. Rolling to his back, he threw his arm underneath his head. The desire to pull her in closely and kiss her wildly until they were both naked and rolling in her bed was overwhelming. Shaking his head, he climbed out from under the covers determined to force his mind back to the case at hand.

Once behind the safety of the bathroom door, Angel stared at herself in the mirror again, noticing the purple bruise was much deeper in the light of day. Sighing deeply, she took care of business, pulled on comfortable clothes and tamed her hair. With a touch of makeup, she attempted to make herself less pale and to hide the dark circles, to no avail. A swipe of pink bubblegum lip gloss was the last thing she applied, more out of habit than anything else. She tried to keep her mind off the intriguing man whose arms held her in the night. Longing to wake up to him in different circumstances filled her thoughts. But she knew he was still angry. *What an idiot I was last night—it could have turned out so badly.* Looking at her bandage taped to her forehead...*or worse than it did.* Straightening herself, she sucked in a cleansing breath. *Time to face the music!*

Monty looked up as she walked out of the bathroom. Her long, blonde, colorful hair dry and tamed into a sleek ponytail. Wearing black leggings with an oversized green sweater, she nervously bit her bottom lip. His eyes dropped to her plump lip and the desire to be the one to nibble on it invaded his thoughts.

Before he spoke, she threw her shoulders back in determination, walked over with her hand outstretched, and said. "We've never been properly introduced. I'm Angel Cartwright. I own the bakery downstairs, Angel's Cupcake Heaven."

His mouth twitched in amusement as he took her hand in his, noting her fingers felt slim but strong. Her grip was firm, *probably from stirring untold bowls of cupcake batter,* but the idea of those fingers around his cock caused him to quickly drop her hand.

"Montgomery Lytton," he replied, shoving his hands in his pockets to discreetly adjust himself. "With Saints Protection & Investigations."

"Yes, you mentioned that last night. I assume you want to talk about...uh..."

"Absolutely," he answered, his voice smooth as velvet.

"Would you mind if we had a little breakfast first? I haven't eaten since lunch yesterday."

"Not at all," he replied, thinking that he would kill for a cup of coffee.

Offering a fleeting smile, she moved into the kitchen and within a few minutes plated a ham and cheese omelet and muffins she heated after taking them from the refrigerator. Serving it with juice and coffee, she set everything at the end of her long table.

He appreciated the bounty she so effortlessly created, and his eyes were drawn to the place settings. Deep purple placemats set off the white pottery plates. Folded pink napkins sat under the forks. He turned, looking back at her.

"What?" she asked defensively.

"Just wondering about your fascination with color, that's all."

Angel sat down at the table, carefully scrutinizing the man across from her. She considered responding to his quip, then decided to eat instead. *Why should I care that he's making fun of my home?* Refusing to let him know that his comment stung, she ate heartily.

Monty realized his observation bothered her and wanted to make it right somehow. "I didn't mean to insult your...um...apartment. It's very nice. I've just never seen... well, that is to say, the color is very...nice."

Angel looked at him for a second before bursting into laughter. "That was the strangest compliment I think I've ever heard," she giggled. Looking around, seeing her place through the eyes of a stranger, she admitted, "Yeah, I like color. It makes me happy."

Smiling at her easy acceptance of his awkward apology, he nodded. *Damn, her muffins are as good as her cupcakes.*

Within a few minutes, they finished breakfast and took the plates back to the sink. Giving them a quick rinse, she placed them in the dishwasher before turning to him as she dried her hands on a yellow dishtowel. "I suppose it's time to talk?" she mumbled, following him to her sofa.

"Yes, but first, I want to know how your head feels." he said, placing a finger on her forehead with a whisper-soft touch.

Battling the desire to close her eyes and lean into his hand, she admitted, "I have a little headache, that's all."

He took her by the shoulders, turned her and gently pushed her down on the sofa, saying, "Hang on."

Within a minute he had brought her more juice and a couple of Advil, watching as she swallowed gratefully.

Pulling up a dining room chair and placing it so he was directly facing her, he said, "Now's the time. I want you to start at the beginning of what the fuck you were doing last night."

She shot him a quelling glare, her lips thinning in irritation. "Look, I'm not some kind of idiot—"

"I'll be the judge of that."

Huffing, she replied, "Do you want me to talk or not?"

Obviously, his hard-ass expression was not going to get them anywhere, so he changed tactics. "Yes. Please tell me what's going on. That's the only way I'm going to be able to piece together what you know in order to help Marcia."

Her eyes widened as she leaned forward. "So you think something happened to her also?"

"Ms. Cartwright, please."

Leaning back, she nodded. "Marcia and I are sorority sisters. She and I stayed fairly close since we still live near each other. There are about six of us who get together every couple of months—oh, wait. That's what you saw the last time we met. I noticed you in the restaurant. And please, call me Angel."

"Yeah, I noticed you also," he admitted, a smile on his face.

Cocking her head to the side, she wondered if that was good or bad. *Oh, hell, that doesn't matter now!*

"Marcia and I would meet for drinks once a week or so." She saw his questioning expression. "Look, if you've been checking into Marcia, then I'm sure you've heard about her reputation. Quite frankly, I think it's more blown up than real but, yes, she's a...liberated woman."

"Liberated?"

Licking her lips in thought, she explained, "Marcia had no compunction about going to a bar, hooking up for the night with a man, and then not seeing him again." Piercing Monty with a stare, she added, "Men do it and are called studs. Players. Sowing their wild oats. Whatever. They get with their buddies, slap each other on the back, and act like they've just conquered the world. Women? They're labeled sluts. Whores. Bitches."

Monty nodded slowly, admitting silently he agreed with her assessment and cursed himself for wondering if Angel did the same.

"I admit bar pickups are not my thing, but I never judged Marcia for her ways."

Threading her fingers through her ponytail, she gazed down at her lap for a moment, sighing heavily. "I was supposed to meet Marcia the night she was last seen. But I ended up having a minor crisis in the bakery and I stayed late with a couple of employees." Lifting her eyes, she added, "I'm sure it wouldn't seem like a crisis to you, but for my business, it was."

He remained silent so she continued, bringing her legs up and crossing them Indian-style. "One of my employees mixed up two orders and we had a huge delivery the next day. So we stayed until about midnight, redoing the cupcake orders so that they would be ready to go. After they left, I stayed another hour creating a quick marketing advertisement so that we could sell the cupcakes not used for a reduced price. I didn't return back up here until almost one a.m."

He said nothing but his intense gaze stayed riveted to her, so she continued. "I got a message from her about eight." She stood, walked over to her large purse, and dug around for a moment. Finding her phone, she moved back toward him. With a few clicks of her fingers, she found what she was looking for.

Monty nearly grabbed the phone from her fingers, looking at the message.

Found a nice one- he's hot! Tall, blond, tashed.

Monty quickly scrolled up and down to determine if there were other texts from that night or yesterday, but found none. His eyes lifted to Angel's. "Did she usually text you about her hook-ups?"

"No, she didn't. When I called about seven to tell her that I could not make it, she joked that she would find a drinking replacement for me for the night. Then she joked that she'd let me know who I got replaced with and teased about me living vicariously through her. I didn't think anything about it at the time until I got a call from her father yesterday to see if I had seen her."

"Why would he call you?"

"It was in her daily planner that we were to meet at Eclipse for drinks at eight."

"Okay," Monty said, dragging the word out. "I get what happened so far. What I want to know is why you went looking for the guy yourself, nearly getting yourself killed in the process?"

"It seemed to make sense," she protested, then saw his incredulous expression. "Well, at first, it did. After Mr. Creston called to ask about Marcia and I told him that she had gone out by herself, he told me he was worried. Believe me, if Marcia doesn't show up for work, especially with a big meeting, there's a reason to be concerned. The police wouldn't investigate until she had been missing for twenty-four hours and since I knew where she had been and a bit of a description of who she had met, I wanted to check it out."

"You were carrying a gun, Angel. That hardly constitutes checking something out," he growled.

"Look, I knew what I was doing. I have a license to carry a concealed weapon. My dad was career Army and so is my brother. Both taught me how to shoot and how to defend myself. I wasn't going to walk into a situation unarmed and unprepared."

His face registered surprise, but his lips thinned in irritation. "Go on."

"I went to the same bar last night that we were supposed to meet at. My plan was to see if anyone fit the description. After all, isn't it true that criminals will go back to the scene of the crime?"

"How many fuckin' detective shows do you watch on TV?" he asked.

Her eyes widened as a blush began creeping from her chest to her bruised forehead. "I'm not stupid," she protested. "I wanted to see if someone matching that description came in again!"

"Then how did you end up in a hotel room with him, may I ask?"

"How do you know all of this? And why were you at the hotel?" Shock registered on her face. "Oh my God, with all that happened, I never asked you how you knew to be there! You were following too, weren't you? I was right! That guy is involved."

"I wasn't following him. I was following you!" Monty shouted, his voice laced with frustration as he rubbed his face a few times in an attempt to re-focus. *Jesus, this woman is infuriating!*

"Following me?" she asked, leaning back on the sofa. Her head pounded, but she wanted answers.

"Yes, you. I was at the bar, asking the bartenders if they had seen Marcia. I'd been to about five bars last night and a partner had been to a bunch of others. Eclipse was the last one and I'd decided to settle back and enjoy a drink. Saw you come in, get busy with some man at the bar, get drunk, and go off with him."

"I wasn't drunk!"

"I know that now, but it sure as hell looked like it then."

"That still doesn't explain why you followed us," she pointed out.

Heaving a deep breath, he forced his reply to soften. "I was concerned. Something about the man seemed off to me." Refusing to divulge that he noticed the man wore a wig, he continued, "I recognized you from the restaurant a month ago and also knew you were a sorority sister of the woman we're looking for."

Seeing her head cock to the side, he added, "Her father has asked Saints Protection & Investigations to work with the FBI in locating his daughter."

"I see," she admitted. Sighing as her fingers touched her

bandaged forehead once more, she said, "I'm sorry. I understand you were just doing your job."

"I still haven't made the leap from trying to see if you could locate the man Marcia met with and ending up fighting him in a hotel room," he prompted.

"I immediately saw that he was the only one in the bar that resembled Marcia's text. He made eye contact and smiled as I walked in. I wanted to get him to talk. You know, see if he came there a lot. See if he was the kind to be looking for a hook-up. I wanted to get him comfortable and then I was going to try to ask if he knew a friend of mine. At least, that was my intention when I first sat down. Right away, I noticed he wanted me to keep drinking. So I had two drinks with him but pretended that I had been drinking before coming to the bar. That made it easier to appear drunk when I wasn't. I tried to intimate I had a friend who I usually drank with but I got nothing out of him. Then I noticed something weird."

Monty's gaze stayed riveted on hers.

Leaning forward, a conspiratorial gleam in her eyes, she pronounced, "He was wearing a wig! And I think his mustache wasn't real." Angel then leaned back, her arms crossing over her chest, smiling. *Now, he'll take me and my suspicions seriously!*

Instead, Monty stood quickly almost knocking his chair backward. Stalking away for several paces he stared out the tall windows. Dragging his hand over his face once more, he suddenly turned, his face red with anger.

"You already had suspicions about this guy. Already thought he might be involved in the disappearance of your friend. And you still went off with him? Are you fuckin' crazy?" he yelled.

Tears of anger and frustration immediately hit her eyes

and she lost the battle to contain them. One after the other flowed down her cheeks as her fingers dashed them away.

Raising his head to the ceiling in a silent plea for patience, he walked over and sat next to her on the sofa, taking her hand in his. "Cupcake, I'm sorry. I'm not trying to be an asshole, but you gotta understand how much danger you placed yourself in last night."

Gulping back her tears, she nodded. After a minute, she became aware of his fingers rubbing gently across her hand in slow circles. The slight connection was calming... and stimulating at the same time. Aware of the handsome man sitting next to her, she once again wondered what it would be like to have him hold her hand out of affection and not necessity.

He leaned forward and grabbed a tissue from the box on the coffee table and handed it to her. "Here you go."

She wiped her eyes and blew her nose thankfully. Turning to look at him full on, she asked, "Why do you call me Cupcake?"

Giving a rueful snort, he explained, "A little over a month ago, my niece had a birthday party and my sister had the whole house decked out in pink, purple, and teal. And then she brought out these huge-ass cupcakes covered in a ton of pink, purple, and teal frosting. Mom talked about ACH and I didn't have a clue what she meant until she mentioned Angels Cupcake Heaven. They coerced me into eating one and, swear to God, I thought I was tasting heaven."

Her brilliant smile beamed at him, causing his heart to skip a beat. Her tired, red-rimmed eyes, dark circles underneath, runny nose, and bruises peeking from underneath the bandage—*still the most beautiful woman I've ever seen.*

"And when I saw you that night in the restaurant, I had

no idea who you were but, when I saw your hair...all I thought about were those cupcakes."

"My signature colors," she explained softly.

They sat in companionable silence for a moment, her hands back in her lap, but wishing his were touching hers again.

"To finish about last night," she said with a sigh, hating to dispel the truce they had achieved. "I could tell he wanted to get away from the bar. I knew I was armed. Knew I could defend myself. I just wanted to get him somewhere to ask about Marcia. I thought as soon as I did, I would be able to tell by the look on his face if he knew who she was and, if so, my plan was to hold him until the police could come. If not, then I would excuse myself, tell him I changed my mind and leave."

Her gaze implored his as she added, "Monty, it seemed like a good plan until he became angry. Not so much at me asking about Marcia as not willing to be there for sex. He made a play for the gun, and I was about to take his legs out from under him." Seeing the doubt in his eyes, she said, "Oh yeah. Believe me, my brother taught me some moves. But when the door flew open and you burst in, I lost my advantage and let him get the best of me."

Before Monty could chastise or question her more, his phone rang. Hitting the button, he answered, "Yes, boss?"

She watched as his face hardened, his grey-blue eyes turning stormy. He disconnected and before she asked, he stood, irritation pouring him. He had been ready to tear her a new one for her dangerous maneuvers in the hotel, but that would have to wait. Sighing, he rubbed his face, fatigue showing in his expression.

Turning, he said, "Get ready and grab your stuff. I've just been called into work for an emergency meeting and I want you to go with me."

She glanced at the clock and then back up to his face. "I can't! I've closed the bakery long enough. I'm late as it is today, so I've got to get downstairs."

"Angel, I don't know what's going on right now, but I want you with me so I can protect you."

"I told you, I can protect myself," she argued.

"Yeah, last night worked out so well for you, didn't it?" he growled.

Standing, she placed her hands on her hips. "Look, I've got a business to operate. I think whoever was in that hotel room is long gone. So unless you plan on kidnapping me, you run off to your little meeting and I'm going downstairs to open my business."

"Don't tempt me."

Cocking her hip, she tapped her toe on the floor. "I told you, I can handle myself."

Stepping closer until his shoes were in front of her pink toenails, he leaned down a breath away from her lips. "Someday, I'm gonna let you prove that to me, Cupcake."

Unable to stop himself, he planted a flash of a kiss on her lips before turning and walking to the door. Calling over his shoulder, he said, "I'll be back with whatever news I can find out and we've got more to discuss." With that, he stepped through the door, closing it behind him.

She stood in the middle of her apartment, not moving except for lifting her fingers to her lips, still tingling from the feathery kiss. *If they're quivering now, what would they do if he really kissed me?* she wondered.

Jolting out of her musing, she ran to change clothes before heading to the bakery downstairs.

8

M onty pulled through the security gate at Jack's and made his way toward the house. During the drive, his mind had been filled with the irritating, frustrating, maddening, and absolutely distracting Angel Cartwright. He tried to tell himself the gentle kiss he gave her meant nothing, but *Damn, if that isn't driving me to distraction!*

Arriving at the house, he met several of the others coming in at the same time. Blaise and Chad were back from D.C. and had already arrived. As everyone gathered around the main conference table, Jack eyed Monty. "Get anything from Ms. Cartwright?"

Reporting as succinctly as possible, he related what happened last night, both from his perspective and what she had explained. As his story came to the incident in the hotel room, the incredulous, and even angry, looks were shared by all.

"I don't care what her dad and brother taught her, going into a hotel room with someone she thought may have done something to her friend was crazy-ass irresponsible," Jude said, with nods of agreement from the others.

His fiancé, Sabrina, assisted the Saints when they were helping her grandmother, but his heart still stopped every time he remembered that she had been kidnapped in the process. Jude decided then and there—no more investigating for her.

Monty continued to explain the subsequent events at the hospital and then this morning's conversation.

"I'm surprised you didn't bring her in with you this morning," Marc added.

"Yeah, well, I tried. She's as stubborn as she is beautiful."

The other saints grinned as Monty drummed his fingers on the table. "Beautiful?" Blaise asked. "Hmmm, maybe I need to check on the intrepid Ms. Cartwright."

Monty's gaze jumped up to Blaise's. "Oh, no you don't. She's mine to take care of." Seeing the grins around the room, he immediately tried to back up. "Not like that," he protested. "I just mean since I'm heading this case, she's mine to...oh, hell, I don't know what she is."

The others laughed; this time, recognizing the signs of another Saint falling. "Don't fight it, bro. If it's happening, there's nothin' you can do to stop it," Cam advised, fist bumping Bart sitting next to him. The two friends had found love with the last two big cases the Saints had investigated.

"Do we need to be concerned about Ms. Cartwright's safety since this mystery guy is still missing?" Jack asked.

"She's at her bakery now and lives above it. I'm going back over there this evening. I did promise to keep her up on whatever we're finding out and she gave her word that she would not attempt to investigate anymore."

That settled, Blaise and Chad began reporting what they found out in D.C. "Marcia Creston's reputation for being driven in the workforce...and driven in the bedroom, extends to her friends outside just this area.

Although, other than her sorority sisters, she really hasn't stayed in contact with too many of her college friends," Blaise said, running his hand over his clean-shaven face.

Chad spoke up, "There was a Colonial Financial Group branch in Arlington and we found a few employees had transferred from the Charlestown office to there when Marcia took over. A couple of the men seemed to hold a grudge."

"You get anything else?" Monty inquired.

"Nah. We knew Luke was running their financials and sent him the names of the few friends we talked to," Chad added.

"What about the security camera from the bar last night?" Jack asked.

"Got it here," Luke replied. "I'll send it to everyone's tablets."

"You looking for the man at the bar?" Bart asked. "Think we can get an ID on him?"

"Gonna try. I talked to Mitch this morning and he's working with the hotel manager and trying to get prints lifted from the room."

Marc quipped, "Fuck, lifting prints from a hotel room would be like looking for the proverbial needle in a haystack."

"Right now it's the only lead we've got. Keep working it, guys. Marcia Creston's now been missing for about thirty-six hours," Jack ordered, his reserved demeanor firmly in place.

The meeting ended and everyone dispersed to their assignments. Monty shifted to a desk, taking his tablet with him. Pulling up Eclipse's security cameras from last night, he watched. His eyes moved over the vision Angel presented. Dressed to perfection. Hair, a riot of her—*what did she call it? Oh yeah, her signature colors.*

The mystery man was good at keeping his face turned toward her and not the camera. *He's been there before. He knows to where to look to avoid the camera.*

He watched the tapes over and over, but the view never changed. *Nothing. Abso-fuckin'-lutely nothing.* Except for her. He paused at the second she threw her head back and laughed. Reaching out his finger he traced over her image, committing it to memory. His phone rang, jolting him from his thoughts and he answered to find Mitch on the line.

"Monty? I wanted to let you know first, although right now, someone is informing the Senator and his wife."

As though plunged into icy water, a cold dread hit him as he waited for the news.

"Marcia Creston's body was found this morning."

"Fuck!" he growled.

"There was nothing we could have done," Mitch added. "It looked like she had been dead about twenty-four hours, but we'll know more when the medical examiner is finished."

"Where was she found?"

"A farmer's field, about five miles outside of town. She was shot at close range."

"Send me what you've got. I'll tell Jack and the men," Monty said, as his mind jumped to the beautiful baker who also needed to be told.

After another few minutes, he disconnected and glanced over at Luke. "Call the others back in. Hopefully, they haven't gone too far."

Thirty minutes later, they gathered around the table once again, with Mitch on the conference video.

"The initial report is in. Marcia Creston had sexual intercourse but there is no evidence of forced trauma. The medical examiner concludes that it was consensual. In fact, other than the gunshot wound, there are no other wounds on her body. No signs of struggle, no cuts, abrasions, or bruises."

"So she knew her murderer," Blaise surmised.

"Or at least, knew him well enough to have sex with him," Bart replied. "He could have been a one-night stand. She might have known nothing about him other than he was a body for a night."

The idea of how close Angel was to the same outcome had Monty's heart pounding. And now...he needed to tell her about Marcia.

Three hours later, Monty entered the bakery, this time, less overwhelmed by the abundance of color. The front was completely glass with the words Angel's Cupcake Heaven scrolling across the windows. The establishment was long, with display cases along the right side. Three walls were done in contrasting colors of pink, purple, and teal. *Of course,* he realized. *When she referred to her signature colors, she meant in everything.* The back wall included a mural of a medieval monk baking in an old stone oven.

Tables lined the left side and as his eyes moved toward the back, he saw a much larger seating area filled with little girls. Recognizing a birthday party in full swing, he watched as Angel came from the back with a platter of cupcakes, similar to the ones at his niece's party. Her smile was genuine and from his distance, he could see that she used makeup to cover the bruises on her forehead and replaced the large bandage from the hospital with a much smaller one.

"Can I help you, sir?" a spritely voice from behind the counter asked.

At first glance, he did not see anyone until he moved closer. A short teenage girl worked the counter and stood on her toes smiling at him. An older woman came from the back, filling the cases. Both women wore pink polo shirts with their names embroidered in swirls over their hearts under the initials ACH.

He leaned closer to the older woman and asked, "Will the party be over soon?"

Helen glanced at the group and then back to him, uncertainty on her face. "I..I—"

"Ma'am, I need to speak to Ms. Cartwright and it's serious. When I talk to her, she'll need to be alone and will need someone to close up the shop today."

"Is this about that friend of hers? The missing one?" Helen whispered. At his nod, she turned, grim-faced, toward the girl. "Chelsea, keep things going up here until I come back."

Helen walked to the back, over to Angel and whispered in her ear. Monty watched as Angel's eyes immediately cut over to his, a question in her expression. Not giving anything away, he willed her to not make a scene.

Smiling at the children that were already finishing the pile of cupcakes, she spoke quietly to Helen, who then moved over to the party. He watched as Angel walked toward him, her smile was in place but her hands nervously fluttered by her side. He stepped closer to the door as she neared, wanting as much privacy as possible. She stopped directly in front of him, her hand reaching for his arm.

"What?" She swallowed hard several times as her voice cracked, but managed to speak again, "What do you need to tell me?"

Monty raised his hand, clasping hers in his warmth. His voice, low and smooth, said, "Cupcake, let's go up to your place." He could see her start to protest, then stopped. Glancing back at Helen and receiving a nod, she turned back to face him again. Her mouth opened and closed twice but no words came out. Finally nodding, she allowed him to lead her to her apartment.

Once inside, Monty, with their fingers still linked, led her to the sofa and sat down, gently pulling her down next to him. She peered deeply into his eyes, both her hands now firmly clasped in his.

"I'm afraid for you to speak," she whispered, searching his eyes for anything other than dread.

"Angel, I'm so sorry—"

"She's dead isn't she?" she cried, her fingers digging into his.

In a flash, all the times as an FBI agent he had to tell a family member their loved one was dead flew through his mind. It was business. Painful, but business. But this? *Fuckin' hell!* Knowing his words were going to cause Angel pain slashed through him.

"Yes, she's dead. Her body was found this afternoon."

For a second he was not sure she had heard him. Her face, motionless. His fingers flexed on hers and he watched as her face crumpled. She pitched forward toward him just as he pulled her into his embrace. No sound came from her at first, then a wail erupted from deep inside as the sobs consumed her. Nothing was said for several minutes as her body jerked against his. He willed his strength into her, knowing it was little he could offer.

"I...I...was...so...a...afraid...this was...going to be... what...you were going...to tell...me," her voice hiccupped between sobs.

He rubbed her back, murmuring comforting words in her ear over and over until the sobs slowed. For a while she sat, her face tucked under his chin, as the steady beat of his heart pounded underneath her palm resting on his chest.

Taking several shuddering breaths, she gradually calmed. "I don't care what anyone else says, she was a good person...a good friend."

"Tell me about her," he said softly. She leaned back and looked at him in doubt. "No, no," he assured. "Not me, the investigator. Just talk to me, the...uh...friend."

Nodding thoughtfully, she looked over his shoulder as memories flooded back. "Her parents were wealthy, but she never acted like it. She could have pledged any sorority, but wanted to be with our group. We were simple, but really did a lot of community service and she said she liked that. She never forgot birthdays and stepped in to help in ways that didn't make you feel obligated."

"How'd she do that?"

Leaning over to grab a tissue, Angel wiped her eyes and nose before continuing. "When I first opened my bakery, she believed in me. Encouraged me. But knew that business would be slow to start. She got her mom to use me to cater some of her parties. She was always doing things like that to help and never asked for anything in return."

Monty encouraged her to talk, to remember, to begin to grieve. He held her close for over an hour as she leaned into his strength. Finally, she shifted back against the cushions, taking a deep breath. Looking to the side, she saw her mascara stained tear trails all over his shirt and weakly moved her hand to touch the wetness. "I'm sorry. Now, I've ruined two of your shirts."

He glanced down at the evidence of her grief on his shirt, usually hating for his clothes to be mussed, and lifted his gaze back to her watery one. "No worries," he promised and meant the words.

Nodding, she heaved another huge sigh before saying,

"I've got a lot to do. I've got to call the other sisters. Talk to Marcia's parents. I'll need to—"

"Take it slow, Cupcake," he said, linking his fingers with hers again as they sat side by side on the sofa. The evening sun warmed the colors in the apartment, as well as glistening off her hair. Tucking a wayward strand behind her ear, he advised, "You've got time to take care of everything." Turning her face toward his with his fingers on her chin, he added, "I'll help. I'll do anything to help."

She looked at him, her brow knitted in confusion. "Why would you help, Monty?" Her eyes sought his as she leaned slightly closer to him.

He brought his face to hers, holding her gaze. "Because I care, Angel. I care." With that, he leaned the rest of the way in, sealing his lips over hers. Her lips were just as he imagined. Soft. Pliant. Tasting of bubblegum.

Angel leaned in further to the kiss. His lips were firm and bold. Soft and strong. She felt his tongue sweep across her seam and she opened for him. He owned the kiss as though he wanted to own her body and at that moment she could think of nothing else but the pleasure he gave. She brought her hands up to his neck, tangling her fingers in the hair at the back of his head, pulling him in closer.

Growling in her mouth, Monty wanted to run his hands along her body, but forced them to just hold her instead. She tasted of heaven and her silky hair caressed his skin as he allowed the colorful strands to slide over his fingers. Moments later, reality pushed its way into his consciousness and he pulled back, resting his forehead on the non-injured side of hers.

Both gulped in air, the kiss having robbed them of oxygen while supplying them with everything that seemed necessary.

"I'm sorry," he mumbled awkwardly, then looked at the

hurt flashing through her eyes. "No, no, I mean, I'm sorry for taking advantage of your vulnerability."

She stared long and hard at his face, dropping her eyes to his lips. "It's okay," she said. "I needed to connect with another human." Then, almost as an afterthought, added, "And I needed it to be you. I wanted it to be you."

9

Standing in his stark condo three days later, Monty checked his navy tie before putting his suit coat on in readiness for attending the memorial service for Marcia Creston. The body had not been released by the medical examiner but the Senator and his wife elected to have a memorial service now and then a private burial at a later date. Pulling on his black overcoat, he anxiously awaited seeing Angel, having not seen her since he left her apartment knowing she needed time to make arrangements and be with family and friends. They had spoken on the phone each day as he strangely concluded he wanted to, at least, hear her voice. No longer forcing her from his mind, he now admitted how much he wanted to be with her again.

Arriving at the massive church, Monty sat near the back, watching as hundreds of mourners paid their condolences to Marcia's parents. The Senator stood at the front, clasping hands as people moved past. His wife, fragile in appearance, occasionally sat in a chair next to him.

Monty's gaze moved through the crowd purposefully before alighting on the object of his interest. Looking very different from when he first saw her, she wore her hair pulled back away from her face, although the striking colors still gleamed. Attired in a dark, modest dress paired with black, heeled boots, she looked every bit the businesswoman that would typically catch his eye. And while she was appropriately dressed for a funeral, he missed the colorful, smiling woman who captured his attention.

She moved among a few of the mourners before settling down with a group of other young women, several he recognized from the restaurant. Forcing his eyes to continue to move over the room, his gaze continually roved to her.

Bart slid into the pew next to him, the two acknowledging each other with a nod. "Anything?" Bart inquired.

"Not that I can tell. I keep looking for a man fitting the description of who Marcia was with last but, honest to God, there are so many people here it's difficult to see everyone."

"Yeah, and if he was in disguise then, or now, we might not be able to tell."

The minister moved to the front of the church and the service began. After the music and prayers, he asked for Ms. Cartwright to please come forward. Monty's gaze followed Angel as she made her way to the front. Her smile was missing. Her colorful clothes were missing. Her face was pale, contrasting with the dark dress. *I miss my Cupcake. Mine?* He blinked rapidly, wondering where the thought came from. *We're friends. I like her. Respect her. Admire her. But mine?* Pushing those thoughts to the back of his mind, he concentrated on her words.

Angel, never nervous in front of a large group, looked down to see her hands shaking on the podium. She breathed deeply and looked out over the congregation. Her eyes immediately landed on Monty sitting near the back.

His gaze pierced hers. *How, in this crowd, did I find him?* Offering him the tiniest of smiles, she felt his warmth sliding over her.

She began her eulogy, extolling the side of Marcia she knew...and loved. Mentioning some of the fun sorority stories, she managed to bring the crowd to smiles several times and won nods of appreciation from Marcia's parents. Ending, she said, "Life is always changing, often in ways we cannot comprehend." Looking down at the pew with the other sorority sisters sitting with hands clasped together, she continued, "Just last month, we lost another sister so tragically. Theresa and Marcia's passings leave us with a tremendous hole in our sisterhood, but we will hold onto their memories forever."

Stepping down, she made her way back to her pew, sliding in and accepting the hugs from the other women.

The Senator stood to speak next, but Monty and Bart looked at each other, both knowing what was racing through their minds. *Another sorority sister died tragically?*

Bart whispered, "Are you thinking what I'm thinking?"

Monty felt his heart pound as he nodded. "This may not be about Marcia at all."

———

After the service, Bart left quickly as he needed to get back to Jack and Mitch about the possibility of a connection between the two deaths.

Monty moved through the crowd toward Angel and stayed in the background until she was free from others. She smiled as she stepped over to him and, much to his surprise—and pleasure—she stepped straight into his arms, squeezing tight around his waist as he pulled her in.

Kissing the top of her head, he said, "How're you holding up?"

She leaned her head back so she could see into his eyes. Sucking in a deep breath, she replied, "Okay. I'm okay. Not great…but okay."

She pressed her cheek against his chest, remembering three days ago when she did the same as her anguish poured from her. Relishing the feel of his warmth and not wanting to let go, she wondered how quickly he had become important to her. *Rescuer admiration? Or a true connection?* Deciding not to worry about the cause, she reveled in his embrace.

Bending down, Monty whispered in her ear, "Do you need to go to the reception?" Feeling her nod against his chest, he said, "Can we talk privately for a few minutes before I leave?"

"Sure," she replied and moved away from his hug while linking her fingers with his, leading him to a small alcove near the back of the church. Looking up, she saw questions in his eyes. *God, please no more bad news.*

"You mentioned another sorority sister had recently died."

Confusion marred her expression. "Uh, yeah. Theresa Constantine. She lived in Richmond but her family is in Arlington. Why are you asking?"

"How did she die?"

"She was killed in a car accident about four weeks ago." Moving back a step, she stared at his face, trying to discern the thoughts behind those intelligent eyes. "Monty, what's going on? Why are you interested."

Leaning down to kiss her forehead, he admitted, "I'm just curious, that's all. It seems odd that two sorority sisters would die within such a close timeframe."

"Theresa's car skidded on some ice. There was nothing about her death that in any way resembled Marcia's."

He felt the stiffening of Angel's body in his arms and recognized the physical response. "Don't worry about it Cupcake. I'm sorry to have questioned you, but you've got to understand that the FBI, as well as the Saints, need to follow up on anything that could be related."

Angel relaxed against him once more, allowing herself to take another minute to feel the strength of his heartbeat against her cheek.

"You go on to the reception, Cupcake. I've got some more work to do and will call you later. Okay?"

Smiling up at him, she replied "Okay." Then, as an afterthought, she added, "If you happen to come by later, I'll be in the bakery. I've got a job for tomorrow I have to get ready for. I gave my staff this afternoon off and I'm going to be working by myself."

"Can you do all the baking yourself? Why don't you have your staff help? Or, at least, call in Helen."

She shrugged a little, her eyes moving to look over his shoulder into the distance. "I...I think I want to be alone for a while." She brought her gaze back to his. "Baking is comforting to me."

Nodding his understanding, he bent to place a whisper soft kiss on her lips, eliciting another smile. He stood, watching as she moved away from his body, their hands still linked. When the only thing left touching was their fingertips, she looked back over her shoulder giving him a wink as she headed toward her group of friends.

His displeasure at seeing her walk away mixed with the anticipation of seeing her again soon. Heart pounding, he tried to remember the last time he ever felt this way about a woman. And came up empty. Shaking his head, he stalked toward his SUV. Time to find out what happened to Theresa Constantine.

Meeting back at the compound, Monty found several of the Saints already gathered and combing through the death of Theresa. He had called ahead, giving them her name. Settling in his seat, he pulled up the latest information Luke had sent.

"Angel said that Theresa slid on the ice and crashed her car," he said.

"Well, that appears to be partially true," Jack replied, giving Monty a chance to catch up. "She was driving in the snow, but there may have been a reason to consider foul play."

Luke took over the explanation. "It seems she was living with a man who had an abusive streak. Geoffrey Daly. Theresa called the police three times in two years for domestic situations but never followed through with a formal complaint. He'd been in juvie years before for anger issues against his parents."

"Got juvie records?" Bart asked, a smirk on his face, knowing Luke's penchant for finding just about anything they needed.

Luke just grinned. "There was a life insurance policy that at one time had Geoffrey's name on it."

"At one time?" Monty inquired.

"Yeah. It seems as though she changed it to her niece about four months before her death. Right after the last police call."

"Who's taking bets she never told Geoffrey he was no longer named as the beneficiary?" Chad quipped, receiving nods from the others.

"He's listed as a mechanic. Did the police check out her vehicle to see if it had been tampered with?" Jack asked.

Luke scrolled through the information he had obtained. "Doesn't look like the police opened a formal investigation at all. It was snowy, icy and they ruled it an accident."

Monty patched Mitch through on conference video and he listened as they relayed the quick version of Theresa's death to him.

"You know the Bureau won't open an investigation into her death based on the two women being sorority sisters, but..." Mitch grinned, "that's where you being a private investigation service can check on things. Just don't tell me how you do it and for Christ's sakes, if you find something, get it to me so I can legally get the evidence."

"On it," Jack agreed as they disconnected with Mitch. Looking around the table, he said, "This gives us a new direction to focus on. Bart, you and Cam know what you need to do. Find Theresa's car and see what you can come up with. Luke, you and Blaise need to work the financials of both women and see if you can come up with a link. Monty, why don't you interview her parents. Chad, see what you can get about her insurance policy left to her niece."

With the renewed vigor of a case that became more complicated, they all headed out. Monty sent a text to Angel asking her to call him as soon as she could. An hour later, she called.

"Hey, Cupcake. I'm going to Arlington tomorrow morning to talk to Theresa's parents, and wondered if—"

"Why?" she interrupted brusquely.

"Right now we don't have any evidence that the two deaths are related, but..." he paused for emphasis, "we don't know that they aren't."

Silence greeted him, so he plunged on. "We want to

know who murdered Marcia, and if there's any chance the two are related, then don't we owe it to her to try to find out?"

"Okay," she said slowly, drawing the word out as her mind raced with the implications. "But Monty, Theresa's parents are having a hard time and I hate to have them suffer more."

"Well, that's why I hoped I could talk you into going with me." He knew she had a large order to fill, so he plunged on. "If I came over tonight, I could...I don't know...maybe help and then, if your staff can take care of things tomorrow, we can drive up right after lunch."

"You want to help tonight?" she asked, a chuckle breaking out. "I'm not sure I see you icing cupcakes in your suit and tie."

"Hey, I have other clothes I can wear," he protested. Sobering, he added, "I know you wanted to be alone but, if I promise to stay out of your way and only help with things I can do, will you consider it?"

Not hesitating, Angel agreed. "Yeah, come on over. Just come to the back door since the front store will be closed."

"See you in an hour," he replied, his heart light. Smiling, he changed into jeans and an old t-shirt hoping it would be appropriate attire for...*whatever the hell I've got myself into tonight.*

The bright lights of the industrial kitchen bounced off the gleaming stainless steel appliances and counters, now covered with an array of swirls of color. Monty began the evening standing awkwardly as he watched Angel move with lightening speed around her bakery's kitchen. Mixing ingredients, pouring the batter into cupcake tins, then lifting the large trays into the industrial oven, she started the next batch.

For the next round, Monty did the pouring under Angel's watchful gaze and laughed as she pronounced him Prince of Pouring.

"Is that a title I can keep?" he teased.

"Absolutely, but you really want to earn the next promotion...the King of Cupcakes," she bantered, smiling as he filled the tins.

Once the first batch came out of the oven, she mixed her frosting and added colors before filling the bags. He watched in fascination as she decorated each one with perfect swirls, some topped with sprinkles. Pink. Purple. Teal.

He wondered if she would resent his presence but, as she worked, they talked. About families, jobs, Marcia...the topics simply flowed from one to the other. He admired her ass in the tight, black yoga pants molded to her perfect form. An apron, sporting a cupcake motif and the letters ACH across the chest, covered her t-shirt but hid nothing of her figure. Her shiny hair was pulled back into a bun with a sheer hair-net holding every strand in place.

"So you didn't become the lawyer, politician, or future judge that your parents wanted?"

Wiping the counters between each batch, he shook his head. "Nope. And believe me, they've never let me or my sister forget it."

"What did they want from her?" Angel asked with curiosity.

"She's a teacher and had just gone back to work full time now that my niece is in kindergarten. But...well, she's pregnant again so she'll go back to part time for a few more years."

Seeing the curious expression on her face, he continued, "Mom and dad would gladly pay for a nanny, but Felicity wants to be a stay-at-home mom while the kids are little."

"Good for her," Angel said. "I think that's wonderful!"

"Well, money is tight. Bob's a high school teacher and coach. My parents would have preferred her to have married someone with more ambition. They've hinted that he should obtain his administrative degree, become a principal and then move up to a school board office position."

Stopping in the middle of a swirl, Angel turned toward him, watching as he leaned his hip against the counter, one leg crossed in front of the other. His slightly faded jeans were tight across his thighs, and delectably faded at his crotch. *Lord, what that man can do to a pair of jeans!* He looked great when he was dressed up—he looked amazing when comfortable. Jolting herself from her lustful stare, she said, "I take it that career path does not suit your brother-in-law?"

Laughing, Monty shook his head. "Nope. Bob loves the classroom. He's good at teaching and is a great coach. He's not about to change that."

Continuing to decorate at record speed, she replied, "Good for him!"

"So tell me about your family. I already know your dad was career Army and he taught you to shoot." He caught her grin and continued, "And your Special Forces brother taught you self-defense moves. What else can I learn about Angel, the Cupcake Queen?"

Throwing her head back in laughter, she said, "What do you want to know?"

Everything, he found himself thinking. *What you think? What you feel? How you take your coffee? What you do on your days off? Every-fuckin'-thing.* "Um, anything you want me to know," he answered, afraid to give voice to his musings.

"Well, you know about my dad and brother. My mom is really great, too. They always wanted my brother and me to be whatever we wanted to be. I went to college to get a marketing and business degree but took culinary baking classes on the side at a community college. I knew I wanted to be a baker since I was a little girl." She turned to him and asked, "Do you remember the first time you wanted to be in law enforcement?"

He thought for a moment and said, "I can't really give you a definitive answer. I knew I didn't want to be a lawyer. It was more catching the criminals than prosecuting or defending them that appealed to me. Why?"

"Because I can remember the very first time I wanted to bake." She finished the last cupcake in the last batch and had Monty move the heavy tray to the refrigerator. Wiping her hands, she sat on a stool as he leaned his hip back against the counter again.

"I was about ten years old and my family was traveling from Arlington to Richmond and we stopped at the town of Fairfield. Driving through the quaint downtown area, we saw a bakery with a pink and white awning outside. Hungry, we stopped. It was Bernie's Bakery and the inside was just as charming. And the pastries? Oh, my God, they were good. Bernadine McDonald was the owner and she came out to talk to us. She took me in the back to show me where she created her magic."

Monty watched as Angel related the tale of the bakery, her hands waving as she talked, her pink lips smiling at the memories. He could easily imagine her enthusiasm in discovering the establishment, much like the little girls who were now feeling the same about Angel's Cupcake Heaven.

"Anyway, years later, I went back to Fairfield and Bernie was kind enough to give me tips about ingredients, suppliers, ways to keep track of everything. She was amazing. I still keep up with her, and when she's in town or I'm passing through Fairfield, we always manage to chat for a while."

Monty pushed off the counter and walked slowly toward her stool until he stopped. Right in front of her. He watched as her chest heaved and her tongue darted out to lick her already moist lips. He lifted his hand to cup her cheek, his thumb caressing her petal-soft skin.

She leaned her head into his hand, closing her eyes as she allowed his caress to soothe her. Opening her eyes, she saw he had leaned down and was a whisper away from her lips. His breath brushed warm against her face as he hesitated long enough for her to decide. She smiled her decision.

10

Seeing her acquiescence, he captured her lips with his, drowning in their taste. Moist sweetness coated his lips and tongue as he plundered her mouth. Tracing the ridges and tangling his tongue with hers, he moved closer, wrapping his arms around, pulling her body until it was pressed tightly to his. Angling his head for better access, he melded his mouth with hers.

She heard a moan, unsure which of them it came from, but regardless it sent a jolt to her core. With one of his thighs pressed between her legs, she moved closer wanting the rough denim to rub against her. *Jesus, how long has it been? I could come, dry-humping his leg.* Another moan was heard and, this time, she knew it had escaped from her. Wrapping her arms around his neck, she lifted herself from the chair, pressing her breasts against his broad chest.

Taking over, Monty stood holding her up with one muscular arm banded around her waist. He walked her backward until her back was pressed against the wall of the kitchen. He used the restraint of the wall to help hold her up while he kept one arm next to her head and the other on her ass.

She wrapped her legs around his trim waist, pulling his erection directly to her crotch. Angel moved on instinct, the rational voices in her head reminding her she did not do one-night stands drowned out by the sounds of her own moans. Feeling the pressure of his jean clad dick pushing against her aching core, she rubbed on him as her body screamed for friction.

His hand slid behind her, giving the strings to the apron a tug, loosening them. With a quick pull, the apron flew over her head and onto the floor.

She was dimly aware of her t-shirt being lifted and her bra cups pulled down, freeing her full breasts. Her dusty-colored nipples were hard, but whether it was from the cool air of the kitchen or the heat from their bodies, she did not know. She did not care.

Monty kissed his way down from her mouth to suck on the wildly beating pulse at the base of her neck. She arched her back wanting her nipples to come in contact with his shirt, but then decided she wanted his shirt off. Reaching down to grab the bottom, she jerked until it cleared his head and joined the apron on the floor.

Needing no other invitation, he lifted one breast to his mouth and, pulling one nipple in deeply, sucked hard, first nipping with his teeth and then soothing with his tongue. Raising his eyes, he saw her head thrown back against the wall, eyes closed tightly, her kiss-swollen, bubblegum lips curving into a smile. Moving to the other breast, he gave it equal attention, not remembering the last time he suckled a woman for the pure pleasure it gave her. Or him, for that matter. Sex had almost become perfunctory—*God, when did that happen?* All he knew was he was unable to remember the last time he was lost in a woman.

Angel, the euphoria of the feelings washing over her, gave in entirely. Her hands grasped his hair as she pulled him in closer. With his mouth finding hers again, she was barely aware of being lowered to the ground until she felt her yoga pants being jerked down along with her panties, before being lifted back up. Now there was nothing between his jeans and her pussy. The sensation was sweet agony. She began grinding her clit on his jeans again and knew she was close to the goal. Dimly aware of his movements, she realized, *I'm going to come just dry humping,* as she heard the sound of his zipper. Then it stopped.

Monty pushed away from her, pausing as he breathed deeply. Seeing her questioning gaze, he said, "I want this, Cupcake. You gotta believe I want this. But not here. Not rushed."

"There are the back stairs to my apartment," she said, her words an invitation.

Smiling, he swung her around and stalked to the bottom of the stairs. Mounting them quickly, he dipped to open the door at the top, leading into the living room.

"I thought this door was a closet," he confessed.

"It's a great way to get to my bakery without having to use the outside door."

"Very convenient," he said, wiggling his eyebrows. "Bed?"

"No. Here. Now." Grasping his face, she pulled him back in, latching onto his lips, desperate for his touch…his taste.

Whirling, he pressed her up against the wall next to the brightly colored curtains. Their tongues tangled once again, stealing his breath. Reaching down he moved his fingers through her slick folds, pressing his thumb against her clit.

Already on the precipice, his touch on her sensitive

flesh plunged her over the edge. Slamming her head against the wall, she screamed.

"Are you okay?" he asked, not sure if her exclamation was from excitement or pain. Or maybe both.

"Yes, yes, yes," she panted, as her orgasm washed over her. Lowering her head so that they were eye to eye, she moaned, "Now. I need you inside me now!"

He reached between them to finish unzipping his jeans, releasing his swollen cock. "Oh, fuck, I gotta get a condom," he swore. *Smooth, real smooth.* Usually suave, he could not remember ever losing control like this. With one hand on her ass and his body pressing hers against the wall, he reached down and jerked out his wallet.

She took it from his hands and with a quick search, the condom was pulled out before the wallet was tossed to the floor. He was able to free his hands to roll the condom on quickly.

Lifting her in his strong arms, he seated her right at the tip of his cock. Pulling away from her kiss swollen lips, he pierced her with his look. "Last chance, Angel."

The roar of passion in her ears, drowning out all other thoughts, had her pulling his head back down to hers. *Whatever comes, I need this now!*

No more hesitation, he plunged his dick to the hilt in her wet pussy, the tightness of it almost making his knees buckle. *Jesus, she's tight...and perfect.*

He watched her beautiful face as her eyes hooded with passion while her pussy grabbed his dick in its vice. Her inner muscles clenched around him and he began thrusting in and out, his control slipping. He wanted her to come again with him but was afraid he could not last. Once more moving his hand between their bodies, he found her swollen nub. Giving it a pinch while sucking on her nipples, he felt her fingernails dig into his shoulders as she cried out her release. With only a few more thrusts, his neck strained as he threw his head back, the veins standing out, and he roared.

She watched as he leaned his head back as his orgasm ripped through him, before pressing it against the wall next to her. She could not decide if she wanted to lick his neck, nibble on his jawline, or kiss the shoulders she bruised with her fingers.

Monty kept his head against the wall until he could catch his breath. *Fuck, she's killin' me. Never. It's never felt like that before.* Fucking her against the wall had not been his intention...at least not the first time, but when she begged, all he wanted to do was give. *Never before has it felt this good. This right. I haven't let go...really let go...with a woman in...never.*

Bodies dripping in mingled sweat, breathing ragged, the two of them clung to each other in the aftermath until slowly the cool air around them began to seep into their consciousness.

Lifting his head to hers, he placed a gentle kiss on her forehead, next to the bandage. "Fuck, Cupcake. I didn't hurt you, did I?"

Moving her lips softly over his, she murmured, "Uh um, Monty. The only way you could hurt me now would be to walk away."

He smiled, loving the way she played no games. No pretense. Just the real Angel. "Not leaving unless you kick me out." He pulled out and set her feet on the floor. "Let me go take care of this," he nodded downward, indicating the condom.

"I'll run down and grab our clothes," she said.

"No way," he admonished. "I'll go get them."

Within a few minutes, he was back in her apartment, watching as she slid his t-shirt over her head. His dick jumped again at the sight of her. Seeing her full breasts filling his shirt and the way it draped over her delectable ass, he knew he would never look at his t-shirts the same again. Stalking over, he smiled as they moved into the kitchen.

Eyeing his naked chest, barely hiding her smirk, she said, "You definitely became the King of Cupcakes."

Laughing, he planted a kiss on her sweet lips. "What're you doing now?" he asked, seeing her pull out a frying pan.

"I thought I'd scramble some eggs if that's okay," she replied.

Realizing he had not eaten since earlier in the day, he nodded. "Sounds great."

Within a few minutes, she plated scrambled eggs, bacon, and toasted bagels. She tried to eat but kept stealing glances at the man sitting across from her. He now looked comfortable in her apartment surround by the colors that made her so happy. Occasionally catching him staring at her as well, she grinned. By the time they finished eating, she began to feel sleepy. He watched as her mouth opened wide, the yawn impossible to extinguish.

"I guess I'd better let you get to bed," he said, regret filling his voice. "I can't remember the last time I had such an enjoyable evening, Angel."

Suddenly unsure, she stood fingering the ends of his t-shirt. "You know you can always spend the night here if you want."

"It wouldn't be the first time," he joked.

"But, this time, you can sleep in my bed from the start," she smiled, turning with the empty plates in her hand as she flounced toward the kitchen, shaking her ass as she walked.

He followed, capturing her around her waist and twirling her back toward his rock hard body. Leaning down, he whispered in her ear, "There's nowhere else I'd rather be."

Waking from a sound sleep, Angel knew the engulfing warmth was from Monty's body curved around hers. Not wanting to turn and possibly disturb him, she lay for a few minutes relishing in the feel of his arm around her waist, his hand curled near her breast. Not one to fall into bed with someone she just met, this felt right. *Slow down, girl. Just because he's handsome, has a rockin' body, is fabulous at sex, is honorable, trustworthy, caring, and helps with making cupcakes, there's no reason to think he wants anything more than this.* Her mind wandered to the last time she felt this way...and came up empty.

Opening her own business consumed all of her time and energy. Working from about four a.m. until late at night left little time for a relationship. Or casual dating. Or going out. Or even sweaty sex against the wall. A smile crept across her face as she remembered last night. He felt different—was different. But whether or not he felt the same stole the smile from her face. *Maybe I'm only part of this case.*

A tight squeeze from the arm banding around her body startled her from her musings. His nose nuzzled her ear and whispered, "Morning, Cupcake. I can hear your mind whirling from here. What's got you thinking so hard this morning?"

She twisted around in his arms, seeing his sleep-tousled hair, stubble on his jaw, and piercing grey-blue eyes focused directly on her. "Um...just business. I always wake up with the business on my mind. You know...um...what needs to be done today, that sort of thing."

Offering a smile, she instinctively moved her hand up to cup his jaw, loving the feel of his rough beard beneath her fingers.

His sharp gaze was taking her in as well. The colors in her hair glistened in the morning sun. The bruising was much less, mostly covered by the small bandage. Her sky-blue eyes were roaming over his face and her smile gave evidence she liked what she saw. "While I have no doubt that you wake up thinking about your business most mornings, Angel, I gotta believe that your mind was on something else today."

She started to deny his observation but found she had no desire to lie. Huffing slightly, she lowered her gaze. "You're right. I was thinking about last night." Once more peering into his eyes, she admitted, "Monty, I wanted what we did last night and the fact that you wanted to stay was perfect. I just don't do...you know...casual. But I know we didn't talk about it beforehand, so um...if I'm only part of the case, then I don't think I—"

With a growl, Monty rolled both of them quickly, pinning her body underneath his. Propping himself on his elbows, he held her gaze. "You're not just part of the case. Getting to know you, Cupcake, has brought a breath of fresh air into my life."

Her smile grew until it rivaled the sun peeking in the windows. "So," she said, once more tracing his jaw with her finger, "I've added some color to your life?"

Chuckling, he moved his nose along hers. "Oh, yeah. You've definitely added color to my rather boring life."

Sobering, she asked, "I've got to get Helen to ensure our delivery is made to the party today before we leave to see Theresa's parents."

"Yeah. I know seeing them is going to be hard on you."

"Can you tell me what you're looking for? Just so I'll understand."

Moving so that he was now leaning back against the headboard, he pulled her so she was tucked into his embrace. "Right now, Angel, it's just a fishing expedition. There may be absolutely no connection between the two deaths. But if there's the possibility there is one, then we need to know that."

Nodding, she wrapped her arms tighter around Monty's waist, giving a squeeze. Looking up into his face, she turned and rolled out of bed. "All righty then, I guess we'd better get ready!"

Watching her gloriously naked body move toward the bathroom, Monty did not even fight to hold back the appreciative grin on his face.

11

A ngel viewed the Constantine's neighborhood as they passed through. Coming to a neat Colonial at the end of a cul-de-sac, Monty pulled into the driveway.

His gaze caught the nervous flutter of her hands and he reached over to give them a squeeze. "It'll be fine, Angel."

Several minutes later, ensconced in the living room, they sat on chairs facing the sofa Theresa's parents were on. Ted and Olivia greeted Monty politely but pulled Angel into a deep hug.

"It's been a difficult month," Olivia admitted, "but we've tried to move through our grief. Hearing about Marcia just brought our agony slamming back."

Ted eyed Monty carefully before saying, "You said in your phone call that you wanted to talk about Theresa's accident. I confess to forgetting the company you said you worked for."

Monty replied, "I work for Saints Protection and Investigations and we are currently working with the FBI on Marcia Creston's murder. Please understand that I know there is no evidence linking her situation with your daughter's, but we would be remiss if we didn't consider all possibilities."

Ted and Olivia peered at each other before turning back to Monty while clasping hands. "We understand. What do you want to know?"

"To begin with, can you tell us about her relationship with Geoffrey Daly?"

The immediate change in Ted's expression shocked Angel. She glanced to Olivia, whose eyes filled with tears, but her face was also marred with a frown.

"That low-life son-of-a-bitch? Jesus, what did our Theresa ever see in him?" Ted bit out. Monty allowed him a moment to gain control of his emotions, knowing he would speak more when able.

"She met him two years ago when she took her car in to get it fixed. He asked her out and they were together ever since."

"I never met him," Angel confessed. "What happened?"

"Three times in the last year, she called 911 because of domestic violence. We knew of the first two because she called us also, but she would never follow through with a complaint. We only learned about the last one after she died," Olivia said.

Ted continued, "He was rough around the edges, but we could have gotten over that. It seemed the longer they were together, the more they fought. His garage suffered financial problems and he constantly nagged her for money. I sometimes wonder if that was why she never took the next step to get married. They lived together and even had a joint checking account, but she kept very little money in it."

"How were her finances?" Monty asked, already knowing what Luke had discovered, but wanting to know what their impressions were.

"She was a teacher so her salary was steady, but not very high. That was actually the reason they moved in together...to save money on rent." Ted and Olivia shared a look before Ted continued. "Theresa did receive an inheritance from an elderly great-aunt that had no grandchildren. My Aunt Liz left a nice amount to both of our daughters. Marcia Creston helped Theresa invest it."

Hearing Marcia's name linked to Theresa's in a way besides sorority sisters had Monty's attention.

"She had an investment account and also took out a life insurance policy. We didn't know about it until she died. The investment account's beneficiary was both of us, her sister, and her niece. Then the life insurance policy was to her niece. Our other daughter only has one child and Theresa wanted to help her with college expenses."

"Do you know if Theresa recently changed her beneficiary on the life insurance policy?" Monty inquired. Seeing the surprised expressions on their faces, he added, "I just wondered. Sometimes those little details can be important."

"No. No, we don't."

"Have you seen Geoffrey since the funeral?" Angel asked.

"He came around about a week later wanting to know where his money from Theresa was. We had no idea what he was talking about so we told him to leave or we'd call the police. Believe me," Ted said, "There was nothing that belonged to him, other than the couple of hundred dollars in the joint checking account, and we let him have all that to get rid of him."

"Was the accident ever investigated as anything other than an accident?"

"Not that we knew," Olivia said. Staring intently at Monty, she asked, "What are you thinking?"

"Ma'am, right now, I'm just fishing. I now know there's a relationship between Marcia and your daughter that went beyond the sorority. And I know that Geoffrey thought he was entitled to some kind of compensation. Neither of those things may add up to anything, but I know more than I did before I came."

Ted squeezed his wife's hand as he held it in his lap. "Theresa was driving in the snow after going out to the grocery store. I always wondered why the hell she went out with the weather so bad. Geoffrey was home...he could have gone. But the police told us she slid on a patch of ice and skidded into the other lane, getting hit by a truck. We had no reason to think it was anything else."

"I don't either, sir. But, as I said earlier, we wanted to check everything."

As Monty and Angel said their goodbyes, Olivia pulled Angel to the side. Glancing over at Monty, she said, "Theresa always loved her sorority sisters. If you find out anything, please let us know. This...well, this whole conversation has opened up more questions."

"I will," Angel promised, offering her a heartfelt hug.

Once back inside the SUV, Monty placed a call. "Tell Bart and Cam to find out what they can about the car Theresa was driving. However they have to do it, we need to know about that car."

The trip back to Charlestown was quiet as classical music played on the radio. Angel glanced sideways, noting Monty's concentration. Not wanting to disturb him, she leaned her head back, letting the elegant instrumental music settle over her.

As they pulled up outside of the bakery he looked over, an embarrassed blush crossing his face. "Sorry, Angel. I wasn't good company on the drive home."

"That's okay," she admitted truthfully. "You needed to think through the cases and I spent the time thinking of what I need to do this week." Smiling at him, she added, "It's all good."

She leaned over the console to offer a quick kiss, but Monty had other ideas. He lifted his hand to cup her jaw and pull her in toward him, taking her lips in a kiss she felt down to her core. Squeezing her legs together tightly, she tried to squelch the tingling. *Oh, down girly parts!*

Monty noticed the slight movement of Angel's legs and would have grinned if his cock was not painfully swelling in his pants.

Pulling away, the two panted for a moment, staring into each other's eyes.

"I've never met anyone like you, Cupcake," he admitted. "Someone who enjoys life, cares for friends, and has a career where making little girls' birthday dreams come true is as important as nailing a large catering job."

Rubbing her nose against his, she whispered in his ear, "Well, if you want to see how much I enjoy life, why don't you come around tonight?"

Taking her lips in another kiss, searing both of them, he muttered, "I'll be here." Backing away reluctantly, he added, "I'll call you later."

Smiling, she nodded before hopping out of his SUV and bounded into her bakery after watching Monty drive away.

The moonless night gave perfect cover for Bart and Cam as they moved through Thomas Auto Salvage on the outskirts of Richmond. Jude's search gave them the location of Theresa Constantine's wrecked car. Following the trail from the towing business, they traced it to the salvage company. Earlier Bart had visited, pretending to be from the insurance company, and was shown which automobile she had been driving on that fateful night. Staring at the crumpled vehicle in the light of day was a stark reminder of the life lost. At night, the entire salvage company resembled an automobile graveyard, the reminders that each vehicle had at one time contained people going about their business until the sounds of a crash interrupted their lives.

Moving stealthily, they arrived at her car. Using night-time vision goggles, they were able to keep the external light to a minimum. Crawling underneath the car, Cam checked the brake lines. Bart crouched next to Cam providing light, as well as keeping an eye out for visitors. A few minutes later, Cam wiggled his large frame from underneath. Nodding to Bart, they left as quietly and unnoticed as they came.

Once inside their SUV, Cam spoke. "Yeah, the brake lines were cut. Looks like they were cut partially and it did not take much for them to tear completely."

"So Theresa went out on a snowy, icy night with her brakes not working?" Bart growled. "Fuck, when she hit the ice, she would have just slid with no way to stop herself."

Cam quickly called Monty, explaining what he saw. "Better get Mitch on it so the FBI will have the evidence."

Angel watched Monty leave her bed as he received a phone call. Earlier she treated him to a back massage, which in turn led to shower sex, which ended up with them both in bed, hot and sweaty all over again.

She tried to listen to his end of the conversation but he kept his words minimal. As he disconnected he turned, seeing her watching him.

"They found something, didn't they?" she whispered.

"Yeah. Right now, the FBI is taking over Theresa's investigation, so I can't give you any details, but Mitch says that I can go with him to interview Geoffrey."

An iron band gripped her chest, squeezing tightly as hot tears hit the back of her eyes, threatening to fall. "I thought it was horrible for Theresa to have an accident, but to have it be on purpose...I...I just...and then to think of Marcia mur...murdered—"

Monty jerked her close, one arm around her waist and the other cupping the back of her head. He settled against the headboard, her body pressed into his side. Watching as she struggled to control her emotions, he recognized the new information would interrupt the grieving process. He let his hand glide over her skin, up her arm, around her shoulder, and down her back before repeating the soothing movement.

His touch was feathery light, yet warm. Barely there, yet comforting. After a few minutes, she lifted her teary face. "I'm so sorry. It seems like ever since we met, all I do is cry on you."

He kissed her forehead, murmuring, "You've got nothing to apologize for. You've had to deal with the death of two close friends within a month. That's a lot to take in."

Pushing away, she shoved her tousled hair back from her face. "Monty, but how can they be connected? I know that's what you're thinking. I just don't get how. Their jobs were different. They lived in different cities. Outside of the sorority, they didn't share the same friends."

He shook his head, a grim expression on his face. "I don't know, Angel. That's what I'm hoping to find out. Were they connected and, if so, how and why."

He lifted her chin with his finger and kissed her lips softly. "I've got to get ready to leave. I need to meet with the Saints and then get with Mitch. What have you got going on today?"

"I'll be downstairs in the bakery," she said. "I've got two catering jobs to deliver, a party this afternoon in the shop, and I'll be accepting some food deliveries later as well."

"Sounds busy."

She gifted him one of her glorious smiles. "Yeah, but I like it. Throwing myself into work will help keep my mind off what you're finding out." She looked down between them, biting her lip in thought. Suddenly glancing back up, she said, "Look, I know there's a lot you can't tell me. But will you promise to tell me whatever you can?"

"Absolutely, Cupcake. Whatever I find out that I can share, I will." *Especially if there is some kind of connection between the deaths and the sorority!*

The Saints sat in the main room with Mitch on video-conference, listening to Bart and Cam describe the condition of Theresa's car.

"The brake lines on both sides had holes in them but, as I checked closely, they were partially cut clean. This could allow her to drive for a little way before all the fluid leaked out, causing her to lose braking power on the slick roads," Cam explained.

"Would it have caused it to happen immediately?" Chad asked.

"No, not right away. The area sliced was large enough to cause leakage, but they weren't slit completely in two. She could have gotten down the street or to the store before losing her brakes."

Mitch nodded. "I've had her car brought in so that I can have it inspected by agents who can document what they find, which I expect to be the same as what you found."

"What did you say to your superiors to get them to impound the car?" Jack wanted to know.

Chuckling, Mitch replied, "I just told them that we now had suspicions about the vehicle based on the boyfriend's expectancy of a life insurance policy payout. And, by the way, good work you all. The police were inundated with accidents with that snow storm and weren't looking for any other reasons for someone sliding on the ice."

Monty spoke up, saying, "Mitch and I will be going today to talk to the boyfriend, Geoffrey Daly. We hope to shake him up a little and see what he gives us."

"I don't get the connection between the two deaths," Blaise admitted. "I know it's suspicious for two women in the same social circle to die within a month of each other, one obviously murdered and the other possibly murdered...but we've got nothing concrete about the two of them."

"Angel said the same thing this morning," Monty reported. "But if Theresa was murdered by having her brakes tampered with, then there's got to be a connection."

Luke, his nervous fingers pounding at the keyboard again, said, "I'm working on it. Marcia's company was small, but had a significant clientele." He looked at Monty, "Can you get the list of the closest group of friends from that sorority? I'll look at all the ties between them that I can find."

Monty nodded and then looked around the table. "I'm sure it hasn't only occurred to me, but if there is some kind of connection between the two murders...we need to find it quickly before something happens to someone else."

The sober expressions around the table indicated each man knew...time was of the essence.

12

_____

Geoffrey Daly's garage stood in an industrial section of Richmond, not far from the riverfront. Mitch and Monty pulled up to the front and parked, looking at the old building. The bay doors were open and they saw four men inside working on vehicles. Next to the bays was an office, the sign Daly's Automotives across the door.

Stepping out of Mitch's truck, Monty noticed the mechanics' eyes immediately shot their way. He knew from years with the FBI, both he and Mitch had the air of law enforcement about them. Following Mitch into the office, they encountered a young woman behind the counter. Her messy bun of bleached blonde hair with black roots, dark eyeliner, multiple piercings, and open-mouth gum chewing greeted them as they approached. Her bored expression perked as she left the counter to go find Geoffrey.

A minute later, a lean man came from the garage, wiping his hands on a towel. A few inches less than six feet tall, built like a runner, his ash-blond hair was neatly pulled into a ponytail in the back. His sharp eyes took them in, quickly assessing.

"Gentlemen," he said. "I'm Geoffrey Daly. I understand you have some questions."

"Yes," Mitch answered, introducing himself and showing his identification before introducing Monty. "Is there someplace where we can speak in private?"

The receptionist, who had returned to her place behind the counter, looked on wide-eyed, popping her gum. Geoffrey glanced her way with a scowl, saying, "Sure. We can talk in my office." He led the way, speaking to the girl as they passed. "Just answer the phones and keep your nose in your own business."

She blinked rapidly before dropping her gaze to the gossip magazine in front of her. Mitch and Monty shared a glance as they made their way into the small, crowded office. Geoffrey sat at the desk, piled high with papers, files, and receipts.

"You'll have to excuse the mess, gentlemen. I haven't been myself since my girlfriend passed away last month and there're things that I'm getting behind in." He sighed heavily, adding, "Fucking tax time."

"We are sorry for your loss, Mr. Daly. We have come into some information and are hoping you can supply us with answers," Monty began.

Geoffrey's eyes darted between the two men. "About Theresa?"

"I know you gave this information to the police, but I'd like you to tell me about the night she died."

Rubbing his hand over his face, Geoffrey heaved another sigh. "Jesus, this sucks. We were at our townhouse that evening. She was a teacher and always got home before I did. We ate supper and I was already in our den watching TV by the time she brought in some schoolwork to grade. I asked if we had any beer and she said we didn't. She headed out to go to the store to buy some. It had been snowing a little and I didn't know it was worse when she left. That was the last I saw her before the police came by."

Monty noticed the succinct story Geoffrey related, giving little emotional details. He sat back, his eyes noting the man's behavior...and the sweat beading on his forehead, as he let Mitch continue the questioning.

"Can you tell me where she parked her car when she was at home?"

Geoffrey's brow furrowed as he answered, "We've got a one car garage at the townhouse. She'd always pull in there. My truck's too big so I always park out on the street. Why?"

Ignoring Geoffrey's question, Mitch continued, "Had her car had any work done on it recently? I assume since you own a garage you would have taken care of its maintenance?"

"Yeah, I'd have her bring it in here when it needed inspection or oil change or something."

Mitch nodded thoughtfully, jotting down few notes. "I saw from the records her car passed state inspection two months ago. Had she complained about her brakes since then?"

Geoffrey sat up straight, his lips thinned in irritation. "No, she never talked about the brakes. What the hell are all these questions about?"

"Was it unusual for her to go out at night to buy beer for you?"

"Now, hold on just a goddamn minute! You're trying to make me out to look like some kind of controlling male who makes his little woman run around after him. That wasn't us at all. I didn't tell her to get the beer. And before you ask, no, there was never anything implied either. I asked if we had any. She said no and that she'd run out and buy some. I never made her go and I sure as shit didn't know the roads were so bad."

"Mr. Daly, I'm not implying anything. I'm simply wanting to get an idea of exactly what happened that night leading to her going out in her car."

Huffing, Geoffrey leaned back in his seat, his expression angry and his gaze distant. "I loved Theresa. No matter what anyone thought, we loved each other and planned on getting married. She had a little inheritance money and we talked about expanding this business. She was a high school marketing teacher and had some good ideas." Running his hand over his scruffy beard, he shook his head slightly. "Her parents never approved of me. I was too working class for them, but Theresa...she and me talked about a future all the time."

"Can you tell us about the matter of the domestic violence calls Theresa made?"

Geoffrey's grimace turned ugly. "How do you know about those?" An expression of dawning appeared and he growled, "I see you've talked to her parents."

"Your arrests are a matter of public record, Mr. Daly," Monty responded.

He sat quietly for a moment and then turned his gaze back to Mitch. "I didn't have the upbringing Theresa did. In my house, if my dad wanted to make a point, he did it with his fist. I even got into trouble as a teenager when I fought back to help keep my mom from dad's anger." He snorted as he shook his head, lost for a moment in the memories. "So yeah, when Theresa and I first lived together, I fucked up and hit her once. I got arrested and that was the last time I ever hit her. The last two calls were unfounded. She felt threatened by what I was saying, but I never hit her. We worked out our communication issues and I got more anger counseling. But her parents never forgave me."

More silence filled the room before Geoffrey suddenly looked back at Mitch. "You said something about her brakes. What were you referring to?"

"It appears her brake lines were cut. Just enough to let the brake fuel leak out slowly. Perhaps just enough for her to drive to the grocery store on icy roads before she lost control completely and was killed when her car was unable to stop at an icy intersection."

Geoffrey stared numbly, his mouth opening and closing several times before his face turned red and he stood quickly. "You tellin' me Theresa's brake lines were cut?" He paced to the edge of his desk before turning back suddenly. "Holy shit, you think I did that? You think I cut her lines and sent her to the store." He leaned forward, placing his hands on his desk, roaring, "You can get the fuck outta my shop! You want me, go through my lawyer." Turning back to the corner of the room, his chest heaving, he said softer, "I loved her. I was gonna marry her."

"What does your gut tell you?" Mitch asked as he and Monty were back in his truck, leaving Richmond.

"He's got a lot to hide. Whether it's about her accident or just the state of their relationship, he's scared right now."

"Yeah, that was my impression also. Did Luke dig up info on Daly's business or personal finances?"

"He was working on it when we left." Monty reached into his suit coat pocket and pulled out his phone. A few clicks later and he had Luke on the other end. "I've got you on speakerphone with Mitch. What do you have for us on Daly?"

"His shop is doing fine according to what I can determine. Steady business, steady income, not great, but okay. Granted, it looks like once all expenses are paid, he puts a lot back into the shop, but he still lives well enough."

"Do you see any reason why he would be desperate to get his hands on a life insurance policy, other than normal greed? Outstanding loans, gambling debts, or something?"

"Not from what I'm seeing, but I'm still digging. You think maybe Bart and Cam should take a look at his office?"

"Jesus, not in front of me," Mitch groused, eliciting chuckles from both Monty and Luke.

Monty clicked off speakerphone and gave Luke a nod. "Contact Bart and Cam. Tell them to find whatever they can, both at the house he shared with Theresa and his business."

"You got it," Luke replied. "Tell Mitch not to get his panties in a bunch!"

Laughing as he disconnected, Monty looked over at Mitch. "You gotta loosen up, man," he joked.

"Easy for you to say. I've got superiors breathing down my neck to make sure whatever we get can stick in court if need be."

"You could always have a change of scenery, you know. Jack would love to have you."

Mitch ran his hand over his jaw but did not answer for a long time. "I'm third generation law enforcement. My grandfather worked as a deputy for a small county in Virginia for most of his career. He never ran for sheriff, saying he wanted to be the one helping folks instead of dealing with the political side of things. My dad spent his career as a police officer and then a detective for the Richmond PD. When I finished training for the FBI, both men were there at my graduation. I thought their buttons were gonna pop, they were so proud."

Monty listened, finding envy sliding over him. "You had respect and pride from them," he commented. "My parents groomed me for a career as a lawyer, with hopes I would someday become a judge. When I headed to the FBI Academy after law school, I thought they were going to have a coronary." Sighing, he continued, "The only one at my graduation from the Academy was my sister."

Mitch glanced sideways, "That's tough, man." He thought for a moment and then said, "I know I could make more money with fewer headaches going private but, for now, the Agency gives me a sense of public duty that was passed down from my family."

Nodding, Monty agreed. "Makes sense. It really does and I gotta say it makes our life easier having you on the inside, understanding how we work and are willing to work together."

Returning to Charlestown, Mitch dropped Monty off at the bakery. Parking behind a pink VW bug, Mitch stared at it for a moment before chuckling. "She ever take you for a ride in that crazy-ass car that looks like a cupcake?"

Shaking his head, Monty laughed, realizing he no longer thought her car was odd, but he quickly explained, "It fits her, but I'd lose my man-card if I showed up at Jack's in that!"

Right then, as though she had been looking for him, Angel opened the bakery door and bounded out toward the driver's side of the SUV as Monty came around the front.

"I brought these for you, Agent Evans," she said, handing a white box tied with colorful ribbons to him.

"They're some of my cupcakes. I thought you might enjoy them."

Staring at the gorgeous woman at his window, her blonde hair with its pink, purple, and teal stripes blowing in the breeze and her blue eyes sparkling, he accepted her gift. Before he was able to thank her properly, Monty had reached Angel, pulling her into a hug while admonishing her for being out in the cold without a coat.

She gave Monty a quick kiss and, with a wave goodbye, she jogged back into the bakery. Mitch looked from the bakery to the box in his lap to the man standing by his SUV with a goofy grin on his face. "You are so fucked," he said to Monty. "That woman is so not like what you used to date and yet everything you ever needed! I think she finally pulled that stick outta your ass that your parents have had there for-fuckin'-ever." Before Monty could retort, Mitch said, "Call me if you get anything," and drove down the street.

Monty stood for a moment on the sidewalk, watching his friend drive away and pondering his words. *Not what you are used to but everything you need.* His instinct was to deny what Mitch had said, but as he turned around to see the swirling words on the front of the bakery knowing who was inside waiting...*Fuck, yeah. Everything I need.*

Once more under the cloak of darkness, Bart and Cam made their way easily into Daly's Automotives. The lax security allowed the pair to get inside with no trouble. Moving through the garage area first, they discovered nothing more than what appeared to be a well-run, organized mechanic's garage. The swept, oil-stained floor was free of tools, which were on the tables and tool chests on the back wall. A search of the drawers provided nothing other than the implements of the trade.

Moving to the reception lobby, it was easy to note the receptionist's duties did not extend to cleaning the area. While the waiting room magazines were neatly stacked on the table by the plastic chairs, the shelves underneath the counter were filled with more magazines haphazardly tossed around, a few empty fast food bags crumpled, a coffee mug filled with moldy dregs from long ago. Gross... but nothing suspicious, just a lazy receptionist.

Bart and Cam moved into the office last. "Does he have his receptionist work in here as well?" Bart commented at the mess.

"Monty said that Daly made the inference that Theresa may have helped in here or, at least, it was better when she was alive."

The two men worked silently, poring over the files and receipts scattered over the desk and what was actually in the filing cabinet.

"Looks like there was a connection between his garage and Colonial Financial Group," Cam said, looking at papers in his hands. "We'll have Luke go through his emails to see if we can find what they were doing but, from this, here is a receipt for financial planning services paid by the garage to CFG."

Finding nothing else of interest, they left the office the way they had found it. Driving by the bar they knew Daly frequented and seeing his truck still there, they visited his house next. Once more, entering was easy and they moved stealthily through the home. Finding the rooms to be neater than his office, Cam looked around with his hands on his hips. Walking to the kitchen, he looked through the cabinets and drawers while Bart searched the bedroom.

"There's still a few women's items in the bathroom in

the bottom drawer, but all other evidence of Theresa is gone. No clothes in the closet but there are a couple of women's t-shirts in his chest, as well as a necklace on top of the dresser."

"Don't know how unusual that is. Some people keep all the deceased's personal items and others get rid of them immediately," Bart commented.

Investigating a few more rooms and finding nothing interesting, they moved to the garage. Cam squatted on the floor and searched the concrete. Looking closely, he rubbed his finger through the oil and antifreeze stains.

"You got something?" Bart queried.

"Could be a bit of brake fluid here mixed in with the other normal stains that come from a vehicle."

"You thinking that if her brakes were tampered with here, it would leave residue on the floor?"

Nodding, Cam said, "We need to get Mitch to get a warrant to scrape this floor and see if it matches the brake fluid in her car."

Having finished, the two friends slipped back out into the night, unnoticed. The natural high from investigating was mixed with the frustration that they were no closer to finding Marcia's murderer...nor Theresa's.

13

The dark romantic lighting in Onyx did not hide the glistening of Angel's hair and Monty could not take his eyes off her. With an uncharacteristic evening free for both of them, he finally managed to take her to dinner. Choosing one of his favorite restaurants, he had smiled as the host seated them at a corner table, next to a large window offering a view of a nearby park. Several of the trees lining the park's walking path twinkled with Christmas lights filling their branches. Monty knew the lights were there all year, having taken a few dates on a walk after dinner in the park.

Funny, but I haven't thought of another woman since meeting Angel. Seeing her sitting at one of his favorite restaurants as his date filled him with pride. Wearing a pastel pink dress, the square-neck modest but showing the tops of her bounteous breasts, tapered to a narrow waist before hugging her incredible ass. Silver hoops adorned her ears, and a necklace with a single charm nestled at the top of her cleavage. *I wonder who gave that to her?* The strange emotion of possessiveness slid through him causing him to lean back in his chair, battling irritation.

Glancing down to where his attention had been, she lifted the charm and smiled. "It's beautiful isn't it? My brother gave it to me when I opened ACH. He was deployed and unable to be there for the grand opening, so he sent this instead."

Seeing the fondness in her expression for the necklace and the man who gave it to her had him smiling in return. "Sounds like a great guy."

"He is. Best brother a girl could hope for."

"Do you get to see him much?"

A shadow crossed her face as she dropped the necklace between her fingers and shook her head sadly. "No. I knew when he went Special Forces he wouldn't be able to come home often, but the last two years have been difficult. I know he's happy and would want me to be as well."

"And are you happy?" he asked. Interested in everything she had to say, he sat entranced as her cotton candy lips sipped the wine. The candle in the middle of their table caught the sparkle in her eyes as she ran her tongue over her lips, making sure to catch every drop of the exquisite vintage.

"I am absolutely happy," she enthused, watching him watching her lips. Unable to hold back a giggle, she added, "You look like a man who would like to kiss me right now."

Sitting at a right angle to her for a purpose, he grinned as he leaned over doing exactly what she knew he wanted to do. Never a man for public displays of affection, he eagerly moved his lips over hers, the familiar taste of her sweet lips with a hint of the wine was a heady combination. Forcing himself to move away tested his willpower… along with gaining control over his swelling erection.

Their gazes latched on to each other, eager smiles indicating they knew what would be coming when the dinner was over.

The waiter brought their meals, both ordering a combination of perfectly seared steak and succulent seafood. Digging in with relish, Angel moaned as the first shrimp passed her lips. Monty groaned inwardly forcing his eyes to stay on his plate, as the idea of her lips around his cock and her moans filling the air, made breathing difficult.

"Tell me about your move?" he asked.

Her eyes lit with enthusiasm and she swallowed her bite eagerly. "I need a larger kitchen. There have been a few catering jobs that I've had to either turn down or had to spend all night baking because I didn't have enough ovens to produce a large enough quantity at one time. I found an empty former restaurant about four blocks from where I'm now located. I'm closing the one as I open the other. So ACH will just be moving locations, not opening another store. I've let the building owner know so he's going to rent out my old bakery to someone else, but I'm staying in the apartment."

"You love what you do, don't you?" he asked, his eyes riveted to her bright smile.

"Who wouldn't love to be surrounded by cupcakes all day?" she laughed. "And as long as the permits go as planned, I can move in a month." She sobered for a moment before adding, "It was Marcia who helped me with the finances to get the loan on the new location. I owe it all to her and now I can't share the success with her anymore."

He reached for her hand, giving it a gentle squeeze. "I'm sorry, babe. But I firmly believe that she's still with you in spirit and knows what you're doing."

Her smile replaced, the two continued eating the delicious meal. Several minutes later, he watched her delight in each bite, making him appreciate the experience so much more. Seeing the tiniest dab of sauce on the corner of her lip had him moving in for another kiss.

"Montgomery?"

Turning sharply, he looked up to see his parents standing to the side of their table...with Claire. *Fuck! Of all the people I don't want to see right now, these would be the top three!*

Breeding took precedence over telling his parents to move on, so he quickly stood kissing his mother's cool cheek, noticing her eyes riveted to Angel's hair. Shaking his father's hand next, he nodded his head to Claire but made no movement to embrace her. Turning back, he held out his hand to Angel and introduced her.

"Mom, dad, may I present my date, Angel Cartwright. Angel, these are my parents, Russell and Lois Lytton. And this is a family friend, Claire."

Smiling at everyone, Angel shook hands but noticed Lois' appraising look and Claire's unmistakable glare. She glanced to Monty, immediately picking up on his mood— unhappy. *Because of them...or me?* "It's so nice to meet you," she said, meeting and holding their gazes.

"Angel Cartwright?" Lois murmured before her eyes suddenly brightened in recognition. "You own Angel's Cupcake Heaven?"

"Yes, ma'am," Angel replied. "Have you had a chance to visit my bakery?"

"Oh, no. I don't go to the downtown area where your little shop is, but I have had your cupcakes before. I believe you catered the desserts at the Women's Legal Society last October. It was held at the Charlestown Country Club." Turning to Claire, she said, "You remember, my dear?"

"Yes," Claire replied, her smile on Lois but her eyes still hardened on Angel.

"I believe your cupcakes were the center of our granddaughter's party last month," Russell added. "They were delicious and Monty, here, had pink, purple, and blue all over his mouth."

"It's teal, Russell," Lois said. "Not blue, but teal."

"Well, whatever it was, it was wonderful and looked just like your hair."

Laughing, Angel smiled at Monty's father and said, "Thank you. I hope you'll come by the shop sometime."

"I've often said that you should expand your business. You could franchise and move into much more lucrative locations," Lois added, ignoring the pointed glares from her son.

"Thank you, but right now the one shop is all that I can handle," Angel replied, trying not to bristle.

"My dear, as a baker you can't expect to understand all of the intricacies of the business world. You should seek the advice of a financial planner and a lawyer. Claire, here, is an excellent lawyer."

"Mom," he growled. "It might interest you to know Angel has a marketing and business degree." He felt the sweat dripping down his back as he waited for the exchange to turn difficult. Hoping to deflect it before anything unpleasant was said, he added, "Well, if you don't mind, we really need to return to our dinner before it gets cold."

"Of course, of course," his father agreed, nodding once more to Angel. "Nice to meet you, Ms. Cartwright."

"Yes, you must return to your meal. It looks very... hearty...and like most of it was eaten already," Lois added, shaking her head. "I, myself, could never eat that much at one time without gaining weight. But you carry it well, Ms.

Cartwright." Taking Angel's hand and shaking it once more, Lois smiled as she said goodbye.

Watching them walk over to another table, Monty sat heavily down in his seat peering at Angel's perplexed expression.

"Cupcake, I'm sorry—"

"I can't figure out if I was insulted or complimented," she said, looking over, grinning at Monty.

Sighing morosely, he reached over to cover her slim fingers with his much larger hand. "Probably both," he answered. "Mom means well, I swear, but she is the most blunt and often socially awkward person I've ever met. She teaches at the law school and serves on numerous committees but, honest to God, she can be abrasive."

"And your dad? I thought you said he was so disappointed when you went into law enforcement but he seemed rather…easy going."

"Dad has definitely mellowed with age. I think it finally got through his mind that his children were never going to be what he desired. Felicity was not going to be a college professor—she loves teaching elementary kids too much. And me? I'll never be a lawyer or judge. And dad seems to have made some peace with that."

"And Claire?" She watched carefully as Monty actually squirmed in his seat. "Hmm," she said, tapping her fingers on his hand. "That reaction would seem to imply that she was a former…?"

Blushing, Monty hated that the evening that started with such promise was now ending in disaster. He had not been out with Claire since that evening when he first saw Angel and yet he felt as though he had been caught cheating. *How the hell do the other guys do it? Banging whomever they want and then ending up seeing those women back at the bar when they're with someone else?*

Meeting Angel's gaze, he was caught off guard by the mirth in her eyes. Cocking his head to the side, he looked at her in question.

Giggling as she squeezed his hand, she said, "Monty, honey, it's fine! I actually recognize her as the woman you were with the night we first saw each other. She's beautiful...in a model sort of way. I used to be jealous of women who were able to maintain that look, but I know now, my curves are what you like. I know we'll run into your old girlfriends. I promise you I won't fly into a jealous rage."

"Then you'll do better than me if we run into an old boyfriend of yours," he retorted.

Throwing her head back, she laughed the deep, throaty laugh Monty heard that night they were both remembering. *Fuckin' beautiful.*

"So...how many old boyfriends am I going to have to be jealous of?" he wondered out loud.

"Not many, I promise. Let's see," she said, holding up her fingers, ticking them off. "There was the high school boyfriend—"

"High school quarterback, I suppose?"

"Nope. President of the math club," she smiled. "Then there were a couple of short term guys in college, but nothing serious." Her brow knitted as she seemed lost in thought for a moment. "Between a double major and the sorority activities, there was little time left over for dating someone when I could tell early on it wasn't going anywhere."

He watched her carefully as her smile landed back on him, their fingers still locked together. Nodding, he said, "Seems we have a lot in common. I have dated women, usually the type that I thought suited me...and suited what my parents would have wanted. But I was never really interested in anyone until you. Ever."

She leaned forward, her lips a whisper away from his. "And you're interested in me, Mr. Lytton?"

He watched as her gaze dropped to his lips before his eyes landed on hers. Moving a hint closer, he replied, "Very interested, Cupcake."

"You want to show me how interested?" her sultry voice slid over his lips.

"Oh yeah," he breathed her in as he closed the minute distance between them. Moving his lips over hers, once more tasting the wine. "I think this was where we were before we were so rudely interrupted," he murmured against her lips.

A slight moan was her only answer before they separated, both smiling once more. The waiter appeared at their elbows and asked if they wanted to see the dessert tray.

Monty cocked his eyebrow in question at Angel, but she slowly shook her head. "I know where you can get the best cupcakes in town," she replied, winking.

Not taking his eyes off her, he called out to the waiter, "We'll take our check now, please."

Laughing, Angel excused herself to the ladies' room. Once inside, she quickly took care of business, but before she could exit the stall, she heard her name mentioned by Lois and Claire at the sinks.

"I haven't been out with Monty in over a month," Claire said. "I assumed he would call, but he must have moved on."

"I'm sure he's just entertaining Ms. Cartwright," Lois declared. "She's not my son's type at all. She's way too… well, curvy, if you know what I mean."

Unable to stop the grin, Angel stepped out of the stall and walked over to the sink next to the women. Washing her hands as they stood, eyes wide open, she adjusted the bodice of her dress before turning to them. "I'm sorry to eavesdrop, ladies. But the truth is I'm just his type." With a nod, she bid them a good evening and sailed out of the door.

Walking over, she allowed Monty to assist her into her coat and slid her arm through his. Giving him a little shoulder bump, she said, "Take me home, babe. It's dessert time!"

14

M onty barely made it to the passenger side of his SUV, after parking outside of Angel's apartment, before she launched herself at him. Tongues tangling, they fought for dominance as their lips met. She wrapped her legs around his waist as he struggled to beep the locks on the SUV and moved them to her door.

"Keffs," he mumbled, their mouths still attached as their heads twisted back and forth, noses bumping.

"Hmm?" she muttered back, not willing to pause the kiss.

Without speaking again, he grabbed her purse from her shoulder and his fingers fumbled in the bag as he attempted to find her keys while pressing her body against the door.

"Ohmph," she grunted against his mouth, slipping her hand in one of the side pockets of her purse while her lips remained firmly locked to his.

Holding her with one hand on her ass and her body balanced against the doorframe, he managed to unlock the door. Opening it, they tumbled up the first two stairs before he remembered to kick it shut and flip the deadbolt.

Angel grabbed his face in her hands, holding him in place as her lips moved over his, sucking his tongue into her warmth. Twisting, Monty set her ass on the steps as he slid his hand underneath the hem of her dress and up her thigh till he found the lacy top of her stockings.

She released him long enough to slide up two more stair steps so he had easier access to her legs. She lifted one leg, offering her high heel for him to pull off and toss behind him. Giggling, she raised her other foot and that shoe went flying down the stairs as well.

Her pink lips were kiss swollen and he leaned over her body as it reclined on the stairs. His hands slid back up her dress, latching his fingers in the tops of her thigh-high stockings. Pulling one slowly down her leg, the silk was tossed to the side. Moving to the other leg, he removed the second bit of silk and lace the same way.

She used her hands to scoot up two more stairs. "You want me, big boy? Come and get me," she teased as she twisted and attempted to scramble up the stairs to her apartment.

She only managed to make it up three steps when he wrapped his arm around her waist, lifting her in his arms. Slamming his lips on hers again, he carried her to the landing. She reached behind her, opening the door to her apartment.

He set her feet on the floor as their hands unbuttoned her coat while attempting to maintain their kiss. Shoving the purple wool garment off her shoulders and down her arms, it puddled on the floor next to the door.

They separated for a moment, breaths ragged and chests heaving. Her eyes twinkled as she slowly turned, lifting her mass of blonde and colorful hair with her hands, presenting the back zipper of her dress to him.

He stepped closer, his nimble fingers unzipping the garment leisurely as though he had all the time in the world.

"Hurry, Monty," she pouted.

"No way, Cupcake," he murmured in her ear, his warm breath washing over her neck. "Like any tasty treat, I want to savor you slowly."

Once the zipper was resting at the top of her ass, he slid his hands into the material at her upper back and parted the dress as it shifted off her shoulders and slithered to the floor. She turned deliberately, now clad only in a violet silk demi bra and matching panties.

Monty slid his hand from her shoulder down her arm, barely touching her skin before he grasped her hand in his, stepping back to admire her beauty. Her porcelain skin appeared luminescent in the moonlight streaming through the colorful sheers on the windows. Her breasts poured over the cups of her bra and he lifted his other hand, trailing his fingers over the delicate lace and soft mounds.

Her nipples, barely contained in the material, beaded against his touch. Their hardened pearls begged for his mouth. Obliging, he tugged the cups down, lifting her breasts. Wrapping both arms around her waist, he pulled one nipple deep into his mouth, watching as her head fell back exposing her long neck.

Her fingers held onto his shoulders, the short nails digging in as his mouth did wondrous things to her breasts. Moan after moan filled the air, barely cognizant that the sounds erupted from her own mouth.

Monty was lost in the feel of her luscious mounds against his face as he moved from one breast to the other, deeply sucking each nipple in, nipping it with his teeth before soothing it with his tongue.

She managed to work her hand between their bodies, unsnapping the front closure of her bra and wiggling just enough to slide it down her arms before tossing it to the growing trail of clothes. With her breasts now completely free, she grabbed his shoulders once more.

He carry-walked her into the bedroom, setting her feet back to the floor before he stepped away. Dropping to his knees, he pressed his face against her silk panties, the scent of her sex rising to meet him. Dragging one finger along the material, he found the evidence of her arousal.

Moving his mouth over the silk, he felt her fingers dig into his shoulders as her legs involuntarily separated. Hooking his forefinger in the top of the flimsy material, he tugged it down her legs allowing her to kick it off once it reached her feet.

With her now completely naked, he placed his large hand in the middle of her stomach and pushed her backward onto the bed. Unable to move, she allowed him to pull her core to the edge of the bed, where he buried his face.

If he thought her bubblegum lips were ambrosia, her wet pussy was a drug. Lapping her juices as he plunged his tongue inside, he knew he was ruined for any other woman. The essence of Angel was now his addiction.

He moved his lips upward to latch onto her clit as he inserted one finger deep inside. Curling it, he found the exact spot that caused her hips to buck off the mattress. Smiling against her folds, he watched as she leaned up on her elbows to watch him, her eyelids half closed in passion.

"Monty...I...I...need..."

Answering her with another suck on her clit, she flung herself back on the bed, her hips undulating against his face. Her insides tightened and her breathing became more ragged. "I...ah..." As he added another finger deep inside her pussy, he lifted the other hand to her breast and rolled her nipple between his fingers while giving one last tug on her clit. Her senses on overload, she flung over the precipice as her orgasm roared through her.

Quivering, she allowed her body to go along for the ride until the last spasm slowed. Angel was aware of her back on the bed with her legs over Monty's shoulders as the cool of the room finally penetrated. Lifting her head to peer down at him once more, she saw his slow, easy smile as he licked her juices from his fingers.

She crooked her finger at him, a twinkle in her blue eyes. "Come here, honey. I want to taste myself on you."

He stood first, unbuttoning his shirt as her eyes watched him eagerly. Agonizingly slow, he undid the buttons at the wrists before moving to the neck and undoing each one as a lazy smile lit his face.

Pouting, she narrowed her eyes. "If you want to keep that shirt intact, you'd better hurry up or I'll rip it from your body."

Laughing, he complied, quickly stripping it from his body. His pants followed, allowing her to focus on his prominent erection. He watched as she licked her plump lips as he crawled over her body. Her curves beckoned and her long hair spilled over her pillows. *Jesus, I'm fucked. Totally. Completely. Fucked.* No woman in his past could compare. And the only woman he wanted in his future was his Cupcake.

Finally at her lips, he latched on, moving deliberately over her. She tasted herself on his tongue—the heady combination of her juices and his own scent had her pussy quivering again. Pulling him in tightly with her legs around his waist and her arms around his neck, she begged, "I need you inside now, Monty. Please…"

He pulled away from her arms as he raised up, twisting his body as he leaned over to snatch his wallet from his pants. Grabbing a condom, he rolled it on slowly. Lifting himself back over her, he placed his eager cock at her entrance.

"I'm crazy about you, Angel," he confessed. "There's no other woman for me."

Her brilliant smile was his reward. Pushing into her tight warmth, he let out a sigh as his body found its home. Moving deliberately, he refused to give into the desire to rush. Thrusting, first slowly and then faster, he found his pace as his cock dragged along the inside of her pussy, the friction causing his arms to quiver as they held himself over her body.

Angel bent her legs at the knees, opening herself as wide as she possibly could to accommodate his body. His pelvis rubbed against her clit, the shivers it elicited starting from somewhere deep inside and beginning to shoot outwards. The pressure built as she climbed higher and she threw her head back on the mattress, her eyes tightly shut, sparks flying in the darkness behind her eyelids.

"Come, baby," he encouraged. "Let go and come with me." His order was gentle, but the meaning was clear. He was holding on by a thread and wanted her going with him.

Still thrusting, he leaned down taking a taut nipple into his mouth, biting slightly as he tugged on the sensitive flesh.

Screaming his name she fell apart, the sparks finally igniting the explosion ripping through her body. He watched as her face tensed with the power of her orgasm as his balls tightened and his own climax roared through him and into her. His arms quivered as they held him up, the muscles in his neck stood out as he strained before collapsing onto her waiting body.

For a moment they lay, their breaths labored, as the euphoria washed over them. Realizing he weighed her down into the mattress, he rolled to the side, taking her with him. Their bodies still crushed together, slick with sweat. Her breasts pressed against his chest, heartbeat to heartbeat.

Slipping out of the bed several minutes later, he hurried to the bathroom to dispose of the condom. Stalking back into the room, comfortable in his nudity, he saw her eyes roving his body. "Like what you see, Cupcake?"

"Mmm," was her answer and she moved to her knees on the bed, patting the mattress next to her.

Lifting an eyebrow at her as his cock jumped to life once more, he stealthily walked toward her. The idea of her pink lips around his dick knocked all other thoughts from his mind. Sitting next to her, she pushed him on his back and threw her leg over his thighs. Bending over, she shimmied down his legs until she was sitting on his ankles.

Monty watched as her breasts hung down, her dusty nipples tantalizingly close. Reaching out, he rolled and pinched their sensitive flesh, eliciting moans from her lips.

Jerking her head back down, she smiled as she leaned her body down further, slipping her full lips around the head of his cock. It did not take long for his cock to respond with her swirling tongue around the sensitive rim. Pressing her hand down on his stomach when his hips bucked up, she moved her lips up and down his impressive girth, relishing in the taste of him on her tongue.

He leaned up, the sight of her mouth sliding up and down his length nearing undoing him immediately. His cock twitched inside her mouth, causing her to giggle. The vibrations from her mouth to his dick had him smiling. The tightening in his lower back alerted him to the oncoming orgasm and he wanted to be buried in her again.

Angling his body forward, he pulled out of her mouth with a pop, surprising Angel with his movement.

"What—"

"Want to be buried deep in you when I come, baby," he growled. He reached for another condom, rolled it on, then, taking her by the waist, hoisted her over his body. Flipping her quickly to her stomach, he grabbed her hips pulling her ass up toward him. Looking down at her heart shaped ass, he palmed the soft globes before plunging to the hilt into her slick pussy.

Glancing sideways to the mirror over the dresser they both watched, fascinated, as her breasts swayed with each thrust. The sight of their joining, as he moved in and out, held their gaze for a moment until their eyes met through the reflection. Her blonde hair, some clinging to her sweaty forehead, rippled as she moved, allowing the colored tresses to catch the light.

Smiling, he leaned over her back, palming her generous breasts, tweaking her nipples. She groaned as she moved backward, pressing against his thrusts.

"I'm ready, baby. Are you close?" he panted, using all his control to keep from blowing his balls before she had a chance to fly again.

With his body pressed against her, he reached around, moving his fingers through her moist folds and pressing his thumb against her clit. She cried out once again, throwing her head back against his neck as the tremors blossomed into a full-blown explosion. He followed her into bliss as his orgasm blasted its way from his body to hers.

His legs quivered with the force of his orgasm,

expending all his energy. Pulling out reluctantly, he disposed of the condom once more. She lay face down on the bed, arms spread out to the side, her breath coming in gasps. He returned from the bathroom, sitting down next to her. Running his hand down her back and over her ass, several times, he worked to steady his own breathing.

"You okay, Cupcake?" he asked.

Nodding was her answer and she was glad it was the only answer required. Chuckling, he lay down, rolling her body so that it was facing his. She placed her head on his shoulder as she looked into his eyes, feeling his arms circling around her body.

"You understand where I'm coming from, don't you?" he asked.

Still drowning in post-coital bliss, she could only suck in her lips, uncertainty on her face.

Brushing her hair back from her face, he rested his hand on her cheek. "Never saw it coming, but I've got to tell you that from the moment I saw you in that restaurant, something about you called to me. I tried to fight it. But it's there and it's real. I'm falling for you, Angel."

The smile on her lips started slowly. Barely a curve of the edges of her mouth. But then it blossomed into a brilliant smile, warming him completely. Nuzzling her nose alongside his, she whispered, "I've already fallen, Monty. I'm already in deep."

Laughing, he leaned down, grabbing the sheets and comforter, pulling them up over their still cooling bodies. He loved there was no pretense with her. *Not coy...just real.* Tucking her in closely, he combed his fingers through her hair, brushing it back over her shoulder. Placing a gentle kiss where his fingers roamed, he murmured, "Sleep now. Round three will come soon."

15

A ngel woke the next morning, the warm body that held her through the night was gone and she sat up suddenly, wondering if she dreamed the whole evening. Hearing Monty's voice coming from the living room had her smiling as she lay back down. Stretching her sore muscles, she luxuriated in the feeling of her first full night's sleep in a long time. Rising from the bed, she moved into the bathroom, brushing her teeth and taking care of business before strolling back out into the bedroom. Bending, she snagged his dress shirt from the previous night off the floor and pulled it on. Buttoning only enough buttons to keep it on her body she moved confidently into her living room.

"Hey sweetie, who was on the phone?" she inquired, stopping dead in her tracks. A tall, dark-haired man was standing with Monty by her front door. His eyes roved slowly from her pink toenails up to her untamed colorful hair, as he grinned from ear to ear making him even more attractive.

"Oh," she said, grabbing the sides of Monty's shirt and

pulling them closed while hoping the large shirt covered her ass.

"Angel, meet a fellow Saint and good friend, Chad," Monty said, moving toward her. Tucking her body into his side, he glanced down to make sure she was covered.

Nodding in greeting and appreciation, Chad chuckled. "Nice to meet you, Ms. Cartwright. I'm sorry to barge in. We needed to have a meeting this morning and Monty wasn't answering his phone."

"Did you leave it in the restaurant?" she asked, looking up at Monty's face.

"Uh...no. It was on the stairs. It fell out of my pocket... along with your shoes and other clothes."

"Oh...uh...Oh! " she stammered, blushing from her neck to her forehead remembering the trail of clothes that started from her front door and led up the stairs to her apartment.

Chad laughed as he turned to head back out the door. "I hope to see you again, Ms. Cartwright. Monty, see you in about an hour."

As they watched Chad leave, Angel turned to bury her face in Monty's chest. "That was mortifying!"

"While I wouldn't want you to make an appearance like that to all my friends, if it had to happen, Chad's a good man."

"I'd like to meet your friends sometime," she said, leaning her head back to look into his face.

"And so you shall," he replied easily. "In fact, as soon as we get a break in this case and get another night off, I'll take you to Chuck's Bar & Grille. It's kind of a Saints hangout."

"Why did Jack name his business the Saints?"

Monty stared over her head for a moment before answering. "The name meant something to him long before he even went into the military. Actually, all the other employees have names that mean something to them as far as actual Saints go."

She watched his face, wondering what his thoughts were. "And you? Does it mean anything to you?"

"Afraid not. I'm not named after a Saint. My name was given to me for family purposes. I suppose my parents hoped I would live up to my name, but I always thought it was pretentious. Montgomery Honor Lytton."

"Honor? That is an unusual name," she agreed, her eyes widening.

"Yep. My grandfather was a mayor and I got saddled with his name."

A slow smile crept across Angel's face as though a secret had just been shared with her. He looked at her with curiosity, but she simply shook her head with the smile still in place. "We'd better get dressed if you've got to go to your meeting and I've got to get downstairs to the bakery."

Kissing the top of her head, he sent her to the shower first, knowing if he joined her he would never make his meeting on time.

Chuckling, the Saints looked at Mitch in disbelief. "You have got to be kidding me?" Monty asked, not sure if the news Mitch was delivering was good or not.

Mitch nodded, unable to hold back a grin, said, "It's true. The man has been identified and, believe me, he's not about to press charges against Angel for pulling a gun on him."

Rubbing his forehead, the beginnings of a headache starting to pound, he looked up. "So some guy from Richmond comes to Charlestown, wearing a fuckin' disguise, just to pick up women in bars because he's married and doesn't want his wife to find out?"

"Yep, that's about it," Mitch said. "And before you ask, he's got an alibi for the time of night Marcia was killed. The hotel's bartender saw the man come from the elevator and into the bar about midnight. Had a drink and then left. The security cameras inside show him leaving alone. Marcia was seen leaving the hotel about thirty minutes later."

"How do we know he didn't meet her somewhere else and kill her then? Maybe she threatened to tell his wife."

"We have a statement from a PI, who's been following him. Seems his wife had hired a PI firm and so we know he was tailed until he got back home. He didn't meet up with Marcia again."

"So, what the fuck was he still doing out prowling with Angel nights later if his wife is having him tailed?" Monty growled.

"The PI was just starting the job and the husband's got no idea he's being followed."

"Soooo...," Bart started, an enormous grin on his face. "Our intrepid cupcake baker...goes undercover...as herself since she made no effort to hide her hair...goes back to a hotel with...and pulls a gun on...a disguised husband who's in town to get some on the side." Leaning back in his chair, he looked over at Monty and chuckled. "Your woman is totally kick-ass, man. I love it!"

"Bet that guy was shittin' bricks when he ran outta there!" Marc laughed, throwing his head back as his mirth joined the others. "God, I wish I'd seen that!"

"That'll teach the cheating bastard to keep it in his pants," Chad agreed.

Monty shook his head again, saying, "Un-fuckin'-believable. I don't know if I'm more relieved that who she was with wasn't a killer or upset knowing we're down a possible suspect."

After a few more minutes of joking, the Saints settled back down to continue the investigation. Monty asked Cam if he had found out anything from the cleaning service from Marcia's condo.

"Yeah, I interviewed the staff that serviced her apartment. Said they were initially contracted to work in the Colonial Financial Group offices and they still provide the service. The manager admitted that Ms. Creston was picky about how she wanted things cleaned. They had been cleaning her condo for about four months every now and again, did a thorough job each and every time. When I asked if they would have wiped down the mantle, furniture, knick-knacks, they said yes. Mentioned she was a neat-freak, as he called it, and they cleaned all surfaces each time."

"I need to have you and Bart *visit* Colonial Financial sometime and see if there's anything there we can use."

Once more, Bart and Cam grinned at each other. "This'll be good," Cam commented. "More of a challenge than her home was."

"We've got a lot of dots here, but so far nothing that's tying them together," Monty added. He pointed their attention to the large screen on the wall as he listed and manipulated the evidence. His FBI agent days were too ingrained. Placing all the pieces of the puzzle up on a board for him to ponder was his preferred method.

"Theresa Constantine died from an automobile accident. We now know her brakes were tampered with and her boyfriend, Geoffrey Daly, was hoping for money from an insurance policy. That gives him motive and opportunity. We also know she had some investments with Colonial Financial. And she was a close friend to Marcia Creston."

Moving down his timeline list, he continued, "A month later, Marcia Creston is murdered, possibly by someone who picked her up at a bar. She had a list of enemies, mostly from the people she worked with...or stepped on. If these two murders are connected, right now the connecting dots are Colonial Financial...or just the sorority."

"The sorority?" Blaise asked. "Someone who's got it out for the members of a sorority that graduated from college about five years ago?"

"Just throwing it out there," Monty replied. "Never dismiss possibilities when all you've got is clues leading to nowhere."

Angel pulled out more trays from the back and set them on the large counter. Helen came from the shop to collect them so she could place them in the rapidly diminishing stock on the shelves out front.

"I swear, with some of the snow gone, people are coming in droves for a sweet treat," Helen proclaimed.

"Good!" Angel grinned. "Let's hope they keep coming in here!"

"You been looking at the new location anymore?"

Nodding, Angel replied. "It's embarrassing how many times a week I drive by. I love this location, but I know the one several blocks over will be better. More traffic—"

She halted, seeing Helen's raised eyebrow. "I know, I know, we're busy enough here, but I really need more kitchen space for the larger catering parties. Now that some weddings have cupcakes instead of traditional cakes, I need the larger kitchen."

She stood, chewing the inside of her cheek for a second then looked up to see Helen's questioning gaze. "I was just thinking...well, last night someone said that I should expand and open more bakeries, like a chain."

"And what do you think?"

"I like being just me. You know, just in charge of this one bakery. If I opened up more, I couldn't be at both at the same time. I'd end up hiring baking chefs to create my recipes and I'd just become a manager/owner."

"How does that make you feel?"

"Honestly? Horrified! Not that I don't think I have the business background to do it. Running my business that way just holds no interest for me."

"So don't you have the answer?"

"Yeah, but—"

"Who put this cockamamie idea in your head, anyway? Surely it's not that nice young investigator you've been seeing?"

"Oh, no. Monty's..." Angel's thoughts trailed off, a smile replacing the look of consternation on her face.

Laughing, Helen responded, "Hmm, by the expression on your face, I'd say there's no problem there!"

"We ran into his parents last night at dinner. They're kind of...um...stuffy, and his mom said I should expand and possibly franchise. I told her that wasn't in my plans... and it's not, but..."

"But what?" Helen asked, her hands on her hips.

"I really like him, Helen. I haven't felt this way about someone in...well, in forever! It would be nice if his parents like me too, but I have a feeling I'm not at all the type of woman they would like to see their son with. A simple bakery owner."

"Who just happens to bake the most kick-ass cupcakes in Virginia!" Helen retorted. She stepped closer to Angel, taking her hands in her own. "Girl, I've known you for five years. And you are no simple baker. You are the dominating force behind Angel's Cupcake Heaven. If this is your destiny, then anyone who wants you to be something different isn't worth having around!"

Steeling her back, Angel smiled at her friend. "You're right. This is where I'm supposed to be. Well, here and then the new location when we get the go ahead to move!"

"Good girl. Now let's move the cupcakes out into the shop before pandemonium strikes because of empty shelves!"

An hour later, the mid-afternoon crowd had thinned and Angel walked back from the kitchen to make sure the eatery was spotless. A lovely dark-haired woman entered the shop, two children in tow. While the children ran to the glass cases to select their treat, Angel noticed the woman seemed to be staring at her, a secret smile on her face.

"Mom, mom! Look at these!" came the excited voice from the little girl. The woman's attention was diverted as she walked over to the cases and leaned down to gaze through the glass at the confection creations.

Angel walked over to the trio, smiling at the little girl. She noticed the boy tried not to show his enthusiasm for the treats, but ACH cupcakes were hard for anyone to resist. The girl stared up, her attention now on Angel's hair.

"Mom! That lady has pretty colors in her hair! She looks like a cupcake!"

The woman blushed slightly and tried to steer her daughter's attention back to the case of sweets. Glancing over, she said, "I assume you're Angel?"

"Yes," Angel smiled back. "And you are?"

The woman stood and lifted her hand out to Angel. "I'm Felicity. Felicity Darwin."

Angel's mind raced quickly, trying to figure out when she had met the lovely woman, but came up empty. "Have you been here before?"

"Yes, but we've never been introduced—"

"We got your cupcakes for my birthday party!" the little girl yelled, her excitement boiling over.

"Chrissy! Use your inside voice, please," Felicity chastised.

"Mom, that is her inside voice," the boy said, smirking at his sister.

The woman turned back to Angel, shrugging her shoulders. "I should have made this trip in by myself to meet you," she joked.

Angel bent down to Chrissy and asked, "Did you like the cupcakes at your party?"

"Oh, yes. They had the same colors that are in your hair. And we made Uncle Monty eat one. He hates to get messy, but he ate every bit and then had pink and purple all over his mouth!"

At that pronouncement, Angel rose and looked at the smiling woman carefully. *Of course! Now I see the family resemblance. Oh, lordy. Is she here to check me out also?*

Before she could worry too much, Felicity grabbed her hand and pulled her in for a hug. "I am so glad to meet you, Angel. You are so good for my brother!"

Surprised, Angel returned the heartfelt hug. Stepping back, she said, "I'm glad you think so. I really...um..." She hesitated as her gaze drifted back down to the children.

"Don't worry about them," Felicity said. She pointed out two cupcakes to Helen, who got the treats for the children. "Guys, let's settle down. You two sit at this table and I'll be over here with Miss Angel."

Angel sat, curiosity overriding her anxiety. Felicity shrugged out of her coat and sat after settling her children at a neighboring table.

"I'm sure you have to be wondering why I dropped in today, but I just had to. My mother called this morning to tell me that she and dad ran into you and Monty at dinner last night." Seeing the tightness of Angel's smile, she rushed on. "Oh, believe me, you made a great impression on dad. He used to be such a hard-ass, but I think he's finally getting to the point where he knows I'll never be a college professor and Monty'll never be a lawyer or judge."

Angel's smile relaxed slightly as she watched Felicity's animated expressions as she talked about her family.

"Anyway, mom said she was surprised to see the two of you together and mentioned she even witnessed a public kiss. Well, I knew then I had to come meet you in person! Any woman who can make my stick-in-the-mud brother relax enough to share a public kiss...well, you had to be someone wonderful!"

Angel burst out laughing at Felicity's description of Monty. The blush crossing her face as she thought about Monty being anything but a stick-in-the-mud when they were in the throes of ecstasy had her bringing her hands to her face.

Felicity noticed and, leaning back with a satisfied expression on her face, nodded. "And it seems there's more to you and my brother than I thought. So," she said, glancing back to her children at the next table and lowering her voice, "I take it you two are an item?"

"Um...yes. I mean...um...yes," Angel stammered.

"Halleluiah!" Felicity exclaimed. "It's about time he fell for a real woman instead of dating those stick-thin, always dieting, high maintenance types that remind me more of mom than someone he really should be with!"

Laughing again, Angel could not help but love Monty's sister. "Thank you for that. I have to confess after meeting your parents with Claire last night—"

"Claire? She was there too? Ugh," Felicity commented. "I only met her once and I got the distinct impression she was one of mom's attempts to sway Monty to give up investigating. Something he'd never do." Giggling, she added, "Plus the one time I met her, I had both my rug-rats with me. We'd just come out of an ice-cream parlor and ran into Claire and Monty leaving a restaurant. I thought she would die before greeting my children who both had melting ice cream on their hands!"

Angel and Felicity looked at the table next to them at the two kids with pink, purple, and teal icing on their lips and cheeks. The women laughed, sharing a look, as they hopped up to assist in cleaning the children's faces.

"Okay, you little monsters. Grab your coats. We've got to get home to fix dinner before your dad comes home."

As the trio was leaving the shop, Felicity turned back to Angel offering another warm hug. "It was nice to meet you and," she added, wiggling her eyebrows, "if my brother can keep his hands off you for long enough, you two will have to come for dinner!"

"I'd love that!" Angel enthused.

Turning back to the kitchen, she saw Helen smiling at her. *Finally, things seem to be looking up!*

16

Angel hung up the phone, her fingers pressed tightly to her lips in an effort to quell the trembling, thinking that would possibly keep the tears at bay. She fought unsuccessfully. The tears slipped down her cheeks until a sob wrenched from her body as she struggled to catch her breath.

How can this be? How can life be so cruel? She bent over at the waist, her face almost to her knees as her body shook with shock...anger...renewed grief.

The past four days had been wonderful. Monty was still working his cases and no new information had come in, but their evenings were filled with sweet words and steamy nights between the sheets.

Monty...I need to tell him. But there's nothing that can be done about this death. This one has nothing to solve. Nothing to question. Another sob broke from her, rising up from somewhere deep inside. Somewhere that was so tired...so fucking tired of hurting.

Sitting up, she wiped her face with the back of her hand and tried to think of what needed to be done. Her friend,

Caroline, had told her she was calling Cynthia and Sally. Sniffing loudly, she moved woodenly through her apartment in search of a tissue. Finally giving up, she headed to the bathroom to grab a long strand of toilet paper.

She glanced at the clock next to the bed and knew Monty would be coming soon. Releasing a shuddering breath, she moved back to the kitchen knowing she should prepare dinner. She found herself standing in the middle of the room, eyes tightly shut trying to stop the flow of tears. She was just as unsuccessful this time as she was earlier.

Grabbing her phone from the table, she called Monty. No longer caring if he were busy, she prayed he picked up.

"Hey, Cupcake," he answered. "I'm finishing at Jack's and getting ready to head there."

"Mon...ty?" her voice hiccupped.

"Angel, what's wrong?" he bit out, instantly on high alert. His eyes cut over to the other Saints in the conference room. "Where are you?"

"At...at home."

"What's wrong, baby?"

"I just got some b...bad news," she answered haltingly.

His first thought was her brother, still serving with the Special Forces. *Oh, Jesus, no!* "Just tell me, baby. What happened?"

"Bet...ty. Betty," she cried.

"Angel, I don't know who Betty is," he said calmly. "What about her?"

"She's another sorority sis...sister," she cried. "She's dead."

Monty's eyes grew wide, both from relief that the news was not about her brother and on alert knowing another sister had died. "Baby, I'm going to put you on speaker right now. Don't be embarrassed. Honest, the guys don't care that you're crying, but they need to hear this." The other men stood around the table, each pair of eyes riveted to Monty. Whether business or personal—what affected one, affected all.

Sniffling, she replied, "Okay, but this has nothing to do with what you're looking into."

With the Saints now listening, he said, "Tell me who she is and what happened, Angel."

She took a deep breath to slow her breathing, before answering. "It's my sorority sister, Betty Mavery. I just got a call that she died sometime last night." Another sob slipped out as she added, "How can this keep happening? It's so unfair. It's like we're cursed."

That thought brought Monty to his knees as he plopped heavily into a chair. Chad moved behind him, placing his hand on Monty's shoulder.

Taking over, Jack spoke. "Ms. Cartwright, this is Jack Bryant. I'm the owner of Saints Protection & Investigations. I know how upset you are and I promise, as soon as we're finished here, Monty will come straight to you. But can you tell us what you know?" He glanced over at Luke and Jude, who were already busy at their computers searching for information.

"Please call me Angel. Betty had a heart condition since birth," Angel explained. "That's why her death can't have anything to do with the others."

"I understand, Angel, but we can't take anything at face value right now. You're right, these could be unfortunate coincidences, but we need to make sure."

Sniffling again, she nodded. Feeling foolish for nodding when she was on the phone and the Saints could not see her, she said, "I understand. Caroline, the sister that called me, said Betty's parents told her she had a heart attack last night. Her parents found her."

Hearing another hiccup from her, Jack nodded toward Monty, who switched his phone off speaker. "Babe, I'm leaving now and should be to your place in about twenty minutes or so."

Disconnecting, he looked around the group. "I don't know whether to be relieved or fuckin' pissed." Seeing the confused expressions, he explained, "She's got an active duty brother who's Special Forces." That received understanding nods from the others. "But now, we've got one more death to investigate to see if it fits in or not. And if it does, how. And are we looking at a vendetta against the sorority?"

Several *fucks* sounded amongst the Saints. Jack interjected, "Monty, go home to your woman. Luke and Jude, see what you can dig up. We'll meet back here tomorrow and add another death to our investigation. And bring Mitch up to date."

As the men filed out of the room after Monty, Luke spoke up. "Just so you know, I've already determined that Betty Mavery had investments with Colonial Financial Group."

"Yeah, well so does Angel," Monty growled. Looking back at the men in the room behind him, he said, "As of now, I'm putting her under our protection."

Every one of the Saints nodded in agreement.

On the way to Angel's apartment, Monty called Mitch to fill him in on the news. "Mitch, I want that body to have an autopsy. I don't care that Angel said Betty had a heart condition. It's simply too convenient for another sorority sister to have a death so soon."

"I agree. I'll talk to the medical examiner and get back with you."

Disconnecting, Monty drove as fast as he was comfortable to Charlestown. As frustrated with the case as he was, his heart was heavy for the grieving woman waiting for him. Bounding up the steps, once inside her door he saw her sitting on the sofa talking on her phone. Her eyes lifted to his, her watery smile shooting straight to his heart.

"Mom, Monty's here now so I'm going to go. Tell dad I love him. Yeah, as soon as I know when the funeral will be, I'll give you a call. Love you," she said before hanging up.

Standing, she stood rooted to the spot, their eyes saying everything. Hers filled with pain. His filled with comfort. Walking toward her, he opened his arms as she rushed in. Wrapping her in his embrace, he held her as tears started anew. Turning around with her in his embrace, he sat on the sofa, pulling her into his lap, arranging her until she was comfortable

He rocked her for a long time, his fingers stroking her silky tresses. She finally lifted her head, grabbed her wad of toilet paper, and wiped her nose. Sniffling, she complained, "I swear if I never cry another tear as long as I live it will be fine with me." Lifting her gaze to his, she said, "I almost never cry in front of people and you've seen me cry a lot."

"I'm not just people," he replied, brushing the damp tendrils of hair from her cheeks. "And when friends die, it's a time to cry. Especially when you can't get very far in the grief process before getting hit again."

Nodding silently, she heaved a huge sigh. Looking over at the kitchen, she said, "Oh, honey, I didn't get anything fixed for dinner."

"I ordered on the way home," he responded.

She smiled weakly, but knew there was little she felt like eating after crying so much. The outer doorbell rang and he gently set her on the sofa and moved to get their food. As he headed down the stairs, she quickly snatched up the various wads of tissues and threw them away. Heading to the bathroom, she washed her face, placing a cold cloth over her eyes. Feeling slightly more refreshed, she walked back to the main room.

He stood at the kitchen counter, dishing out soup into two bowls and placing soda crackers by the side. Looking up, seeing her curious expression, he shrugged, "I figured you wouldn't feel like eating much, so I ordered soup from the deli down the street. It's their special chicken noodle." Holding the steaming bowl out to her, she smiled as she reached for it.

"It'll cure what ails you," she said softly. "That's what my grandmother always used to say. A bowl of soup will cure whatever ails you."

Setting their bowls on the table, Monty pulled her in for another embrace. "I hope it does," he whispered into her hair.

Two days later, Monty received the dreaded phone call from Mitch. "You're not going to like this, but I got the word from the medical examiner."

Monty held his breath, waiting for Mitch to deliver the crux of his news.

"Betty Mavery did have a heart condition and she did have a heart attack. But the medical examiner found high doses of pseudoephedrine in her system."

"Plain English, Mitch," Monty ordered.

"It's basically like Sudafed. The decongestant you'd take for colds."

"So that's not really much of a find, right? She got sick,

took over the counter medicines and it reacted to her heart?"

"According to her cardiologist, she knew the dangers and would have never, under any circumstances, taken any OTC like that."

"What does her family say?"

"I'm heading there now. Want to join me?"

"Absolutely," Monty confirmed. "Give me the address and I'll meet you there."

Forty-five minutes later, the two men sat in the small, but comfortable living room of the Mavery's. Betty's father, Charles, was a tall, thin man, his face pinched with emotion. Brenda Mavery's hands shook as she attempted to pour tea.

Monty leaned forward, gently taking the teapot from her, saying, "I'll serve, Mrs. Mavery."

She smiled in gratitude before sitting back on the sofa, tucked tightly next to her husband. "We...we're still in shock, you understand," she said.

"Yes ma'am, we do understand. We know your daughter had a heart condition and took medication. Do you have it here?"

Brenda nodded. "Betty was between homes and staying with us for a few weeks. She sold her condo and had bought a small house, but the closing was not for another month. It was nice to have her in our home again." She stood, saying, "I'll go get her medications."

Mitch jumped to his feet quickly and stilled her with his hand on her arm. "If you would show me the locations, I'll bag them for evidence."

A flash of pain sliced across Brenda's face but she turned and led him down the hall. Betty's father leaned forward in his seat toward Monty and asked, "Do you think there's something in her medication?"

"Sir, we don't know, but we want to find out everything we can. Tell me, do you or your wife have any over-the-counter cold medicine in your house?"

"No, none at all. I have high blood pressure and my wife makes sure to watch my medications very carefully. Plus, neither of us have had a cold in a couple of years."

Brenda and Mitch came back into the room, his hand full of plastic evidence bags with Betty's medications. Sitting back down, he asked, "Can you tell us about anyone who would have wished your daughter harm?"

The two parents shared a glance, easily caught by the two investigators. Charles heaved a huge sigh and said, "Maybe. It's complicated, though."

"That's why we're here, sir. Take your time."

"We were unable to have children on our own and adopted Betty when she was about three months old. We never knew anything about her parents, but we were always up front and honest with her about being adopted." He stopped and looked at Brenda, a wistful smile on his face. "We told her we wanted her and God graced us with the opportunity to have her in our lives."

At this time, Brenda took over the story. "About a year ago, Betty was contacted by a man named Bill Bradley. He said he was her brother and had been adopted by another family. He had gone after his birth records and found their parents were now deceased. He wanted to connect with his birth family. Betty was cautious. She had a very lucrative engineering job and was making good money. As much as she wanted to know her possible brother, she was uncertain he was who he said he was."

"They did genetic testing," Charles said, "and it proved they were related. She was ecstatic and we were happy for her. We had Bill over numerous times, welcoming him into our family as well."

Monty watched carefully, sensing the story was about to take a dark turn.

Brenda licked her lips as her hands clasped each other in her lap. "About six months ago, Betty came to talk to us. It seemed even though Bill worked as a pharmaceutical technician in a local drug store, he was short of money. He claimed he wanted a loan from her so he could go to college."

Charles looked over at Mitch and Monty, quickly assuring, "Betty was hesitant. She had worked during college, taken out a few loans, and always said she was sure having that responsibility made her a better student. She didn't mind loaning Bill some money, but it seemed he wanted more. I believe there were some debts that he needed to pay off first. And they began to argue about it. The more he pressured, the more she backed off."

"A few weeks ago, they were both here for dinner when the subject came up again. Charles and I wanted to stay out of their business, after all, they were both adults, but we saw a change in Bill's attitude. Bill accused her of making a killing with her investments from Colonial Financial and surely she could spare some. I mean it was no secret that she had investments, but it was just the way he said it."

Monty, alert as ever, lifted his gaze to Mitch. The room was silent for several minutes, the investigators allowing the Maverys to tell their story in their own time.

"Yesterday afternoon, Bill came over here as we were making funeral arrangements and made a comment that just...well, it...um..." Brenda's voice cracked.

Charles took over as he squeezed his wife's shoulders. "He said he knew we would grieve Betty, but he'd try to fill her place in our lives." Charles exhaled, his last words barely more than a whisper, "It was as though he thought he would now be our son since our only daughter was gone."

Brenda looked back at the men and said, "Then this morning we get a call telling us our daughter was poisoned. My husband and I are barely holding on so I won't give voice to my fears. But you can imagine what they are."

Monty and Mitch soon left the Mavery's house and walked back to their vehicles. "This fuckin' case gets stranger by the minute," Mitch said.

"So once again, we may or may not have any connection to Theresa or Marcia's deaths. They could be three coincidences or...three murders tied together. And the only link is Colonial Financial Group and a sorority."

17

M onty, Luke, and Jack stood in the compound's conference room, once more looking at the board on the wall with the case notes Luke had projected. Moving them around on the screen, they tried to see patterns with the new information. Chad walked around the corner and into the room, seeing what the others were viewing. "What a fuckin' mess," he exclaimed, seeing the various lines and connections.

"We keep looking at Colonial Financial Group, but do you think it could be the sorority? Someone with a grudge? Someone trying to get a payback...even years later?" Jack pondered aloud. Like Luke, he meticulously sifted through every angle in an investigation.

"I've mentioned this to Angel, but she swears nothing was going on with the sorority," Monty replied. "According to her, they were a small sorority, made up mostly of studious women, and their activities centered around community service. They didn't have a house together to live in. It was a small chapter...only about twenty girls each year."

Luke asked, "So no disgruntled girl who didn't make it? No one kicked out?"

"Nope. Angel said they were so geeky, almost no one wanted to pledge with them."

"Hey, nothing wrong with being a nerd," Luke added, his lips turning up. He had fought against the geeky reputation as an adolescent but, once in college, found a group of other like-minded computer nerds.

Chad laughed, saying, "Yeah, well I'll bet your intelligence didn't keep you alone on Saturday nights in college."

"Hell, I didn't get my growth spurt until I was about seventeen and by then I was a freshman in college," Luke ruefully admitted, a smirk on his face. "Before then, I was a ninety-pound, nerdy weakling."

The others laughed, now looking at Luke's height and lean, muscular, runners' build, before turning back to Monty.

"Angel said having a small sorority allowed them to get to know each other and the ones that graduated with her stayed close. There were about seven of them and now three are dead within a two-month period."

"Too much of a coincidence," Blaise said, walking into the room, having heard the last part of Monty's explanation. He looked at Monty and added, "She's still at the bakery. Never left today. I stayed until Jude took over. He's parked outside."

Jack asked, "Does she have a clue she's being watched?"

"I told her that she was under our protection, but I doubt she knows we have a tail on her. Honestly, most days she's in the bakery's kitchen by five a.m. and stays until about seven or eight at night."

"I've been digging into the finances of the sorority women and not just the victims," Luke said, eyeing Monty.

"I want you to remember that includes Angel. I don't want any misunderstandings."

Nodding, Monty agreed. "Thanks for the reminder. Yeah, I understand she's got to be checked as well." He twisted to look at Luke. "You find anything pertinent?"

Luke held his gaze for a second too long. "Only that Colonial Financial is her investment brokerage as well, but you knew that."

By now, Bart and Cam had entered the room as well. Bart leaned his large body against the doorframe and said, "I'll be glad to do more interviewing."

"How about you two making a trip to Colonial Financial...after hours, of course. I don't know what exactly to have you look for, but maybe anything that isn't showing up on Luke's electronic trail." He grinned as Bart and Cam fist bumped at their assignment.

"Jack, can you and Chad see Bill Bradley, Betty's newfound brother?" Monty asked. Receiving their nods, he jotted down the address and handed it to Jack. "Luke and Jude are checking into him, but I'd like your take as well."

Glancing at his watch, Jack replied, "We can leave now and probably get him tonight."

"Mitch is having the labs put a rush on her meds. He'll call me as soon as we know if there was anything wrong with her prescriptions."

Chad smiled at Monty as he passed Jack to head up the stairs. "Don't worry. We'll just lean on him a little."

Bart smirked as he threw his arm over Cam's shoulders, saying, "And we'll be just as quiet as little mice tonight breaking into the offices!"

The others laughed as the two largest of them headed out the door. Monty said, "I'd like to talk to Scott at Colonial Financial again. I'll call Marc and see if he's up for a chat as well."

Blaise, pouring more coffee, said, "He should be available. He was just coming in behind me. By the way, I heard the forecast as I was driving here. We're right in the path of a huge snowstorm."

"What else is new for central Virginia?" Jack chuckled.

"Well, this one is huge. They're calling for over two feet."

The men in the room whistled. It had been a couple of years since they had snow that large. "When's it supposed to hit?" Marc asked, coming in around the corner. An outdoorsman, he had no fear of a large storm.

"Day after tomorrow."

Monty, rubbing his chin, said, "Then we need to step things up. We need to work these interviews in. Blaise, you meet with the Senator and his staff again. Marc, you and I will head over to Colonial Financial. Jack and Chad are interviewing a possible suspect in Betty Mavery's killing. Jude'll watch Angel and, Luke…you know what to do."

"With all of you interviewing, send your intel in and Luke and I'll add it here. We'll coordinate virtually," Jack ordered.

With nods all around, the men moved out.

———

A small group of woman were meeting in the back of Angel's Cupcake Heaven. Helen came into the kitchen where Angel was finishing the specialty desserts for the assembly.

"You fixing your designer cupcakes for the women in the back?" Helen asked.

"Yes. A woman who runs a wedding venue called to say that she wanted to taste-test some of my newer creations and that we could talk about her using me as one of her preferred businesses that she would recommend to brides." She looked up at Helen and cocked her head while wiping her cheek, leaving a pink stripe. "Why? Is there something going on?"

"Oh, no. They keep asking when you'll be out. They seem anxious to meet you."

With a last flourish of the icing bag, Angel placed it on the counter and announced, "Well, I guess I should get this show on the road then." She and Helen each picked up a tray and made their way to the back of the bakery.

Approaching them, Angel saw four women sitting at one of the oval wooden tables covered with heavy glass over the pink tablecloths. She saw smiles from the four, but noticed their faces also held curiosity in them as well.

"Ladies, here is a sampling of my latest creations. I hope you enjoy them."

"Can you sit with us?" The question came from the fresh-faced woman whose honey-blonde hair was pulled back in a long braid hanging over her shoulder. She was dressed for comfort in khakis and a forest green sweater.

The others immediately scooted their chairs together, making room for another seat. Another blonde, her designer clothing noticeable, but comfortable. A petite, dark-haired woman leaned back, her pregnancy obvious in her pale pink maternity sweater. The fourth woman, her face soft with a gentle smile stared intently at Angel.

"Um, sure. I thought you might want to eat in private first and then, if you're still interested, we could talk."

"Oh, no. Your reputation speaks for itself. This is really just a formality. Um…sort of a chance to get to know you."

"O…kay…" Angel said, seeing the huge smiles on the other women. Turning to grab a chair from a neighboring table, she placed it between two dark haired women in the group.

The speaker said, "I'm Bethany Bryant. I own Mountville Cabins and Wedding Venue. These are my friends, Miriam, Sabrina, and Faith."

Shaking their hands, Angel turned her attention back to Bethany as she served the various deluxe cupcakes for them to try. She tried not to notice the women's glances at her and each other, but it was hard not to be aware of the undercurrent of curiosity.

After several minutes of orgasmic moaning over the various melt-in-your-mouth, moist goodies, the women leaned back in their chairs, satisfied expressions on their faces.

"I would love to work with you," Bethany said. "If you would be agreeable, I would offer your bakery as the go-to business for wedding cupcakes in my advertisements."

While Bethany and Angel discussed the particulars, the other three women sat observing the exchange. "Listen, Angel, I feel the need to make sure you understand who I am before we finalize any deal. My husband is Jack Bryant...of Saints Protection & Investigations."

"Monty's boss?" Angel asked, surprise on her face.

"Yes, but please don't think this offer has anything to do with that. But I have to say..." she continued, looking at the other women, "we really wanted to meet you."

Angel looked around the table as each woman re-introduced themselves and the Saint they were with. Smiling, she said, "Monty speaks of the other Saints with such respect and I've heard him mention you, too."

Focusing her attention back to Bethany, she said, "I would love to partner with you, but in another couple of weeks, I'll be moving to a different location and it will take at least a week to get up and running. I'll have the kitchen going quickly, but will need to decorate the new space."

Sabrina's eyes lit up. "I just happen to be an interior

decorator. I'd love to help. In fact, I was just noticing the unusual mural painted on your wall." She nodded her head to the muted painting of a medieval man in long robes, using a flat paddle to pull loaves of bread from a domed stone oven.

Angel smiled, but offered no other explanation other than, "I saw that in a book once when I was in culinary school and thought it was fitting."

"It's certainly apropos." Sabrina turned back to Angel, "Here's my card if you're interested in talking about decorating the new shop."

"I'd love to...as long as it would involve my signature colors," Angel said, waving her hand around, at the pink, purple, and teal colors splashed all over her walls.

"I can definitely do that!" Sabrina laughed.

As the women stood to leave, Angel hugged each one. Sabrina turned to the group and said, "I'll catch a ride with Jude since he's on duty outside. We'll only have to wait just a bit for until Monty comes."

Angel cocked her head to the side, confused by Sabrina's words. "Duty? What duty? And I don't know that Monty's coming tonight."

"Oh, sure he is. He's here at night and the other men rotate during the day," Miriam said, beaming at Angel.

Angel stood, tapping her toe with her hands on her hips. "I still don't understand what the duty is all about."

The four women glanced nervously between each other and Angel. Just then, Monty walked into the bakery.

"Oh, good. Monty's here," Bethany exclaimed and with another round of quick goodbyes and promises to see each other soon, the women hastily left.

Monty looked in surprise as the foursome greeted him as they flew by on their way out the door. He turned to smile at the beauty in the back when he saw her stance.

Arms crossed, hip cocked, toe tapping. He walked toward her, not stopping until his shoes were directing in front of hers and wrapped his arms around her stiff body. Planting a kiss on her unyielding lips, he leaned back.

"You want to tell me what's got you in a tiff? I see you met the women...what happened?"

"They were great, but you want to tell me what they meant by Jude on watch outside my shop?"

He rubbed the back of his neck as he stared down at his feet. "Cupcake—"

"Don't you cupcake me, Monty!"

He placed his hands on her shoulders and bent down to look directly into her eyes. "I told you that you were now under our protection." Before she could protest, he continued, "and that means that when you're not with me, I want someone on you."

"You don't think that's just a little bit over the top?" she queried.

"Nope. Babe, I've got three deaths that are all close to you and we're no closer to solving them than we were. Bottom line, I want you safe." Sighing, he pulled her in tightly, nodding at Helen, who was locking the front door and turning out the lights.

"Angel," Helen said. "I'll close up tonight. You go on upstairs with Mr. Lytton and I'll see you in the morning.

Nodding, Angel and Monty made their way up to her apartment. Reaching the top of the stairs, they both began to apologize at the same time."

Smiling, she said, "You go first."

Taking her hand and leading her to the sofa where he pulled her down next to him, he said, "I'm sorry I did not tell you about the men watching over you, but please understand I'm not sorry that I'm doing it."

"And I'm sorry that I jumped down your throat. I

realize this is difficult. I just don't see how the three deaths can be related. It just makes no sense to me."

They sat in comfortable silence for a few minutes, before she spoke. "Monty, I'd like to help."

"Help?"

"You know, with the investigation. These were my friends."

"Oh, no fuckin' way, Cupcake. You remember what happened the last time you tried to get information?"

Slapping his shoulder, she said, "Don't remind me! I ended up scaring some poor man who was trying to just cheat on his wife."

Monty glared. "And don't you even think that it was anything less than you taking a huge risk that could have played out very differently if he had been a killer."

The silence was no longer comfortable and she moved to rise from the sofa. He captured her hand before she moved away and gave it a little tug. Turning, she gazed back down at him, regret in her eyes.

"Baby, we've got this. I know it may seem like we're not making progress, but we'll figure it out." He silently hoped he could keep that promise.

Bill Bradley opened the door of his apartment, his eyes wide at the two huge men standing in the breezeway. "Uh...uh..."

"Mr. Bradley, I'm Jack Bryant and this is Chad Fornelli from Saints Protection and Investigations. I called earlier to meet with you."

"Yes, yes," the much smaller man said, backing up so that Jack and Chad could enter his home.

A quick glance gave evidence that Bill lived simply, but

not frugally. A large, flat-screen TV was perched on a nice cabinet, the multitude of wires behind connected to a DVD/Blueray player, an X-box, a sound system, and a cable box. The sofa facing the TV was not new, but not worn. The dining room table was older but appeared unused for eating, with its tabletop covered in papers and a laptop.

Jack turned his attention back to the owner. Bill Bradley was about five feet eight inches, with a slender body. His brown hair was trimmed neatly and his dark-rimmed glasses were constantly pushed upon his face as they slid down.

As the three men sat down, Bill shifted his eyes nervously between the two men. "Can I get you anything? I've got soda and tea?"

"No, thank you," Jack said. "We're here to ask you some questions about Betty Mavery." When Bill just nodded but did not say anything else, Jack continued. "We understand that you recently discovered your relationship with Ms. Mavery."

"I was adopted and decided to see if I could get information on my parents. It took a while, but I finally did and discovered I had a sister. I contacted Betty and, well, the rest is history. Her adoptive family made me feel real welcome and it finally felt like I had a whole life."

"How would you describe your relationship with Betty?" Chad asked.

"Relationship? Uh…well, we got along good. We'd have dinner sometimes and, about once a week or so, I'd go to her parent's house for dinner too."

"How did the Maverys compare to your adoptive family?"

Seemingly surprised by the question, Bill appeared thoughtful. "The Bradleys were nice people. They didn't have much money, but we got by okay. They were a lot older when they adopted me and Mr. Bradley had a stroke when I was about fifteen. Things got real tight then...with money. I worked part time at a grocery and helped out. He died a year later and Mrs. Bradley was lost after that. They weren't bad to me, but when I hit eighteen years old, I left."

"And compared to the Maverys?"

"I know they're not rolling in a ton of dough, but it was obvious that Betty had pretty much anything she wanted growing up. She went to college and got a good job." Bill grimaced as his lips tightened.

"But you've managed to obtain training and a job as a pharmaceutical technician?"

"It pays the bills and allows me to have more money than I've ever had before," he admitted. "This is the nicest place I've ever lived."

"Tell us about the last meal you had with the Maverys. The one where you and Betty argued," Jack stated.

Shifting his eyes down to the floor, Bill's face turned red. "I see the Maverys have been talking." Silence moved over the occupants of the room, seeming to unnerve Bill. "Betty had a lot of money. She had a big job and made twice what I make in a year. Plus she had money that she invested and I know it was doing good. I overheard her talking on the phone one time to one of her friends about the money. I tried to get her to understand how inequitable it all was."

Jack and Chad said nothing, but Jack's lifted eyebrow gave evidence to Bill that more information was needed.

"You know?" Bill implored for understanding. "We came from the same parents. By a stroke of luck, she gets adopted by a family that can give her stuff and by that same stroke of unluck, I get adopted by an older couple who can't give me much at all. If that's not inequitable, I don't know what is! All I asked for was some money to help me get ahead."

The room filled with silence once more as Bill slumped against the chair he was sitting in. "All I was asking for was some financial equality."

"Did she ever help you out financially?" Chad asked.

"Yeah. She gave me some money occasionally and then gave me the name of her investment broker." Giving a derisive snort, he added, "I talked to the person she told me about but they were going to let another person handle me. It seems the amount of money you want to invest determines which person will help you."

"So you two fought?" Jack prodded.

"No, it wasn't no fight," Bill protested. "We discussed it…loudly, but it wasn't no fight. I backed down like I always did and figured I'd just keep saving to get more money to invest."

"And then your sister died."

Bill glumly looked up at both men. "Yeah." His voice carried a mixture of grief and wistfulness. "I know the Maverys are hurting real bad. I told them that I'd try to take her place."

Jack and Chad shared a quick glance, first at each other and then back at Bill. He was still slumped in his chair, the appearance of a kicked dog visible in his countenance.

"Do you think the Maverys will have you be a continued presence in their family?" Chad asked, caution tinting his voice.

Bill's face changed from downtrodden to indignation in a flash as he sat up quickly. "Of course. Why wouldn't they? I'm Betty's brother after all. That's almost like being their son. I'm sorry about Betty, but they're gonna need someone to take care of them and I'll be that person."

Changing gears, Jack asked, "Did the pharmacy you worked at fill Betty's prescriptions?"

Bill hesitated a half-beat too long in answering. "Um, yeah. Sure. I'm sure we did. Why? She'd had a heart condition since birth and it was just her time. Maybe she skipped some pills or something. I could...um...check for you...if you want."

Bill's nervous rambling motivated Jack to increase the pressure on him. "Oh, don't worry about it. The FBI is already checking with the pharmacist." He watched Bill's face carefully before dropping his bomb. "And, they've collected all of her medicines from the Mavery's house for analysis."

Bill's eyes grew wide at that proclamation. "Whatever for? She had a bad heart!" he squeaked, chewing on his lip.

"Oh, just normal procedure in a suspicious death."

"Suspi...." Bill's voice tapered off as he looked down at his clasped hands. "I just thought she died from a heart attack."

"Do you think that you will be in Ms. Mavery's will?" Chad asked.

Bill's eyes darted up to Chad, his face now a mask of anger. "I don't know what you're implying. I've got no idea if I am or not. If I am, then that'd only be right since I'm her brother." He looked over at Jack before adding, "I think I've answered all the questions today I'm gonna answer."

Nodding, Jack and Chad stood and walked back to their SUV. Once they were driving down the road, Chad looked over at Jack and said, "He's guilty. Of what, I don't know. But he's guilty of something."

Jack nodded, his mind racing as to how Bill Bradley fit into their puzzle. The increasingly convoluted puzzle.

18

Monty and Marc walked into Colonial Financial Group once more, this time, met by a slender receptionist, her smile seeming etched permanently on her face. They sat as directed in the comfortable leather chairs in the waiting room, cooling their heels for several minutes. The door to the hall opened and Cindy walked through.

"Gentlemen, if you'll follow me," she requested, her smile forced. Leading them to Scott's office, they noticed her name on the desk outside his door.

"I see you've stayed here," Monty remarked.

Her eyes sought his as her mouth turned down. "Yes. I...I like the work here. I'm trying to..." she sucked in a deep breath before continuing, "it's hard." She knocked on Scott's door and then opened it, stepping to the side to allow Monty and Marc to enter.

"Gentlemen, good to see you," Scott greeted affably, his eyes jumping to the large, mountain man. He shook Monty's hand before being introduced to Marc. Indicating the chairs in front of his desk, he walked to his chair and sat. "Were you offered refreshment?"

"No, but that's all right. We're fine," Monty replied, noting Scott's flash of irritation.

"I'm trying to be patient with Cindy, but I confess it isn't easy," Scott said. "She and Marcia were very close. Almost unnaturally so."

Monty raised his eyebrow at this statement.

Scott caught the expression and quickly moved to amend his comment. "Oh, no, I didn't mean to suggest *that*! We all know Marcia loved the men too much." He tried to chuckle but it fell flat. Blushing, he stuck his finger in the tight neck of his shirt, giving a little jerk. "What I meant was Cindy was the consummate assistant for Marcia and now that Marcia's gone...well, I'm kind of stuck with her and she lets me know she's not crazy about how I'd like the office to be run."

"If you're not happy with her, can't she be assigned to someone else?" Marc questioned, wanting to understand the office politics.

"Marcia was the president of our branch and her assistant had a certain seniority with that. For her to be assigned to someone else would be seen as a demotion. So, for now, I'm stuck with her." He looked at the two stone-faced men sitting in front of him. "I'm sure you're not here to talk about my assistant troubles. What can I do for you?"

"You've heard of another one of your client's deaths— Betty Mavery?" Jack asked.

Scott's face registered surprise and his gaze shot between the two. "I'm not familiar with that name. I don't think she was one of my clients."

"So if she were the client of another investment broker in Colonial Financial Group, you wouldn't recognize her?"

"To be honest, no I wouldn't. We're not a huge firm, but

we are diversified enough that with five investment brokers on this staff alone, and then with the branch in Arlington, I really only deal with my clients. Well," he amended, "I know the more prominent clients with our firm even if they aren't mine."

A silence slid over the group as Scott turned to his laptop and, with a few clicks, located Betty's account. "Oh, of course. She was Marcia's client. I took her client list and divided it amongst the rest of us until we hire another broker."

He turned back to Monty and said, "She's dead, you say?" Gaining Monty's affirmation, he shook his head.

"We're concerned because that now makes three women, all from the same sorority, who have died within a two-month period."

"I understand your concern, gentlemen, but I fail to see how that relates to Colonial Financial," Scott replied.

"All three were clients of your company," Marc pointed out. "With one of them being the investor, it would be unwise for us to not take into consideration their finances."

Scott sat up straighter, his face flushed with indignation. "Are...what are you...do mean to say you suspect... I..." he sputtered.

Monty eyed him carefully. "We're trying to find a common denominator amongst the deaths and this company keeps coming up."

Scott leaned back heavily in his chair, his face a portrait of conflicting emotions. Rubbing his forehead, he said, "I don't know what to tell you." Sighing again, he said, "One of the ways Marcia was able to get ahead so quickly is she was a very social person and had a ton of friends. Considering who her daddy was, she naturally brought a lot of clients into the company. I was jealous at one time...here I worked for every client I could get and she waltzed in with a huge portfolio of friends...or daddy's friends, ready to give her business."

"Was that jealousy hard to handle?" Marc asked.

Scot snorted ruefully. "Honestly? It was hard to stay mad, because the more clients CFG got, the more bonuses that were shared by all of us."

Monty's eyebrows shot up. "So everyone benefited from Marcia's extensive client list?"

"Yes, indeed. The company's owners wanted it set up that way. Now, of course, the broker with the most clients got the extra commission, but we all benefitted from Marcia. I think it was the all-for-one attitude of the owners."

Scott eyed Monty and Marc speculatively for a moment. "Gentlemen, I'd be a fool to not realize you are considering someone from CFG as a possible suspect. But I can assure you that the loss of our top broker, and then two of her clients, hurts all of us. There's no one here who'd want to lose their bonuses."

After a few more minutes, Monty and Marc left Scott's office. As Cindy rose from her desk to walk them out, they stopped in the empty reception area noting the receptionist had already left. "How are you holding up, Ms. Bartley?" Monty asked. He watched as Cindy's face contorted and appeared to battle back tears.

"These...leeches," she bit out. "Ms. Creston was brilliant. She may have had a huge social circle that brought in business, but she knew what she was doing. They all rode on her coattails." Steeling her back, she said, "You want to know how I'm doing? I miss her." With that, she escorted them to the door and locked it behind them.

Marc looked over at Monty as they drove away. "Don't even ask," Monty declared. "Just when I think I might have a direction to look at, we're thrown for a loop and the new information doesn't fit in with where I thought the investigation was going."

Blaise sat in the Senator's study, looking around the room as the Senator poured them both a drink. The fireplace crackled on the chilly night, casting illumination as well as shadows about the room. Several family photographs in wooden frames sat on the mantle, keeping company with a large clock. The windows on the far wall were covered in dark green drapes, closed to the setting sun. The Senator walked over, handing Blaise a tumbler filled with amber liquid. The scotch went down smooth as Blaise appreciated the quality. The Senator finally settled in a leather winged-back chair, opposite of its twin where Blaise sat. He pulled off his tie and unbuttoned the top button on his shirt. Nodding to Blaise, he said, "You're more than welcome to relax as well, Mr. Hanssen. I've had a long day and I have a feeling you investigators have too."

Blaise nodded but kept his suit jacket on, glancing down to ascertain there was no cat or dog fur on his coat. "What I'd like to ask you about is your daughter's sorority. You know now that Betty Mavery has died. We'd like to understand more about their relationship."

The senator sighed heavily, the weight of his grief bearing down on him. "When Marcia was in school, she could have joined any organization. Her mother was a legacy with a more popular sorority and we assumed she would want to follow in her mother's footsteps." He smiled indulgently at the memory. "But Marcia was determined to go her own way. The first time we visited her after she joined, I will say her mother and I were shocked. We expected to see a large brick sorority house, but instead, there was no house. The girls occupied a corner wing of a dorm."

The Senator continued, "Marcia was so proud to introduce us to her new sisters. The whole group was only about twenty girls...maybe not even that many. But it was a small group of her pledge sisters that resonated with her. And such a diverse group."

"Diverse, sir?" Blaise prompted.

"Mrs. Creston and I taught Marcia to never judge a person by how much money their parents made and that showed in her sorority. Theresa Constantine attended there on full scholarship. Betty Mavery acted just as geeky as she could," he smiled as he remembered. "Angel Cartwright took baking classes on the side and Marcia spent a lot of time doing community service. There were about four others making the core group." His face fell as the weight of grief once more settled on him. "All good women. Good women," he said, his voice suddenly tired. "We were real proud of Marcia...and quite frankly were very fond of all of her sorority sisters."

Carlton walked into the room, then halted when he saw the Senator had company. "Oh, excuse me, Uncle. I wanted to inform you dinner is almost ready." His eyes darted to Blaise, seeking an introduction.

Blaise recognized Carlton from their investigations, but kept silent, waiting on the Senator, who simply acknowledged Carlton with a slight hand wave. Carlton stood, uncertain for a moment, before leaving the room. Blaise noted the door to the study stayed wide open and he had not heard Carlton's footsteps continue down the hall.

"I'm sure my reminiscing about the sorority isn't helping your investigation," the Senator added.

"Actually, sir, it does. We're talking to the other women,

but anything we can find to tie in the three women is helpful."

The Senator turned his intelligent gaze to Blaise. "You think the three deaths are related? I thought Betty's was a heart condition. And Theresa's a car accident."

Blaise nodded noncommittally. "Yes, sir, but there's evidence we cannot ignore. We have to look at all three cases as possibly related. Or, if not all three, then two of them and one an unfortunate coincidence."

The Senator sat motionless for a long minute, the only sounds in the room were the crackling firewood burning in the fireplace and the tick-tock of the clock on the mantle.

"I can't think of one single thing that tied the women together other than their friendship and I know Marcia had a few of them as clients." He looked up quickly and added, "Marcia was a complete professional and never discussed her clients with me, but that came out in casual conversation."

Blaise nodded and then stood. "I don't want your dinner to grow cold, Senator Creston, so I'll take my leave. I appreciate you seeing me on such notice."

As they shook hands, the Senator added, "Feel free to ask me anything. I not only want my daughter's murderer found, but if the other two women did indeed meet an untimely end, then I want their cases solved as well."

As they stepped into the hall, Carlton rounded the corner once more. "Oh, there you are Uncle. Would you like me to see Mr. Hanssen out?"

"Yes, thank you," the Senator said before disappearing down the hall.

Blaise turned toward Carlton, a smile on his face. "I don't want to keep you from your dinner."

"Oh, don't worry about that. I'm just here to check on

my aunt and uncle. I'll be eating at the club later." The only sound was their shoes clicking on the entry foyer. Just as they reached the front door, Carlton asked, "So, um... how's the investigation going? I know the FBI have kept my uncle up on their findings but I was curious about the others. Is there a tie-in?"

"We don't know, yet, but as I told your uncle, we have to look at all possibilities." Blaise let the silence sink into the space between the two of them. "Is there any information you can give us that you think will help?"

Startled, Carlton immediately jerked and said, "No, no. I didn't meet any of Marcia's sorority sisters."

Blaise offered his hand before turning to walk out the door. Standing on the stoop for a second he looked back through the glass at the side of the door and saw Carlton still in the entry foyer, his phone already at his ear.

The black of the moonless night aided Bart and Cam, although they would have had no difficulty if their way had been more illuminated. Easily disarming the building's security system, the two slipped into the Colonial Financial Group offices.

Their footsteps made no sounds on the dark burgundy carpet as they moved down the ivory painted hallways. Peering into the dark paneled offices, they became acclimated to the layout of the company. The front held the reception room filled with chairs and an ordered receptionist's desk. The building was bifurcated with a hallway straight down the middle, with three offices on either side of the hallway. The hallway ended in a cross hall, the left leading to Scott's office. As the now acting president of the branch, he enjoyed the largest office with an assistant desk sitting in the area outside of his door. To the right were the workroom, several closets, and another space for the second assistant.

Splitting up, they moved from office to office, searching for anything that might give them insight into the inner workings of the employees. Bart had spoken to Monty and knew he was particularly interested in Scott's office. A thorough search gave him nothing. The office was neat and organized, although not as neat as Marcia's apartment had been. Going through his files and drawers turned up nothing, other than a roll of antacids and a strip of condoms. Smiling, he wondered if Scott ever used them at work or if they were there for his after hour's activities.

Turning on Scott's computer, he slipped in the special flash drive Luke had given him. Sending Luke a text on his phone, he waited until he received the signal. Scott's computer flared to life, the login bypassed. Leaving it running for a moment, he then shut it down, making sure to pocket the drive. Stepping back into the hall he ran into Cam, who had been performing the same task in the smaller offices of the other brokers.

"You get the info from their computers?" Bart asked.

"Oh yeah," Cam whispered back. "Just the receptionist and the two assistant desks are left."

"I'll get this one," Bart volunteered. "This is the assistant that used to work for Marcia. We'll see what information Luke can gain from her computer."

Nodding, Cam moved silently down the hall. Bart checked out her desk, but there was not a paper-clip out of place. Firing up her computer, he did the same thing. He moved to the other assistant's desk, finding it much messier.

By the time Cam returned from the front reception

area, the two met in the back hall. "What are your impressions?" Bart asked.

"The place is extremely clean," Cam noted. "Even the workroom is neat. I remember the same cleaning company that works here, was also hired by Marcia Creston for her condo. I'm also struck by how little personal effects I found in the receptionist's desks."

"Same for the assistants' desks," Bart commented. "We know Marcia Creston was a neat-freak, but it seems her legacy for order has been passed on.

As they slipped back out into the dark night, resetting the alarm system, they moved to their vehicle. In the still moonless night, the only illumination came from the headlights and streetlights. Cam leaned over and peered at the sky. "The big storm is supposed to hit tomorrow. They're calling for more snow than we've had in a couple of years."

"It'll make getting around hard for a few days. I'm sure Luke'll just stay at the compound and work on what he can pull up from the computer drives we copied. I'll get them to him tomorrow morning at our meeting."

"I have a feeling once the storm hits I'll be at home with Miriam for a day or so."

Bart could not hold back his grin. There was a time when he had a hard time imagining spending days indoors with one woman. Now that he had Faith—*bring on the storm.*

19

The morning rush over, Angel filled the cases again with the more decorative cupcakes. It had been Marcia who encouraged her to add muffins to her menu, therefore drawing a breakfast crowd. The result had Angel getting up much earlier to bake and open the shop by seven a.m., but the financial rewards had been excellent. Even though her present location was not great, a lot of customers discovered her treats were just what they wanted as they headed to work.

It seemed with the impending storm, more customers were flocking in to grab their muffins and cupcakes to have in case they were snowed in for a couple of days.

She looked up as a few more customers came in and she welcomed them. Her eyes landed on the last woman entering and she blinked in recognition. *Claire. Monty's former...something.* Turning her attention back to the first customers up, she assisted them before they made their way to the cashier. Glancing over at the counter, she plastered on her best ACH smile.

"Hello. Claire, I believe? Welcome to Angel's Cupcake Heaven. What can I get for you?"

She watched as Claire's gaze searched the glass case, the shelves filled with the healthy muffins and delectable cupcakes already on display. Claire had taken off her overcoat and had it laying across her arms, exposing her thin frame covered in designer silk.

"I don't usually eat anything for breakfast other than a piece of whole-wheat toast," Claire said, her eyes riveted to the case. "But I decided to bring in treats to my office today. To celebrate my promotion," she added.

"Well, why don't I pack an assortment for you and then your office will have choices?"

Claire looked up, surprise in her eyes as she stared at Angel. "That would be lovely."

Monty happened to take that moment to step from the kitchen where he had come from the apartment above by way of the back stairs. Still tightening his tie, he called out, "Hey babe, I'm on my way. Make sure to let us know if you're going anywhere today." He grabbed Angel from behind, no longer inhibited from public displays of affection. Leaning around to kiss her lips quickly, he let his hand slide to her delectable ass, making sure none of the customers could see the gesture.

Lifting his eyes, his gaze landed on Claire. Straightening stiffly, he looked at her with a mixture of irritation and curiosity. "Claire," he stated. "I didn't know you shopped here."

Claire's surprise at seeing Monty so naturally at home in the bakery, as well as his arms around Angel, had her uncharacteristically stunned. So much so, she stood, silent with her mouth open, for a few long seconds. Blinking, she said, "Monty? How nice to see you." Her eyes darted back and forth between the two, as she replied, "I'm here to pick up treats for my office. As you know, I don't add extra calories to my diet." Her eyes skimmed down Angel's frame, landing on Monty's hand resting possessively on her hip. "The extra pounds would be so unattractive. Of course," she laughed, "some women don't care about such things."

If she thought Angel would be intimidated, she was wrong. Laughing the throaty laugh Monty loved, Angel said, "Thank goodness or I'd be out of business. Here's your box. You may pay at the register and I hope you have a lovely day." With that, she handed the white box, tied with pink, purple, and teal ribbon, to Claire before turning back to Monty.

He nodded stiffly to Claire before walking back into the kitchen with Angel. She wrapped her arms around his waist, kissing the underside of his jaw.

"Mmm. Are you sure you have to work today?" she purred, now licking his neck.

He felt his knees almost buckle and grinned at the top of her head. Kissing each colored stripe, he then pulled back slightly to look into her eyes. "Thank you," he whispered. Seeing the unspoken question in her eyes, he added, "For putting Claire in her place...in such a classy way."

Laughing, Angel said, "She doesn't bother me." Lifting her arms from his waist so she could cup his cheeks, she said, "Honey, if you wanted her, you would be with her and not me. Since you're with me, then I assume you either like my tits and ass...or you just like waking up over a bakery that always smells great! Either way, I win!"

Laughing with her, he leaned down to kiss her pink, glossy lips. "You're right. I love being with a woman who bakes such incredible treats, whose place always smells good, who kisses like nobody's business, whose tits and ass are unrivaled...and who rides around in a hot pink VW convertible."

Offering another quick kiss, she turned him around and gave a slight push toward the door. "Go! I've got to get to baking!"

With a final wink tossed over his shoulder, he walked out of the bakery toward his SUV. Nodding toward Chad parked outside, he stepped to the driver's door. His thoughts on the woman inside, he was surprised when Claire stepped up next to him. Her face was pinched as she looked at him.

"I don't understand, Monty. She's not your type."

He cocked his head to the side, staring at the woman looking like the perfectly coiffed professional—everything he used to think was for him. And suddenly Felicity's words came slamming into his memory. Last Christmas she said she would be glad when he finally met a real woman. Someone who made him feel. Someone who made him live. When he tried to protest, she accused him of subconsciously dating women that would meet their parent's approval. And it was safe because he would never let one of those women get too close. He remembered as Felicity stooped to pick up one of her children and at that moment, she turned back to him with a smile, saying, "When you meet the woman that's right for you, I'll bet anything she's not like the women you've been with."

At that memory, his gaze shifted from Claire's face to the storefront behind her shoulder. The one with the huge pink, purple, and teal swirling letters declaring Angel's place. *Felicity, you were right.* Feeling more alive than ever, he looked back at Claire. "I know you weren't that into me, Claire, so I know you're not jealous. What's the real reason behind this visit?"

Claire's head snapped back as her lips pursed. "You're

right, Monty. I'm not jealous of her," she bit out, glancing over her shoulder. "At first, I wondered if it was some kind of latent rebellion on your part. It's embarrassing to have been thrown over for a shopkeeper."

"Shopkeeper? You're serious? Jesus, Claire, you want to know what's crazy? I dated women like you for several years—women easy to keep at arm's length because I wanted nothing more. I've just now discovered how fuckin' great it is to be with someone real. Someone who makes me laugh. Someone who accepts me for me." He leaned over her slightly, using his height for emphasis. "So if you're embarrassed to have been thrown over for someone so incredibly amazing...then you need to get the fuck over yourself."

With those parting words, he hopped into his SUV and drove down the street leaving Claire standing on the sidewalk, her ACH decorated box in her hand. And grinned all the way to Jack's.

Bart walked in early, his hair already standing on end from running his hand through it, and handed the special thumb drives to Luke, who was already on his second cup of strong coffee. "You're gonna get an ulcer slamming down that strong stuff the way you do."

Luke just grinned as his fingers tapped on the desk. Taking the drives, he tucked them away securely. "I've already been going through the data of CFG, but it's taking a long time. I'll go over it when everyone gets here."

About fifteen minutes later, the Saints gathered to look over the updated intel. Blaise reported on his visit with the Senator. "Put cousin Carlton on your list to check out. He's definitely shady and looking to move into a more supportive role with the Senator. His tie-in with CFG as Scott's best friend also makes him a suspect...at least for Marcia."

Jack and Chad sent their interview notes on Bill Bradley to the other's tablets. "He had motive, opportunity, and means...at least for Betty's death. And he's shittin' bricks knowing her meds are at an FBI lab. I've already contacted Mitch and the FBI will be detaining him until they have a chance to get the results so that he doesn't fly."

Marc leaned his seat back, stretching his long legs out in from of him, and added, "And we know Geoffrey Daly had the means, motive, and opportunity for Theresa Constantine's death."

"So are we looking at three, entirely independent murders?" Monty growled. "I know we've considered this, but it's too fuckin' neat." Something hovered in the back of his mind, but he could not pull his thoughts together. "My mind's firing all over the place," he complained. Turning to Luke, he asked, "Did you make the coffee this morning?"

Luke's grin was his answer.

"Fuck! How do you operate with this much caffeine in your system," Monty complained as he walked over to the sink, dumping his cup. Whatever thought flew through his mind quickly disappeared, much to his irritation. Sitting back down, he said, "There's a tie in here somewhere and it's got to be CFG."

Bart looked up and said, "Cam and I did a thorough search of the offices last night. We got their computer drives copied for Luke and Jude to pour over. Other than that, there was almost nothing. The offices were clean, almost sterile. We did not find any paper trail that would offer us any more information."

Monty added, "I don't get a good feeling about Scott, but I don't see him masterminding anything. He's made it back to the top at the office because of Marcia's death, but I don't see him being able to plot and plan what it would have taken to make this happen."

"Does that mean you're leaning toward Carlton?" Jack asked.

"Right now, I'm not leaning toward anyone, but neither am I ruling anyone out."

Blaise asked, "If the three murders are linked, where do Bill and Geoffrey fit in?"

Monty heaved a sigh as he ran his hand over his trimmed beard. "I don't know. I don't believe either of them could have arranged all of this," he indicated with a sweep of his hand toward the large board in the room, filled with pictures, connecting lines, and data. "But maybe, just maybe they were there just to do a part of an overall plan."

The attention of the group landed squarely on him. He continued, "It would take someone with money, the ability to plan in great detail, and motive. But what the motive is for all three deaths is beyond me at this point." Leaning back in frustration, he eyed the rest of the group. "Suggestions, anyone?"

The Saints continued to process the cases, but in the absence of new information, the meeting concluded, and new assignments were handed out. Jack said, "This is still our top priority, so Luke and Jude will stay on the computer end of it while Monty will continue lead. There are a few new contracts that have come in for security and investigation. You'll find new assignments on your tablets. I don't expect any of those to be too taxing, so you'll still assist with this case as needed."

As everyone stood to leave, Jack reminded, "Stay safe out there. Until I can plow the driveway, I won't call another meeting here. According to the weather forecast that will be at least two days."

With goodbyes and good lucks all around, the Saints headed out. Monty watched as the single men left, making plans to meet at Chuck's Bar and Grille as soon as they could get their SUVs there. He noted the Saints with women were hustling out, ready to be snowed in for a day or so with the ones they loved. He stood on Jack's front porch for a moment, breathing the cold mountain air deeply. His thoughts moved to Angel and of this morning's confrontation with Claire.

Felicity once accused him of dating women that their parents would approve of as though that would soften the blow to them that his career was not what they wanted. He thought her accusation was completely wrong. Now he knew she had been exactly right. Now, with Angel in his arms, he realized what he had been missing all those years...*living*.

With a smile on his face, he jumped into his SUV and followed his friends down Jack's driveway, anticipating being snowbound with the woman he loved.

Monty stepped into his apartment and the plain interior startled him. Smiling, he realized that after spending most nights at Angel's place, his home looked very bare indeed. Walking through to his bedroom, he moved to the closet. His dress pants and suit coats hung neatly in a row. His ties hung perfectly even from a tie rack. Bypassing them, he moved toward the back where his jeans were hung neatly.

Neatly. A fleeting thought passed through his mind and then nothing more. Focusing on what he would need for the next couple of days, he continued with packing. Grabbing a small duffle bag, he packed jeans, thick socks, thermal shirts, as well as a couple of flannel ones. He found his heavy boots and packed them as well. His toiletries were mostly at Angel's place so he did not need to worry about those items.

Moving to his hall closet, he pulled out his winter coat and a heavy winter parka. Gloves, knit hat, and a scarf finished out what he thought he would need. It only took one trip to place everything in his SUV, but he made another trip back up just to check.

He walked to the bank of windows overlooking the small skyline of Charlestown with the Blue Ridge Mountains in the distance. He loved this view—at least, he always had. Now it seemed distant. Remote. Just like he had been.

As an FBI agent, it was necessary to maintain a distance between himself and the victims' families. He loved the analytical aspect of crime investigations. Never get personal. Never get too close. It might interfere with objectivity. But Angel had changed all that. The victims were people, not to only be investigated, but to be mourned.

As his gaze moved back to the distant mountains, he smiled as he remembered Angel hosting a party for a group of little girls and their moms. The girls were enamored with her colored tresses as she flitted around serving them. The oohs and aahs rang out when she appeared with a platter of her famous cupcakes. When he asked her if she personally saw to each party, she replied, "I need to get up close and personal with life."

Closing and locking his door behind him, he headed to her place to wait out the storm. With an eager grin, he knew he planned on getting up close and personal tonight.

Arriving in the early afternoon, Monty entered the bakery noting it was still busy. Seeing Helen behind the counter, he nodded his greeting as she jerked her head, indicating Angel was in the kitchen. Walking through, he saw her busy pouring batter into the tins and one of her assistants taking out what finished baking. Glancing down, it appeared to be muffins instead of her usual afternoon cupcakes.

Angel looked up as he entered, a huge smile on her face. Seeing the grocery bags in his hands, she cast a questioning gaze his way.

"I figured we wouldn't starve since you own a bakery, but I brought over some other food for us to eat during the snow storm besides your amazing cupcakes."

Laughing, she admitted, "I haven't had time to go to the grocery store, so thank you!"

He ran the grocery bags upstairs to her apartment and placed the cold items in her refrigerator as well as the dry goods in the cabinet. Heading back downstairs, he moved to take a large tray of muffin tins from her hands and set it on the counter. With a quick glance, he saw more muffins than she typically made in several days.

"Angel, why the baking frenzy?" he asked, placing his hands on her shoulders. Gently turning her as he leaned down, he kissed the corner of her mouth.

She grinned and whispered, "I think you missed."

"Nope, just aware your assistant is in the room. And..." he said with a slow grin, "that's just a preview of what's to come."

Laughing, she shoulder bumped him out of the way as she took the baked muffins out of the tins.

"You didn't answer my question," he reminded.

She looked around the busy kitchen and said, "Don't worry, they'll get eaten. You'll see."

Assuming she would have the shop opened for limited hours even in a snowstorm, he shrugged. "You need any help?"

"I can always use the help!" she agreed.

As the first flakes of snow began to fall, she dismissed Helen and her two assistants for the day. Monty made sure they were in their cars and on their way before locking the back door to the alley. He then joined Angel in the main bakery and assisted her wiping down the tables and counters. He noted she had turned on the closed sign. *I guess she's not going to stay open.* Looking back toward the kitchen, he wondered, *then who the hell are all those muffins for?*

Before he could question her further, she turned out the light in the shop and moved toward him. He opened his arms as she walked straight in and cupped his face in her hands. Pulling him down, she stopped her lips a breath away from his. "And this is a preview of what's to come from me."

She stood on her tiptoes, latching her mouth onto his. The touch of their lips ignited a firestorm. His cock swelled painfully as he took the kiss deeper, his tongue tangling with hers. Her hand slid between them, palming his length.

"Mmm, babe," he muttered against her lips, "let's take this upstairs."

The kiss continuing, she mumbled back, "We don't have time. I've got the timer going off in five minutes. Another batch is in the oven." Feeling the length of his erection pressing into her stomach, she giggled, "Can't you wait?"

"With you, it appears that it has a mind of its own," he growled as she pushed him back against the door to the stairs.

She heard his moan deepen as she worked his zipper down. "Well, let's see if we can do something about that," she purred, kissing a trail from his lips downwards until she circled his swollen cock with her lips.

He sucked in a ragged breath as she slid his length into her warm mouth. Too large for her to take all of him in, she fisted the base with her hand. Working her hand and mouth in rhythm she continued, noticing with pleasure as his balls tightened.

Monty held her shoulders in his hands, looking down at her pink, glossy lips sliding over his cock. He could not remember the last time he had a woman suck him off. *Jesus, I've been dating some seriously uptight women!* Fighting the urge to move her up and down even faster, he panted, "I'm close. Come here." He tried to lift her, but she just smiled as she grabbed his ass with both hands and held on as her tongue continued to swirl around his sensitive head in between of sucking his length deep.

Shaking her head while not breaking rhythm, she continued to suck until the hot semen hit the back of her mouth. Sucking until the last drop came into her mouth, she slid off looking satisfied.

He was not sure his legs could hold him up as he lay back against the door. The tingling sensation from his lower back through his balls had him panting to catch his breath. He was barely aware of Angel tucking him carefully back into his pants and re-zipping them.

He lowered his head to gaze into her face. She ran her tongue over her still-pink lips before rising on tip-toes to kiss him once again.

Just then the oven timer went off and she twirled away from him, laughing. "Perfect timing," she sang as she washed her hands before taking another tray of muffins out of the oven and placing them on cooling racks.

Monty took his duffle bag up to Angel's apartment while she finished the baking. When he had asked why she was still baking, she grinned and told him to come back down when he was done. Walking over to one of her windows, he pulled back the red sheers and looked out at the rapidly falling snow. Dusk was coming early this evening and as he looked down the street, the snow had already covered the ground. Movement at the edge of the corner of the building caught his attention, but he was unable to see what it was.

Rapidly moving to another window overlooking the front of the building, he saw a large group of people shuffling through the snow toward the front of Angel's bakery. Leaning his forehead against the cold window pane to gain a better view, it appeared as though they had congregated at her doorstep.

He sprinted to the stairs, jogging down and into the kitchen before he heard voices coming from the front. Flying to the front, he skidded to a stop, seeing the front door open and Angel standing in the doorway. People walked by and she was handing muffins to them as they thanked her profusely. *What the hell is she doing?*

Just then she turned, hearing him coming up behind her. Her blonde hair glistened with the snow pouring behind her as her smile shot straight to his heart. "Hey, sweetie. You're just in time."

Stepping up to her protectively, he looked at the faces of the men and women moving by. Leaning down, he whispered, "Angel, what are you doing?"

"When I know the weather is going to be bad and some of these people might not be staying at the homeless shelter, I open up for an hour or so to give out muffins." Turning back, she smiled as heartfelt "thanks" came her way once more.

Torn between pride at her thoughtfulness and anger at the risk she was taking, he stood stiffly behind her for a moment, his breath coming in spurts. "Babe, I don't think this is a good idea. You're encouraging...I mean, you're—"

She whipped her head around, her colorful streaks flying out behind her, the smile replaced with a glare. "What? What are you saying," she hissed under her breath. "I'm encouraging these people to be homeless? Jesus, you sound like my brother." Huffing, she added, "He's always worrying."

Right then, Monty felt a kinship with her Special Forces brother even though he had never met him. Taking a deep breath, he stepped to her side, saying, "I didn't say that."

"No, but you were thinking it," she accused.

He did not deny it, but stayed by her side, if for no other reason than to keep an eye on the group of people. He watched diligently but saw nothing untoward. The group did not rush the door or create a scene. They formed a single file and came by accepting the offered muffins, most expressing gratitude. He watched as Angel's face shone with a heartfelt smile for every person. She reminded them that the homeless shelter was only a few blocks away and there was a cold-weather refuge in one of the churches down the road.

Monty kept his eyes peeled in case someone had a weapon or nefarious intent, but his concerns were unfounded. After about half an hour, the last of the visitors had moved on and Angel pushed her almost empty cart back inside the bakery, shutting and locking the door.

He remembered his parents' efforts at community service. Twice a year, his mother collected his and Felicity's clothing that no longer fit and took them to a facility that could use them. Drive up. Drop off. Done. He thought of the charity event Claire had invited him to last summer for a charitable board she served on. The dinner cost hundreds of dollars per plate, there was an auction for various items, and he won two theater tickets. The money was for...*I don't even remember what it was supposed to benefit.* Later that month, he took Claire to the theater and she remarked that it was so nice that they could enjoy the finer things while helping the unfortunate. He remembered, at the time, it seemed an incongruous statement to make but had spent no time pondering it further.

And here was Angel. Businesswoman. Entrepreneur. And philanthropist, by giving of herself to people she could actually see. Actually touching their lives in a personal way. Accepting them, where they are—not demanding they change for her.

Sighing, Monty stood back watching her in earnest, wondering what her attitude toward him was going to be. She avoided eye contact as she stepped around him, pushing the cart with only a few muffins left on the trays. He followed her into the kitchen as she took the surplus muffins, wrapped them in cellophane, and then placed them in the refrigerator. *Shit, she's not talking to me.*

"Babe," he called out softly.

"Hmm?" she asked, still not looking at him, busying herself with unnecessary tasks. She remembered her brother's visit last summer when he was in-between assignments. The temperature was reaching over one hundred degrees for a week and she passed out muffins and water bottles. He came by and lectured her mercilessly. He claimed her heart overruled her head. *Wasn't that what Monty had said when she tried to find Marcia's kidnapper by herself?*

"Angel, look at me," he ordered, his voice softer.

She turned to face him, keeping her eyes on his chest. He walked over and lifted her chin with his fingers.

"I'm sorry," he said.

Her eyes grew wide at his apology. "You're sorry for...?" she asked, watching his face carefully.

He ran his hand over his face, before trusting himself to speak. "I'm sorry for not understanding what you were doing. You have to understand where I'm coming from, Cupcake. I was an investigator with the FBI for years. I've seen things I wouldn't want you to even know about and, believe me, you can't imagine. So I'm suspicious by nature. I'm fearful for those I love. I'm not trusting of the motives of many."

"You do sound like my brother," she admitted, still holding his gaze.

"Sounds like someone I'd like to meet," he said.

Unable to withhold her smile at the thought of the two of them meeting, she nodded and said, "I'm sure you will sometime when he comes home again." Then, remembering what he had been saying, she continued, "I can't live my life with that much fear."

"I know we're different in that respect," he admitted. "But for every down-trodden, hard-luck story that came by your bakery tonight, there can also someone with issues so that you cannot be certain of how they will react in situations." He heaved another sigh. "You gotta see it from my point of view, babe. A woman. Alone. Handing out food in front of a shop that could have had some money here. That was dangerous."

"You think I should just stop?" she queried, pushing her hair back as her voice vibrated with renewed frustration.

"No," he said, surprised at his gut-reaction answer. "But I do think that we can come up with a safer solution. Maybe have them meet you at the church that you said has the cold-weather refuge. It might even encourage them to stay there and utilize the facility."

She considered his answer thoughtfully, chewing on the inside of her cheek. "I can do that. As long as you're not trying to stop me from doing something that I care about, I can compromise."

He smiled as he gazed at her face peering up at him so seriously. Sliding his hand to cup her cheek, he smoothed his thumb over her skin before lifting his other hand to follow the same action. "Compromise? I like the sound of that."

"You ready to go upstairs?" she asked, her voice low and sultry once more.

"Oh yeah," he responded, leaning down to touch his lips to hers. Soft. Gentle. With a promise of more to come. "Let me double check the locks and I'll be up."

Grinning, she lifted up on her toes, kissing his jaw. With a wink and a toss of her colorful streaks, she sashayed up the stairs leaving him staring at her gorgeous ass. *Damn.* Checking the front and back door locks as fast as he could, he sprinted up the stairs after her.

21

Entering Angel's apartment, Monty noticed the overhead lights were off and the only illumination came from several lit, scented candles placed around the room. The door to the bedroom was open and he saw candlelight there as well.

Angel walked into the room clad in only a short silk robe, the swirling colors of the silk catching the light. With her hair flowing down her back, his fingers twitched to run through the shiny strands.

She walked straight toward him, her hands at the belt's tie on her robe. Smiling, she ran her tongue over her lips as she approached.

He stood his ground, watching as she continued until she was right at his body, the robe hanging loose, showing her deep cleavage. *That's my girl...knows what she wants and goes after it with everything she's got!* He gazed into her blue eyes, her gaze never wavering. *And thank fuck she wants me!*

His hands went to the lapels of her robe, pushing them until the top gapped open and more cleavage peeked through. Placing his hands on the soft material at her shoulders, it took little movement to have the silk land in a pile at her feet. Dragging his eyes down, he perused her full breasts, her tapered waist, and full hips. Her legs, long and toned...*Damn, I want them wrapped around me when I'm buried deep inside.* With a quick lift, he carried her into the bedroom, laying her on her back, her breasts bouncing with the motion. His dick, already pressing into his jeans, was straining, leaving him to wonder if his zipper was creating a permanent mark.

Leaning up on her elbows, she watched him as he divested himself of his clothes as quickly as he could. When he was down to his tented boxers, she lowered her gaze to travel slowly over his body. His dark brown hair was clipped neatly, as was his trim beard. She followed his body with her eyes, from his muscular chest to his defined abs. He had a smattering of chest hair that tapered down to the waistline of his boxers. "You're absolutely gorgeous. You know that, don't you?" she said, marveling at the muscles flexing with each movement.

Lifting his eyebrow, he took her in. "Seems like you've got that backward," he countered, his gaze traveling down her luscious body. He lowered his hands to his boxers and kicked them down his legs and onto the floor. Finally out of its constraints, his cock stood at attention as he ran his fist up and down its length. He knelt on the floor pulling her feet toward him before placing a kiss on each instep.

Angel raised up on her elbows and watched as his bearded face kissed her feet. Trying to jerk her legs back, she could not contain the giggle that erupted. "I'm ticklish," she gasped, but then his mouth began to move higher and her mirth ended as her pussy clenched in anticipation.

Kissing up her legs, he then slung them over his shoulders as he moved his lips to the prize. With the flat of his tongue he licked her moist folds, memorizing the taste of her. *I want this. Every night. Forever.* Plunging his tongue in, he grinned as she jumped, jerking her hips off the bed. "Easy Cupcake, we got all night," he said. Using his mouth in tandem with his fingers, he nipped, licked, sucked, and worked her into a frenzy.

He latched onto her clit while sliding a finger deep inside, crooking it as it hit the spot that he had been aiming for. The one that he knew would throw her over the edge. With one last suck, he was not disappointed as she screamed his name and he felt her hot pussy clench his finger as he continued to move his tongue around her clit prolonging the orgasm until she fell boneless back onto the bed.

Gasping for air, she moaned, "Oh God, Monty. You're going to kill me." A giggle erupted as he kissed his way up her body. "I can see it now," she laughed. "The rescue workers come in after the snowstorm when the bakery doesn't open and they find our naked bodies, stretched out here on the bed." She grinned, leaning up to look at him and continued. "There it will be, on our death certificates. Death by sex."

"Is that such a bad way to go?" he joked, as he made his way to her breasts, latching onto one dusty nipple.

"Ummm," was her only response.

He continued to move between breasts, his mouth on one while his fingers gently pinched the other. Remembering the first time he saw her in the restaurant wearing the green dress showcasing her breasts to perfection, he had wanted to know what they looked like naked. The soft, natural mounds were even more impeccable than he imagined. His hand skimmed down her body, memorizing her curves as he moved over her waist and landed on her hips.

"Babe, are you on the pill?"

"Hmmm?" she murmured, her fingers trailing over his abdomen.

"Are you on the pill?"

Her fingers stopped their movement and her eyes sought his. "Yeah, I am. Do you want to—"

"Fuck yeah," he said, leaning down to capture her lips. Hotly moving over them, he felt the scorching heat of her body pressed close to his. Lifting his head, he held her gaze. "I'm clean. We get tested—"

"I believe you," she breathed against his lips. "I am too."

Rolling over on top of her he grabbed her hands in his, pulling them over her head, exposing her beautiful body to his perusal. Moving his straining cock to her entrance, he looked down at her expectant face.

"Tell me what you want," he ordered, teasing her pussy with the head of his cock. Moving it slowly through her wet folds, he closed his eyes briefly, forcing himself to go slow. His cock strained to move inside, as though it had a will of its own. *Slow down, boy. You'll get there.* Sucking in a deep breath, he opened his eyes, carefully watching her flushed face as she held his gaze.

"I want you. Now," she answered, her breasts heaving with each pant as her hips bucked upward.

Dipping his lips to hers, he whispered, "My pleasure," before plunging his dick into her hot, tight pussy and his tongue into her warm mouth.

Moving both in rhythm, he started slowly, his cock stretching her as it hit every nerve along the way. In and out, creating the friction that drove her to distraction. He moved his tongue along her neck, sucking on the tender area at the base where her pulse throbbed.

Her hands wrapped around his back as her legs entwined around his waist, opening herself up more. Digging her heels into his ass, she heard him groan as she met him thrust for thrust. She felt the power of his muscles underneath her fingertips as they moved over the ridges of his arms and back as they flexed with each stroke.

"More. Harder," she moaned as the friction built to a crescendo. She squeezed her eyes shut as the world around her fell away, feeling only the rocking of her body as he powered into her. He changed the angle of his hips, grinding them against her clit. Feeling the world tilting as tremors began in her core and exploded outward, she suddenly felt his dick swell even larger inside.

Monty watched as her perfect teeth bit into her kiss-swollen bottom lip, her head thrown back against the mattress as he felt his balls tighten. Her breasts moved with each thrust and her breath came out in pants.

Much to her surprise, he rolled, flipping her on top. "Ride me, baby," he ordered, and she immediately complied. Moving to her knees, she placed her hands on his chest as she met his every thrust. She tried to control the pace but quickly found herself slowing as the sensations overwhelmed her. He took over the pace, using his hands on her hips to lift her up and down in rhythm to his movements.

"Open your eyes. I need to see you when you come," he ordered. Her eyes popped open in obedience, their blue orbs focusing on his. Her plump lips were smiling as he felt her pussy walls clenching on his dick. Reaching down, he tweaked her clit and watched with satisfaction as she screamed his name again, feeling her milk his cock.

She watched as his normally serious expression changed as his orgasm rocked through him. With his head thrown back, she watched as the veins stood out on his neck as he powered through his orgasm. Looking back down, he held her gaze...neither speaking...neither needing to. Words were not necessary. Love flowed between them. Between their bodies. Between their gazes.

He felt the difference. He wanted her again as soon as one orgasm passed. He wanted to make the next one better. Sex with Angel was soul rocking. Sex had always seemed perfunctory. Always an action. Not an emotion. But now, emotions were not only involved—they were as necessary as breathing.

He dropped his head back to the mattress as he tried to catch his breath, as she dropped onto his chest. Rolling to the side, he pulled her along with him. Their sweat-slicked bodies cooled slowly as their heartbeats continued to pound.

Pushing her silky hair from her face, he watched her as her breathing slowed. After a few seconds, her eyes opened and focused lazily back at him, a lazy smile crossing her face.

"Hey, you," she said, stroking his face, her fingers tracing his beard.

"Hey back," he added, tucking her in tightly as he pulled the covers up over them, not wanting her to become chilled.

They lay for a while watching the snow fall, the flakes glistening in the illumination of the street lights outside. Peace descended…Calm. As though the cares of the world could not touch them as they rested in their cocoon.

Monty pulled her tightly, wrapping his arms around her body, his hand resting on her breast. Throwing a leg over her as well, she was as protected as he knew how to make her.

She twisted her head and whispered, "Are you any good at snowball fights?"

Not sure he heard her correctly, he raised up slightly and said, "What was that?"

"Snowball fights. I asked if you were any good. 'Cause no matter how expert you are at giving orgasms, I was trained by my brother in snowball warfare, so you should expect to be beaten tomorrow."

Chuckling, he pulled her in tighter. "You're on, Cupcake. You're on."

Splat! The icy wetness hit the back of Monty's capped head and slid down his neck. *Jesus, her aim is accurate!* He was thankful Angel insisted he wear a scarf or he had no doubt the melting snowball would be working its way down his back.

He quickly turned and dropped to one knee while scooping another handful of snow. Packing it into a ball, he then twirled while running, throwing it with equal accuracy right at Angels back as she tried to get away in the deep snow. He watched as it hit directly between her shoulder blades. *Score!*

Screaming, she laughed as she threw another snowball. This time, her aim was off and it landed on the side of the building. Monty jogged over as fast as he could which, with fifteen inches of snow on the ground, was not very fast. Coming upon her, he reached out only to have her attempt to turn to run away. Unable to lift her booted feet in the deep snow, she tripped, falling on her back.

He heard her laughter as he stumbled closer and did not hold back his mirth. The more she attempted to stand, the more her feet slid out from under her, creating another spasm of giggles. Towering over her, he watched as she moved her arms and legs.

"What are you doing?" he asked.

"Making snow angels." She looked up seeing the

confused expression on his face. "You never made snow angels?"

"Afraid not," he replied, taking the offered hand reaching up to him. As he pulled her out, he looked down at the pattern she created in the snow. *Snow Angel.*

"Now it's your turn," she proclaimed. Seeing him about to protest, she walked up to him, a sultry expression on her face. Placing her hands on his chest, she leaned up to kiss him, then surprised him with a shove backward while kicking the back of his knee. Laughing when he landed in the snow, she leaned over him and said, "Your turn. Wave your arms and legs."

He lay for a moment, stunned at the turn of events, but could not take his eyes off the woman now towering over him. Her blonde hair was tucked into a purple knit hat with a matching scarf wrapped around her neck. Her cardinal red parka came to her knees and, paired with polka-dotted snow boots, she once again looked like an explosion in a paint factory. *And fuckin' gorgeous.*

With the sun glistening on the pure white snow, he did not think the day could possibly get any brighter. And then she smiled. The world lit and his breath was stolen as he looked at her flushed cheeks and pink lips.

"Come on," she implored. "Your angel will be right next to mine."

Grinning back, he waved his arms and legs the way she had earlier. Lifting his hand, he allowed her to pull him out as well. They took several steps back and he saw their impressions in the snow. Two angels. Wings touching.

The world was silent, no cars on the street and no pedestrians attempting to come out. The sun was brilliant in the blue sky, but the cold kept everyone at bay. Monty could not remember the last time he had played in the snow. *Probably not since he and Felicity had been children.*

Sucking in a deep breath of cold air, he reveled in the freshness of the day and was thrilled Angel had insisted they came out to play.

Taking her hand, he trudged around the side of her building, assisting her over the drifts. Stepping inside, he grabbed the snow shovel propped up next to the alley entrance door. "I'm going to work on the sidewalk in front of your shop," he said.

"You don't have to do that," she protested. "It's my sidewalk."

Tapping her red nose with his gloved finger, he looked down, saying, "You think there's any way I'm going to let you shovel the sidewalk when I'm here?"

"Isn't that kind of chauvinistic?" she retorted, her hip cocked as her toe tapped on the floor.

"Yep," he replied, and with a wink was out the door.

Grumbling, she tried to toe off her wet boots but slid down on the wet floor in the process. Finally getting her boots off, she hung up her coat and tossed her hat, scarf, and gloves onto a small table near the door. Walking through the kitchen into the shop, she peeked out the front glass window and saw that Monty had almost finished with the sidewalk in front of her bakery. She had to admit that he shoveled much quicker than she could and smiled as she made her way back into the kitchen.

Within five minutes he joined her, propping the snow shovel in the corner. She walked over, two hot cups of cocoa in her hands. Setting them on the counter, she took his coat and hung it on the hanger next to hers.

"Be careful," she warned. "I slipped on the wet floor and landed on my ass."

His eyes jumped to hers and then, as he took off his gloves, he tossed them to the side and grabbed her shoulders twisting her away from him.

"What?" she asked, trying to peer over her shoulder to see where he was looking. "What's wrong?"

"Nothing," he replied. "I just wanted to make sure that perfect ass was unharmed in your fall."

Laughing, she twisted around, pressing her body in close to his, allowing his hands to slide down to her hips. She felt his fingers slide over the globes and give a little squeeze.

"Yep, still perfect," he murmured in appreciation.

"Come on, you," she said, his words warming her. "Let's take the cocoa upstairs. And then I'll let you check out my perfect ass."

22

In the middle of the night, Monty rolled over and the coldness of the bed sunk into his consciousness. Opening his eyes, he verified what he already knew—Angel was not in bed with him. A quick glance at the dark bathroom and he saw she was not in there. Throwing his legs over the side of the bed, he slipped into his flannel pajama bottoms and wandered out into the large main room of her apartment.

She was standing in front of the window overlooking the corner of the street and alley. The moonlight and streetlights provided the background illumination, casting a glow over her form. She was wearing his flannel pajama top, its length coming to her mid-thigh. She appeared lost in thought, not turning as he moved stealthily toward her.

"Babe," he murmured, not wanting to startle her. She jumped in spite of his care and he slid behind her, encircling her with his arms. Wrapping them around her chest, he pulled her back into his warmth and nuzzled her hair.

"What are you doing up?" he asked.

"Look down there," she said, pointing to the ground. He

leaned over her shoulder to see what she was indicating. Underneath the streetlamp were the two undisturbed snow angels, wings barely touching.

He glanced at her reflection in the window and knew she saw more than just the evidence of their fun in the snow. "What's on your mind, Cupcake?"

She turned in his embrace, pressing her cheek against his heartbeat, wrapping her arms around his waist. For several minutes they stood together, hearts beating as one. He slowly moved one hand to caress her back while the other hand slid through her silky hair. He knew something was on her mind, but determined to give her the time to know when to unburden herself.

Finally, she leaned her head back and sighed. "I was thinking about the girls. I mean today was so phenomenal, Monty. We had a winter picnic here on the floor on blankets, in front of a video of a fire on TV, with a space heater on so that we felt warm. We played games. We had a snowball fight. We've made love." Her voice drifted off for a moment as her gaze slid to the side, the day's memories playing through her mind.

"But I can't help but feel guilty. Marcia, Theresa, and Betty will never have a day like this again. They were my age...we only graduated five years ago from college and our lives should be starting out. Not ending."

He continued to hold her, letting her work through the grief. Kissing the top of her head, he rocked her back and forth for a few more minutes.

"I don't have that gut-wrenching feeling of grief right now. That's passed for the moment. But what's left is just a pervasive sadness. And guilt."

"It's called survivor's guilt," he said. "It's what you feel when someone you love died and you didn't. You're happy to be alive, but feel guilty about the fact that you're here and they're not."

She nodded, her cheek rubbing against his chest. "I'm so happy to have you in my life." She leaned up and held his gaze. "Does that make me a horrible person to have found happiness among so much sadness?"

Tightening his arms around her, he shook his head. "No, Angel. Your friends would have wanted you to be happy. They would not begrudge your life. Or our coming together. Nor would they want any harm to come to you either."

"Take me back to bed," she whispered.

With one last look down at the snow angels, they turned in unison, walking back through the large room into the bedroom.

Angel did not open the bakery since the city had not plowed her road, so she decided to work on her books. Monty sat on the sofa, his laptop balanced on his knees as he reviewed the notes of the three cases while also staying in contact with the other Saints.

Sitting at her desk, fingers flying over her laptop and business files spilling from the desk to the floor, she began the monthly payroll, business plan, and started working on the taxes. It helped to have an accountant so she could turn all of her files over to him for both the business and her personal taxes.

Monty glanced over, hearing her huff and puff in the corner. Grinning, he watched as she sat, frowning at the disarray of papers. Her long hair pulled up in a sloppy bun on top of her head, melding the colors all together in a rainbow. Black yoga pants and one of his sweatshirts with the letters FBI emblazoned across her generous chest had his gaze moving slowing over her form. Glasses perched on her nose, he realized he had never seen her in glasses. Dark purple frames. *Of course,* he thought, the broad smile breaking out across his face.

Another sigh from her corner, and he asked, "Babe, you okay over there?"

"I hate this aspect of the business," she lamented. "Payroll is easy, to be honest. I keep such good records for the bakery, I just have to have them organized for the accountant to do the business taxes. But I'm afraid my own records are a bit of a mess."

"You want any help?" he asked.

She peered over her glasses at him sitting on the sofa. He looked so comfortable in her apartment amidst the color and chaos, she grinned back. "Nah, but thanks. Something's just not adding up, but I know what you're working on is much more important than what I'm doing."

"Maybe," he shrugged, "but it does keep me over here when I'd rather us both be—"

"Oh, no, big boy. You stay over there. If you get within a few feet of me we'll start going at each other like weasels again, and if you give me another orgasm, I'll combust!"

Throwing his head back, he laughed as she giggled as well. As their mirth slowly ended, they held each other's gazes for a moment, no words spoken. It seemed as though an eternity passed as emotions moved between the two.

"I told you I was falling," he said, watching her carefully from across the room. She said nothing, but held his gaze, licking her bottom lip. "I wanted you to know that I fell."

Tranquil silence flowed through the room, his words hanging out there as she stared, her heart pounding in her chest. Suddenly, on wings, she flew across the room. He barely had time to set his laptop on the floor before she landed on him.

Tossing her glasses on the coffee table, her sky-blue eyes, bright with happiness, held him captive. "Me too," she whispered. "I love you too."

He lifted his hand to the back of her head, pulling her forward until his lips met hers. Tongues tangled, fighting for domination before he angled her head to take the kiss deeper. She felt consumed as the heat of his kiss shot straight to her womb. She lay, pressing her body full length on his, her breasts crushed against his broad chest.

He slid his other hand into the waistband of her pants, moving to clutch her ass. Moaning, she wiggled, grinding herself on his erection.

A buzzing sound slowly broke into their sex-induced haze. It finally stopped before starting again. Aware his cell phone was vibrating across the coffee table, he reluctantly pulled away from her lips to lean over, grabbing the irritating device. She mewled in protest but shifted so he could answer the call.

He groaned as her body pressed against his swollen cock as she tried to move away, legs and arms flailing. Finally, she moved off him as he answered. He mouthed *Jack*, so she nodded and walked back to her desk.

A moment later he was off the phone, but stood with his laptop. "Cupcake, if it's okay with you, I'm going into the bedroom for a bit. Jack wants to set up a video conference call to go over new information from Mitch."

She smiled as she nodded. "Take your time," she sighed, looking back down at her piles of paperwork. "I'll be right here still slogging away on this mess!"

The Saints continued their meeting for a while and Monty went to the door of the bedroom, seeing Angel hunched over her desk once more. He re-shut the door to give her privacy as Luke talked about what he was finding from CFG.

"They may be a small company, but their client list is long. I tried to find out something about why Marcia was keeping her friend's as clients when you discovered that she was supposed to have given them to another broker. Can't seem to dig up any emails about that. What I am learning, so far, isn't suggesting anything unusual. I've only skimmed the surface, but I'm peeling back layers at a time. I'm looking at their client investments and trying to see if there are any discrepancies between the other clients and what Theresa and Betty had."

"So it's slow going."

"Yeah. Gotta tell you, it would help if I had someone with investment knowledge on this with me, but until then, I'm running comparison programs through every-thing I've got."

As the meeting ended, the Saints acknowledged they would be housebound for at least another day. Shutting off his laptop, Monty continued to sit on Angel's bed for a few more minutes. *What is it? What are we missing? There's got to be a link between the three deaths...and it's got to be with CFG. And what does that mean for Angel?*

Going through the monthly investment statements she received from CFG, Angel added the figures for the third time. The numbers almost matched up perfectly. Almost. But one of the investment company's tax statements did not correspond to her monthly tally. *I wonder if it was like this last year and I just did not notice?* Pulling out her file for last year's taxes, she looked at the numbers. *Same thing.* She knew there was no reason to check two years ago since she had only been investing for the past year.

Chewing on the inside of her jaw, she pondered the discrepancy but sat back huffing once more. *This is like trying to understand pig-Latin! That's why I had someone do investing for me, 'cause I don't understand it at all!*

She heard Monty finishing in the bedroom so she sent an email to Scott at CFG, asking for a meeting.

Sorry Scott. I need to meet with you concerning the discrepancy in my monthly investment statements and the tax statement sent by CFG. Let me know when we can meet. Thank you, Angel Cartwright.

Closing her laptop, she shoved all the files into one large pile and met Monty as he moved into the living room. She walked straight to him, not stopping until her body crashed into his. Arms wrapped around each other, she leaned her head back, searching his face. "Are you all right?"

"I never told you that the man you met with at the hotel is no longer a suspect. He had met with Marcia, but witnesses say he left alone and then she was seen leaving later."

She sucked in her lips, saying, "So I pulled a gun on an innocent man?"

His chuckle could be felt through her chest as he shook his head. "Cupcake, that was the craziest thing I've ever seen...the craziest thing you could have ever done...and hope to God you never do anything so risky again!"

Huffing, she lowered her eyes. "I won't," she mumbled. Lifting her gaze to his again, she said, "But you have to admit, I got you all a clue!"

"Jesus, Angel," he said, touching his lips to her forehead.

"Remember, you bake world-class cupcakes and leave the gun-toting investigations to me!"

Giggling, she agreed. Standing on her tiptoes, she kissed the underside of his jaw. "You know, we were somewhere nice when Jack's phone call rudely interrupted," she reminded. "Do you want lunch first or to get back to business—"

Angel grabbed onto his shoulders as Monty lifted her effortlessly in his arms. Striding quickly into her bedroom, he latched his lips onto hers, igniting the sparks that immediately flamed throughout her body.

I guess we're eating lunch later, she grinned.

Luke sat alone at his secure computer in his house. The small bungalow set away from the street suited his needs perfectly. The house was comfortable, containing three bedrooms, although the smallest one was used as an office. When he left the CIA and first joined Jack's Saints, he rented an apartment in Charlestown. It served his needs, but he hated the close quarters. A loner by nature, Luke felt constrained with noisy neighbors on all sides. Finding this house sitting on three acres had been perfect. Surrounded by trees with a small creek running through the backyard, he could sit out on the back deck and not hear his neighbors.

The snow blanketed the vista, the brightness almost blinding. After filling the bird feeders in his yard, he tromped back inside, stomping his snow-covered boots off by the back door. Glancing over, he noticed his coffee was ready and headed over to pour his first strong cup of the day when his laptop alarmed, indicating incoming mail.

Having set his alerts to different sounds, he recognized

the email came from his secure network. Walking over, his heart pounded as he noticed the incoming message. With their last case, Luke had been contacted by an anonymous source, someone even more tech savvy than himself. This person told him that they could not divulge their identity, but their assessment of the intel Luke had been searching for helped lead them to the kidnappers. He wanted to know who his secret internet associate was, but they managed to hide from him, saying it was too dangerous.

And he had not heard from them since...until now. Clicking open the email, he read:

I'm back. I've watched your searches. Follow the money. The answer is there.

Sitting down quickly, Luke immediately typed, **You're back? Any chance you'll let me know who you are?**

Not a chance. Sorry. Too many eyes around. But follow the money.

Luke, frustrated, typed, **I'm trying, but I don't have a background in investments. Data analysis is ponderous.**

I'll send something that will help. Good luck.

Before Luke was able to ask more, the connection was lost. He did not even attempt to discern their identity. If this person was as careful as before, it would be a waste of his time. And with three murders to solve, time was not something he had.

Plus, he admitted to himself, there was something strangely comforting in knowing someone was out there willing to help. *Even on their own terms.*

23

The next day, the city's snowplows finally made their rounds clearing the streets and Angel prepared to open the bakery. Typically up early, she decided to sleep in, opening the shop later to allow her employees a chance to get to work safely. Sleeping in with Monty had not been a hardship and she grinned thinking about the last two days. His presence in her apartment had felt...right...perfect. She smiled to herself as she thought about their declaration of love.

Standing in front of the bedroom mirror, she brushed her long hair before pulling it up into her work-day bun. Monty had already left for the day and she hurried to finish getting ready. Checking her watch, she knew she only had an hour before Helen would be coming in. Walking back through her living room, she looked at her still-messy desk. Grabbing the files, she shoved them in her filing cabinet to neaten the area.

Heading downstairs, she turned on the ovens so they could pre-heat and quickly mixed up a batch of batter. Reaching into her pocket for her phone, she realized she left it on her nightstand. *I think my brain's on sex overload,* she grinned. After placing the first batch into the oven, she ran upstairs to retrieve the phone. Stopping at the top of the stairs, she grinned as she saw a goofy text from Monty. Loving the idea of their personalities melding together, she realized *I'm more careful and he's more free.* Shoving her phone back into her pocket, she walked to the steps leading down to the kitchen.

Before she could take the first step down, a roar filled her ears the instant before the building shook on its foundation. A fiery blast blew burning air up through the stairwell from the kitchen, knocking Angel backward onto the floor. The roar continued as the sounds of glass breaking ripped through the bakery below.

Trying to make sense of what happened, she rolled over and attempted to crawl to the closest window. Pictures were shattered on the floor. Her kitchen cabinet doors flung open, their contents spilled out. Twisting back, she saw flames licking up the stairwell proceeded by thick, black smoke.

She shook her head, trying to hear what was happening, but the roar did not dissipate. *Fire...fire in the kitchen.* Fighting the urge to try to get to her beloved kitchen, she forced her body to move to the window.

The building shook again, bricks now tumbling loose from the walls and pieces of ceiling falling all around. The choking, black smoke curled up the stairwell, licking its way into her apartment. Reaching the window at the outside fire stairs, her fingers fumbled with the latch. Looking desperately around, she grabbed her office chair and hurled it toward the window. It shattered outward and she continued to bang the glass around the edges until most of the window was open.

Shoving one leg out onto the metal landing she thought

she heard sirens, but the roaring in her ears kept her from hearing anything distinctly. Attempting to reach out to the railing, her shaking hands were unable to grasp the metal. Her breath came in short gasps, her mind trying to catch up to what was happening. Sliding forward, she tried to pull herself up, but the building shook once more, sending her flying back down on her ass.

Scooting forward, she moved toward the fire-stairs. Her gaze caught a fireman below. He appeared to be speaking, but she could hear nothing but the continuous roar. Turning her head, she realized she could barely hear him from her left ear.

"We're coming up!" he yelled.

Looking down, she now saw two firemen making the quick climb to her landing. One began speaking to her, but she could only shake her head, pointing to her ears.

Arriving at the top, he knelt as he shifted down to her face and said, "Ma'am. This building is now unstable. We're going to get you down."

She nodded, her body shaking more. One fireman pulled out a shock blanket and wrapped it around her. It dawned on her that she was in freezing temperature wearing only khaki pants and a pink polo—her standard bakery uniform.

One of the men lifted her up after assessing her injuries. Carrying her down the flight of metal stairs, she was quickly moved to a waiting ambulance. The firemen handed her off to the EMTs before turning to rush back to the building.

Chad ran over to her, his face bleeding from glass cuts as well. "Angel?" he yelled. He had been on duty sitting in his old truck across the road. He noted her glazed eyes and spoke to the EMTs. "Nah, I'm good. I've just got a few cuts. Take care of her," he ordered.

Sitting on the stretcher in the ambulance, Angel was vaguely aware of someone putting a blood-pressure cuff on her arm and another brushing her hair away from her face as they wiped her forehead. Her eyes dropped to the swab in their gloved hand. Red. Blood. *I'm going to have more stitches in my head.* She giggled out loud but heard nothing. She saw the expressions on the faces of the two EMTs now staring at her, concern in their eyes.

They think I'm losing my mind. Maybe they're right.

Leaning forward a few inches allowed her to see the front of her bakery. What was her bakery. All she saw was shattered glass, broken bricks, and black smoke billowing from the windows. Angel's Cupcake Heaven. Gone.

The Saints gathered for the latest information from Luke. Monty had spent a few minutes staring at the working board, pouring over the intel and links.

"They're back," Luke proclaimed, immediately gaining the attention of the group as they all turned their gazes to their intrepid computer genius. Before anyone could ask who he referred to, he sent the email messages between he and the mystery assistant to their tablets.

Low whistles were heard amongst the *Fucks, Damns,* and *No shit* comments.

"I don't know who this person is or how they can hack into my system without me being able to trace them. I don't know if they're CIA or some crazy-ass fucker sitting in a hut somewhere in Montana," Luke proclaimed. "But they were legit with our last case and I'm willing to take a chance that they're legit on this one."

Jack sat back in his seat, rubbing his hand over his beard thoughtfully. "I've got no reason to doubt this person and, although I admit, there were times in the Special Forces when we got intel from someone who wanted or needed to stay out of the picture. We always had to evaluate it, but more often than not it helped our missions."

Jude and Bart nodded. "Same in the SEALs," Bart confirmed.

Monty looked over at Luke and said, "I trust your judgment, man. If you think it's legit info, then I say check it out."

"Well, after they sent the messages I showed you all, they then sent a program that is helping me disaggregate the data from CFG. Without it, I don't know how long it would take me to go through it all."

"What have you gotten so far?"

"Roy had the investment accounts for Theresa and..." Luke looked up at Monty before he continued, "Scott had Betty's and Angel's."

Bart's head jerked up. "Scott said he didn't know Betty. So the fucker lied."

Monty's gaze shot up, but he kept quiet, forcing his heart to find a normal pace when it wanted to gallop.

"About three months ago, when Marcia was made the president of the branch, she took them back as her own clients. I did find one email from Scott questioning her about the trade, but the only answer she gave him was she wanted to take care of friends."

"If that went against the company's policy that seems odd, considering she was such a stickler for doing things by the book," Blaise noted.

"So what would be the purpose?" Bart asked. "Unless she was doing something to their accounts and didn't want anyone else to know about it?"

Monty shook his head. "No, she was too close to the

other women. They were good friends, at least from all we can tell."

"I didn't get a good feeling about Scott or Carlton," Bart said. "My money's on those two doing something illegal with some of their accounts and Marcia found out."

"What I have found so far is that there are discrepancies in the account statements that were sent to the three women and what was reported to the IRS," Luke said.

Monty straightened quickly, his hand slamming down on the table in front of him. "Angel was working on her business and personal taxes the past couple of days. She got frustrated because she said there were problems she noted and couldn't reconcile."

Luke confirmed, "I'm finding discrepancies, but haven't had enough time to figure out what I'm looking at."

Jack's phone vibrated and he looked at the caller. His eyes shot to Monty. "It's Chad."

"Fuck," Monty cursed, knowing nothing good could be coming from the Saint watching Angel's bakery.

Jack immediately put Chad on speaker. "You're on speaker. Monty's here." Before Chad had a chance to answer, the sound of sirens shrilled through the phone.

"What the hell's going on?" Monty yelled, already out of his chair and grabbing his coat.

"An explosion...a goddamn explosion," Chad gasped, his voice raspy.

Monty fell back into the chair as Marc clasped his shoulder for support. "Angel—"

"She's alive. She was upstairs and able to break out of the window. The firemen are bringing her down now."

"Oh Jesus," Monty said, his breath leaving his body in a rush. "What...where..." He stuttered, trying to still his racing heart.

Jack took over, giving orders. "I want everyone there. Chad, we'll be there in fifteen minutes."

"I'll be here. I want to see what the fuck happened."

Jack agreed, knowing his former ATF Saint would be able to let them know what caused the fire. "I want the rest of you to head to the bakery. Assist Chad and find out what you can. Luke, you go as well. I know you want to get into the records but, for now, I need all of you there." Looking over at Monty and then Marc, he said, "Marc, get Monty there. Stay with him."

The Saints dispersed, Jack stopping to call Bethany before he left. Explaining the situation, he said, "Babe, get the girls. I don't know what Angel's going to need, but from what Chad said...her whole world just blew up."

24

Marc pulled as close to Angel's damaged block as he could, Monty already leaping out of the vehicle before it stopped. The other Saints parked nearby, running toward the chaos as well. Dark, billowing smoke poured from the building, sending the ashes into the sky. The police attempted to barricade the area, but Jack's Saints flashed their investigator badges and managed to make their way closer.

The corner of the building was destroyed. The glass front was shattered, colored shards littering the area. The former shop, now a blackened cave, dripped with water as the fire hoses continued their aim. The second-floor apartment had shattered glass on the front, blackened bricks now facing the street, which was littered with debris.

Monty's gaze darted through the police, fire, and rescue vehicles, searching for the one holding Angel. Seeing Chad standing next to one, he charged over, the other Saints following. Chad was talking to the fire Chief and a detective. As they approached, Monty was vaguely aware of Chad introducing his boss to the other investigators.

Monty's sole focus was finding Angel. Rounding the back of the vehicle, he looked inside, his heart in his throat. *Thank Jesus!* She sat on the stretcher, her arms covered in cuts. Her khaki uniform pants were shredded and bloody. One of the EMTs was in the process of cutting them off high on her thighs and Monty could see her legs were in the same shape her arms were.

"Baby," he called out, attempting to enter the ambulance. When one of the EMTs attempted to stop him from climbing into the vehicle, he started to shove back. "She's my fiancé!" he shouted, willing to say anything to be able to be with her, as Marc appeared behind his back.

Moving to the stretcher, he reached for Angel but halted when he saw her eyes. Dull blue stared back at him, a blank expression on her face. "What's her condition?" he asked, his voice much softer now.

"She's suffered multiple cuts and abrasions, mostly to her hands, arms, and legs. She's got a cut on the side of her forehead that will likely need stitches, but we've treated it here for now. We were getting her prepped here as much as possible before transport, but she's telling us she doesn't want to go to the hospital. She keeps saying she needs to open the bakery."

"Angel?" he said cautiously, sitting on the stretcher next to her. "You need to go to the hospital. I'm here and I'll go with you."

Jack, Bart, Cam, Blaise, and Marc appeared at the opening of the ambulance to check on her situation. Looking her over, Jack turned his eyes to Monty. "How is she?"

Monty looked down at his friends, uncertainty written on his face. "Still checking. Cuts, bruises, but right now, she's in shock."

One of the EMTs asked, "Sir, does your fiancé have a hearing problem? Is she deaf?"

Monty's head jerked around, "No, why?"

"She doesn't appear to be able to hear out of her right ear. This may be temporary, but we need to get her to the hospital and have her checked out."

Monty moved off the stretcher and squatted in front of her. Leaning slightly toward her left ear, he said, "You're going to go to the hospital and get checked out. There's nothing you need to do here, Cupcake."

At the world *cupcake* her eyes flared to life momentarily and her raspy voice croaked, "I have to open up the shop."

"Angel, look at me," he ordered gently. "You're going to the hospital and don't worry about the shop."

Monty turned and hopped out the back of the ambulance to talk to the other Saints for a moment. "She's in shock...she doesn't seem to understand what's happened. I'm riding with her." His eyes looked up at the building, fear mixed with rage inside. He turned to Chad, saying, "What do they think? Gas fire?"

Chad's grim face held his friend's eyes. "Too early to tell, Monty. But my experience tells me this was no ordinary gas fire." Seeing Monty's rage begin to rise to the surface, he quickly said, "You take care of her and let me do my job here when I'm allowed in. I'll be able to tell if it was a gas explosion or an incendiary device."

Behind them, Angel did not say anything but turned her head toward the group, a question in her glazed eyes. She looked out on the chaos once more, the area swarming with firemen and police. And a blackened hole where her bakery used to be. Suddenly, her breathing came faster, heavier and her eyes cleared. The roar in her ears continued but she fought against the fog that filled her mind. *Smoke. Fire. Explosion. Broken window. Escape.* Sucking in a gasp of air, she lunged forward, propelling herself toward the open back door of the ambulance.

"Nooooo!" she screamed, startling the men standing in their huddle. "My shop!" her raspy voice screeched. Her bandaged hands clawed out, fighting an unknown enemy.

Monty whirled around, catching her as she tried to leap away from the EMTs. He clutched her shaking body close to his. The warming blanket had fallen away and Blaise grabbed it off the ground, wrapping it around her from the back as her front pressed to Monty's chest. Her rage morphed into sobs as her mind registered the devastation of her world.

"Baby, baby," he soothed. "It'll be fine, I promise." He turned slightly and nodded to the others. "I'm riding with her." He looked at Jack and said, "Can Bethany get—"

"Already taken care of," Jack answered. "She's getting the women together. They'll get some clothes and other things. We'll get them to your house."

Nodding, Monty turned and climbed into the back of the ambulance with Angel still in his arms. Depositing her gently onto the stretcher once more, he glanced back at the Saints as the doors were closing. Their rage mirrored his own.

Waiting in the ER, Monty had a sense of déjà vu as he was reminded of his last time in with Angel. Before, he was concerned. Now…he was petrified. *Is this what love does? Make you scared shitless when something happens to someone you love? What will it be like when we have kids?* As soon as that thought crossed his mind, he shook his head. *Kids?* Continuing to pace up and down the hall, he realized that as scary as it was, he wanted everything with Angel. Life. Love. Marriage. Family.

Hearing his name called, he jogged to her room. The curtain opened and a doctor was just stepping out. The older, grey haired man, stethoscope around his neck, had a calm countenance Monty picked up on.

"Are you seeing Ms. Cartwright?" Monty asked, his voice strangely quivering.

The doctor looked up into his face and nodded. "And you are?"

"Her fiancé," he said. He knew Marc, standing behind him, would back anything he said.

"She's quite lucky. We did not have to treat her for smoke inhalation, due to her quick thinking in breaking a window and getting to the fire escape. She does have cuts and abrasions on her arms and legs, which were treated. Our primary concern is that she appears to have lost her hearing in her right ear. The ear drum ruptured and the hearing loss hopefully will be temporary."

"Can I see her now?"

The doctor smiled and nodded. "Yes. We have an audiologist coming down to evaluate her and then she'll be ready to be discharged." Putting his hand on Monty's arm, he said gently, "She was very lucky, but has been through a trauma and is shaken. I'm going to suggest she see a trauma counselor."

"Absolutely," Monty agreed, his eyes darting to the room where she lay. As the doctor moved on down the hall, Marc clapped Monty on the back.

"You heard what he said," Marc reminded. "She's going to be fine. So when you go in there, don't scare her to death."

Nodding, Monty steeled his spine, sucking in a deep breath. Pushing back the curtain, he stepped in. As prepared as he tried to be, seeing Angel in the bed halted him in his tracks. More bandages were on her forehead and her arms and legs were dotted with cuts. Wearing a hospital gown, he glanced to the side to see her ripped and bloody khaki pants and pink ACH polo shirt. Her hair, dull and tangled, was pulled back away from her face.

Alive. She's alive. He wanted to sing it over and over, but when she turned her blue eyes up to him, he was not sure she felt it.

Her eyes filled with tears and he rushed to her bedside. Gathering her in his arms, he gently scooted her over so he could sit on the narrow bed next to her.

"What happened?" she asked. "Please tell me. Was it a gas leak or did someone do this to me?"

"I don't know, babe, but I promise we're working on it," he murmured as he held her.

She felt the rumblings in his chest, but his words were garbled. Turning her head, she faced him, watching to see if his mouth was moving. "I...I...can't hear you very well," she said. Reaching up, she touched her right ear. "There's just some dull roaring in here." She knew the doctor was sending an audiologist down to see her. *Please don't let this be permanent,* she prayed.

Monty shifted so that his mouth was closer to her left ear. "We don't know what happened yet," he spoke deliberately. Watching her eyes, he knew she understood. "The Saints are working the scene with the Fire Inspector. Chad worked for ATF...he's an expert."

My shop is gone. My apartment is gone. Everything I own in the world is gone! Once again, she nodded. *Deep breaths. In... out...in...out.* The ER nurse had breathed with her when she began to hyperventilate. The antiseptic odors of the hospital mixed with the smoke on her body hit her nose, and she choked back a gag.

"It's all gone," she said, her voice laced with fear and anger. Her fingers gripped the sheet so tightly her knuckles were white.

"Cupcake, look at me," he ordered, turning her face to his with his fingers on her chin. "You're safe. You're alive. And I'm going to thank God every day for that miracle. All the other things can be replaced. You've got insurance. You've already got a new building that you were moving to in another week or so. And your apartment? There's nothing there that can't be replaced."

Offering a shaky nod, she noticed Monty looking toward the door. She watched as he called out "Come in." *Damn, did someone knock? I didn't even hear it!*

Jack stuck his head in the ER bay, his eyes scanning Angel before moving to Monty. "The police are wanting a statement. I've held them back, but needed to know when a good time would be."

Angel turned her head slightly to the right so that her left ear was closer as she kept her eyes on Jack's mouth. Shooting a glance over to Monty, she watched as he spoke.

"An audiologist is coming to do an eval. I'm taking her home when we're done here. We'll meet at my place and she can be questioned then."

Jack nodded and with a head jerk toward Angel, he backed out of the room. Before Angel was able to speak, a woman entered the room. Walking over, she stuck her hand out toward Angel and introduced herself. Speaking slowly and clearly, she explained the auditory evaluation she would be conducting.

"I will be putting earphones on you and you will simply lift your hand when you hear a tone. What it will measure are the faintest tones you can hear in both ears. I will also evaluate you with tympanometry. The ER doctor looked at your ears with an otoscope and determined that your eardrum perforated."

Angel, her face tight with anxiety, merely nodded. Monty squeezed her hand and she responded with her fingers digging into his slightly, but did not take her eyes off the audiologist. The evaluation did not take too long and soon the audiologist was back in the room after conferring with the ER doctor.

"Okay, Ms. Cartwright. Your right ear is confirmed to be ruptured. This is not an unusual occurrence with a loud noise or change in air pressure." The audiologist stopped to make sure Angel was understanding. Assured that she was, she continued, "What you can do for the pain is use warm compresses against the ear and over-the-counter pain meds. You will need to keep the ear canal dry, so you will place cotton balls in your ear when you shower or wash your hair. No swimming or putting your head underwater."

"How long?" Angel asked, her mind whirling with all of the information flying at her.

"The eardrum should heal itself in about two months. If not, then surgery may be needed. Right now, you have a moderate hearing loss in the right ear and, if you call my office, we will check you weekly. We are anticipating a complete recovery."

She shook Angel's cold hand before she left the room, leaving Angel to slump against Monty's back. *Building destroyed. Home destroyed. Hearing loss.* Her body began to shake, the tremors overtaking her. Monty wrapped his arms around her, willing his warmth to spread through her body.

"Baby, talk to me," he implored, speaking on her left side.

She shook her head for a moment, unable to put her

thoughts into coherent words. Swallowing deeply, she finally replied, "It's all gone. I can't believe it's all gone."

Pulling her face to his, he pressed his warm lips on her cold ones. He moved his hand over her hair, brushing the colors back from her face. His eyes roved over her shocked beauty. "Baby, you're alive. You gotta focus on that."

Her gaze held his, not wavering, as his strength seeped into her consciousness. The fog began to clear, gratitude edging out the shock. "You're right. I've got to focus on that." She allowed him to assist her from the bed and then she walked over to look down at her clothes. Holding up the ripped khaki pants and the pink polo with ACH embroidered over the breast, she turned, grim-faced to him. "But if I find out this was no accident I will hunt down the one who took this from me."

He observed her determined face, remembering the woman holding a gun to a man she thought hurt her friend. *Jesus, I've got to keep her safe and find out what the fuck is going on or she's going to go rogue again.*

Monty drove Angel to his home, glad the snow covered roads had been scraped. Pulling into the underground parking garage of his apartment building, he glanced over at her. Pale, quiet, dressed in borrowed clothes from Bethany.

Bethany had dropped the clothes by the hospital, offering a warm hug, and told her not to worry about anything. Angel had been grateful, but her thoughts were less accommodating. *Sure. Don't worry. I don't see that happening.*

Realizing the vehicle came to a stop, she looked around. Turning toward Monty, she said, "Are we here?"

"Yeah, baby." He jumped down and hurried to the passenger side. Scooping her out of the seat, he planned on carrying her up, but she wiggled.

"I can walk," she insisted, meeting his gaze.

"I know," he agreed. Leaning in, his voice hoarse, "But when I think how closely I came to losing you now that I've found you...please, let me do this."

She relaxed in his arms, the first smile in hours sliding across her face. "You're right. There's nothing I've lost that can't be replaced." She nuzzled his neck as he carried her to the elevator and up to his apartment.

As he opened the door, he hesitated. Searching her eyes, he confessed, "Angel, I know this place won't remind you of home. It's really just a place for me to retreat to, but you can do whatever you want to make it seem like yours."

Her puzzled expression was replaced by understanding as they entered his apartment and he set her feet on the floor. The space was minimally furnished, with clean lines and no clutter. *And no color. No personality.* She grinned as she turned to him, remembering the Monty she first met. *Very much like this apartment.* "It's fine, Monty. Thank you so much for having me here."

It dawned on her that he always spent the night at her place. She had assumed it was so that she could be closer to her bakery but now realized that, while this place may have been his home before he met her...*I am now his home.* She raised up on her toes, kissing his jaw. The tangy taste of his aftershave plus his own scent was home to her. It was then the overpowering smell of smoke filled nostrils. *My hair,* she realized ruefully.

"Do I have time to shower?" she asked.

Never wanting to deny her anything, he glanced at his watch. "Yeah. The others will be here in about thirty minutes and so will the detectives and Fire Marshall. But remember, you need cotton in your ear."

He escorted her through his apartment, giving her a quick tour. "The second bedroom is an office for me and there is a small bathroom down the hall." He led her through the master bedroom and into the large master bathroom. A soaking tub was in the corner with a large, separate tiled shower stall next to it. A double sink graced the other wall and a door led to the private toilet.

He laid out a thick, plush towel and dug around for the cotton balls. "I don't have anything here that would even remotely pass for feminine," he confessed as he showed her the shower soap and shampoo.

Grinning, she admitted, "I think I'm really glad about that."

Chuckling, he slid the shirt over her head and then clasped his hands to her hips. Moving them downward, he tucked his thumbs into the waistband of her pants and skimmed them off her legs. Her body, naked and glorious, was marred with cuts and bandages.

His smiled slipped as his fear poured through him once more. She noticed the change and lifted her injured arm to cup his face. "Hey, remember what you told me. I'm here. I'm alive."

His lips found hers in a barely-there kiss. Pulling back, he heard her mewl of disappointment. "Gotta get you in the shower, babe." He stayed in the bathroom as she stepped into the warm water, listened to her moans of delight as she washed her hair, and cringed at the whimpers of pain when the water touched her injuries. As the water turned off, he heard the doorbell.

"I'm going to go let in whoever's gotten here first," he said, handing her the thick, soft towel. "I'll be back."

"Go on," she encouraged. "I'll be out in five minutes."

Angel dried off quickly, then slipped the borrowed clothes on once more. Standing in front of the large mirror, she perused herself. Her eyes dropped to her various injuries, then slowly moved upward. When she finally met her gaze in the mirror, she peered deeply into the shadows. *If it wasn't an accident, then someone tried to kill me. And it's got to be the same someone who killed Marcia, Theresa, and Betty.* Holding her gaze, she vowed, *Don't worry, girls. They will not get away with it!*

25

Several minutes later, Angel stepped out of the bathroom and heard voices in the living room. Steeling herself, she walked down the hall and halted when she saw the crowd of men and women. Jude and Chad she recognized, along with Bethany, Miriam, Faith, and Sabrina. The other men filled the room with a wall of angry testosterone. They all seemed to be talking, but their voices ran together. The roar in her right ear had not diminished, but only served to irritate her more.

Monty, seeing her from across the room, immediately sought her out. Pulling her in closely, he spoke into her left ear. "These are my friends and co-workers, baby. The police and Fire Marshall are here also."

Her eyes roved over the now silent crowd, their eyes all pinned on her. "Hello," she said, offering an off-kilter smile.

Warm greetings and introductions were made before everyone settled into the spaces available. The detective and Fire Marshall sat in chairs directly in front of her. She noticed Mitch, the tall, dark-haired FBI agent, sat to the side. He appeared physically fit and his sharp eyes were filled with concern. Her mouth curved into a gentle smile and was greeted with his warm smile in return.

"Ms. Cartwright, we need to know what your actions were this morning, please."

She noticed the Fire Marshall spoke clearly and somewhat slowly. *Looks like everyone knows I'm deaf.* Her irritation disappeared quickly as she realized he was trying to make things easier for her. Taking a deep breath, she gave a succinct description of her morning.

"After Monty left, I went downstairs about eight. That's much later than I normally begin my day, but I wasn't expecting to open for the breakfast crowd. I mixed the batter and then turned on the ovens."

"You did not preheat the ovens first?" the detective asked.

"I did, but not then." Seeing their confused expressions, she explained. "The cupcake batter needs to rest about ten minutes before I put it in the oven. So I mixed it up and then turned on the oven."

"Then you went upstairs?"

"I realized I had forgotten my phone, so I ran upstairs to get it. I had it in my hand and had just gotten to the top of the stairs when..." she faltered. Monty's arm gave her a squeeze and she leaned back into his strength.

Taking a deep, cleansing breath, she continued. "There was an enormous exploding noise. I heard glass shatter and then there was a ball of heat that swept up the stairs." She lifted her hand to her face, rubbing the bandage on her forehead. *At least this cut is on the other side from my other scar.*

Monty's fingers massaged her neck, allowing her to slowly relax. "How are you holding up, baby?" he said in her good ear.

She turned to face him, admitting, "The roar in my ear is still there. It doesn't hurt but is giving me a headache."

Monty's eyes searched the room, landing on Miriam. She nodded and reached into her purse, pulling out ibuprofen. She grabbed a water bottle from the refrigerator and walked over to Angel. "Here you go, sweetie."

Grateful, Angel took the proffered pain reliever. Looking back to the detective and Fire Marshall, she asked, "Now it's time for you to talk to me. Was this an accidental gas explosion or was my oven—in my kitchen—rigged to explode?"

Her voice sounded harsh, her eyes boring into the men sitting in front of her. She noticed Chad shifted and her eyes moved to him. His expression was one of barely disguised rage. Shooting her eyes back to the Fire Marshall, she pierced him with her gaze. "I want to know exactly what happened to my bakery...and my home."

"Ms. Cartwright, please understand that our investigation is just starting. I will say that our initial consultation with the investigators and the gas company is that it was not an accident. But that is all we know at this time."

The detective looked at Chad. "I'd like to suggest that we be able to use your expertise in this matter."

Chad agreed. "Absolutely. I'll be heading back to the site this afternoon."

The detective scribbled Angel's statement and then proceeded to talk to Jack about the case they were working before he left.

She felt exhausted and the group of Saints and their women, while kind, were all talking amongst themselves and she could not hear their conversations. Bethany approached Angel, taking her hand and leading her over to where the other women were standing around the table. Looking down, Angel's eyes widened in surprise. The table was covered in bags the women were emptying. Shampoo, conditioner, bath oil, body wash, underwear, t-shirts, sweaters, yoga pants, socks, and even some shoes.

"It's not everything you need, but it will take care of you for a bit," Miriam said.

Her eyes filling with tears, Angel looked around at her new friends, assuring, "Oh, this is amazing. Thank you so much!" Touched by their generosity, she embraced each one. The women took the bounty back to the bathroom as she turned around to watch Monty interact with his co-workers.

Each man, different in appearance, shared the same determined expression. Picking out the boss was easy. Jack's somber expression matched the personality Monty had ascribed to him. It was interesting to see his face when his eyes landed on Bethany. There was no doubt the man loved her when his eyes lit and his expression relaxed. *The bigger they are, the harder they fall.* Looking at Bart and Cam with Faith and Miriam, she understood the meaning of that saying. Jude was the only other Saint who had a woman with him. *What was it that Monty said? Oh yeah, Sabrina was Bart's cousin and engaged to Jude.* Besides Chad, there were four other men there, all discussing the explosion.

Monty observed as the other women came back into the room and noticed Angel standing alone, her eyes moving over the group. He watched as they landed on him, and she smiled. *She's been through hell and she still smiles at me. If I had already solved this case, maybe I could have stopped this from happening.*

Marc watched the emotions cross Monty's face. "This is not on you," he said. The other men heard and agreed. "Or if it's on you, then we all share in that guilt."

Monty's face was tight with anger and frustration.

Angel walked over, looking up at his face as she approached. As usual, she walked straight into his arms, not stopping until her body hit his. Kissing the top of her head, he then pulled her face back so he could peer into her eyes. "I know you're tired, Cupcake. I'm so sorry."

"Monty Lytton. You have nothing to apologize for! The guilt rests squarely on whoever is after us girls. And I'm going to let the rest of the sorority know."

"Angel," Jack said, then waited as Monty turned her gently toward his boss. Making sure she looked at him when he spoke, he continued, "We're going to let you know that it's our feeling that it's not just the sorority that is tying these cases together, but it has something to do with Colonial Financial Group."

Monty sucked in a deep breath, hoping to have been able to keep Angel from knowing what they were investigating since it possibly implicated her friend.

Cocking her head to the side so that she could hear better, Jack recognized the maneuver and apologized. "I'm sorry. I should have spoken clearer. We don't think your whole former sorority is in danger, but rather those of you connected to Colonial Financial Group. And that's what we're working on."

"I don't understand," she confessed, her mind grappling with the possible implications. Suddenly looking up at Jack and then twisting around to Monty, she said, "You think Marcia had something to do with this?"

"We're considering her involvement since she was the broker for the other three of you," he admitted.

"No! You have it all wrong," she protested, shaking her head. "There's no way Marcia would have done anything to hurt us."

Monty quickly added, "Angel, we don't know anything

for sure. But we're looking into the finances and practices of the group."

She lifted her hand to her pounding head, sighing heavily. She looked back at Monty, proclaiming, "I'm done for today, sweetie. I've lost three of my closest friends, my shop, my equipment, my building, my home, my possessions, my hearing, and now I have to face the possibility that one of my friends may be involved in something I don't want to have to face. I've got no more fight left in me."

Leaning into his arms, she grunted as he swept her up, carrying her into the bedroom. He set her feet on the floor and pulled the covers back. Assisting her into bed, he tucked her in tightly. "I want you to rest. I'm going to talk to the others for a few minutes and then I'll be right back."

She nodded, but as he kissed her forehead and started to walk away, she tugged on his arm. "It wasn't Marcia," she implored. "And I know you'll catch them, whoever they are."

Kissing her head once more, he left the room.

The next morning, Monty lay awake as the pink, pre-dawn sky filtered into his bedroom, bathing the room in a soft pastel glow. *Why have I never noticed that before?* He knew the answer as he watched the light stretch across the room, offering a slight illumination over the woman sleeping in his bed. *She brought the color into my world.*

She· had been restless during the night, at times throwing her arms up as though to protect her face from the explosions in her nightmares. He had slept little, preferring to watch over her. His mind had wandered to the final conversation of the Saints before they left yesterday.

Luke had headed back to Jack's to pore over the financial records, hoping to use his new mystery contact to wade through the data quicker. Jude had left with Sabrina but was joining Luke in his searches.

Bart and Cam had decided to head out last night, taking another look at Geoffrey Daly. Blaise said his money was on Scott and Carlton. Jack had wanted to delve into Bill Bradley more. Chad and Marc had gone back to Angel's apartment to see what else they could find.

Before Monty had a chance to ponder if his co-workers found any more evidence, his attention was diverted by Angel waking.

She slowly opened her eyes, flinching as her strained muscles and abrasions twinged when she stretched. The white walls were unadorned and she sat up quickly, trying to determine where she was. *Monty's place.* Remembering why she was here sent her flopping back to the bed. Turning her head, she saw his worried face.

"Don't be worried, sweetie," she whispered. "I'm alive, remember?"

"I don't want to ever feel like that again," he said, his voice rough with emotion.

Smiling, she cupped his face. "I'm here with you." Her eyes shifted beyond his shoulder as she made a decision. "I want to go back to my place today. I need to see it."

"Oh no—," Monty started to protest, but she interrupted.

"I have to. I need to do it for lots of reasons. I need to sort through to see what can be salvaged. I need to check on my new location and see if I can hurry that along. I need to talk to my employees. And I just need to see it. It was my shop...my apartment...where I worked and where I lived. I need to see it again."

Monty had to admit that her reasons were valid, so he agreed. "But I'm going with you," he declared. "And if it's too overwhelming—"

"I've been taking care of myself for a while now, so I'll be fine," she assured. "But thanks for caring."

They lay for another minute, pressed together, arms tight around each other. "I love you, you know," Monty whispered into her left ear.

Smiling, Angel nodded against his chest. "I love you, too," she whispered back.

Standing in front of the burned out bakery, Angel felt her anger rise again. Grimacing at the destruction, her hands fisted at her sides. Yellow caution tape encircled the area with Keep Out signs plastered on the brick walls.

Not heeding the warning, she stepped inside, looking around. The shop area still stood, the glass windows and cases shattered. The colorful walls were blackened and water damaged. Stepping over rubble, she walked to the back of the shop and stared at the damaged mural. Placing her hand on the painting, she noticed the face peering out at her was still barely visible. *Thank you. You kept me safe and I'll make sure you go on the new wall.* Turning to walk away, she glanced back over her shoulder. *If it's possible, can you please help Monty find the killer? Please.*

Moving on to the other wall, she peeked into the kitchen seeing nothing but destruction. Sighing heavily, she realized there was nothing she could save. She had planned to take the baking tins, mixers, and all of her kitchen equipment to the new site with her. *Looks like I'll be buying all new items.*

"You can't go in there," Monty chided, pulling her back slightly. "I know Chad has been looking around, but I don't want to take a chance with you."

She nodded her agreement, knowing there was nothing to salvage. Stepping back out, she made her way to the side of the building and walked toward the fire stairs. She stopped and looked down; the little bit of snow that had not melted was dirty.

Monty followed her line of vision, knowing she stared at the spot where their snow angels had taken shape. Squeezing her hand, he leaned down and promised, "Those will only be the first snow angels we make together. We'll have lots of winters to do the same each time."

Smiling at his thoughtfulness, she started for the stairs but stopped as Chad rounded the corner.

"I've been up there," Chad explained, "and the floor seems sound, but I wouldn't trust it."

She pierced him with her gaze. "Tell me the truth, Chad. Is there anything salvageable in my apartment?"

Sighing heavily, he looked at Monty first before facing Angel straight on. "The fire did get to part of your apartment, but what ruined almost everything was water damage from the hoses and smoke damage. None of your clothes or furniture will be salvageable. If you had pots, pans, dishes…maybe those would be able to be used again. But honestly, Angel, the insurance company will pay you for everything lost."

"We can go on a buying spree," Monty promised, trying to steal the sadness in her eyes.

After a moment of pondering what she had upstairs, she looked up sharply. "I have a filing cabinet up there…

near the door actually. My dad bought it for me and it was fire resistant."

Chad looked at Monty and asked, "Do you want to give it a try?"

Thrilled to be able to retain something of hers, Monty agreed. The two men carefully made their way up the fire stairs and disappeared into her former apartment. After only a minute, they emerged, each carrying an end of the metal drawers.

Feeling a sliver of optimism for the first time in twenty-four hours, Angel smiled. "Oh, thank you. This holds both my work and my personal business papers. I was working on taxes the day before all this happened."

As they walked back to Monty's vehicle where the men put the cabinet, she turned to Monty and whispered. "You saw it. Was Chad right? Is it all gone?"

Hating to break her heart more, he turned and cupped her face, allowing his warm hand to press against her cold cheek. "I'm so sorry, Cupcake," he said, "but Chad was absolutely correct. There is nothing salvageable."

She closed her eyes against the blinding rage that poured over her, but his voice brought her back.

"Angel, I promise to get whoever did this. And I promise to be with you as you start over...and would love it if we could do it together. Blend our lives...join our homes."

Looking up, she watched as he brought his lips to hers. A warm kiss...one of the promise of a new future.

26

"Scott, I'm so glad you were able to see me today," Angel said, smiling at the familiar broker sitting behind his desk. *The desk that used to be Marcia's. Stop! It's only right that he should have her office now.* Forcing her mind to remember that life goes on, she hoped her barrage of emotions did not show on her face.

Having taken her hand in a warm greeting and ushering her to one of his deep leather chairs, he called out to Cindy for coffee. Settling himself down behind his desk, he expressed his condolences at her recent losses. "I'm shocked and angered for you, Angel. With the loss of dear friends and now your business…" he appeared to search for the right words. "Well, I hardly know how to express my feelings. But please know that CFG is here to assist you with anything you need."

"Thank you for replying so quickly to my email," she responded. Placing several files on his desk, she said, "I know we have a lot to discuss today. We need to take a look at the discrepancies in my statements and also I should be getting my insurance check by the end of the week."

"What would you like to start with?" Scott asked, his conciliatory voice smooth.

"Well," she pondered, "I suppose there really isn't much to say about the new store. I won't be investing any of the insurance money until I have bought all of my new equipment. I planned on taking my furniture, cases, and kitchen supplies with me. Now I'll have to buy all new everything for the shop." Sighing heavily, she admitted, "It really won't be hard to replace everything for the new bakery…it's all of my personal belongings that will be difficult."

"Yes, what will you be doing about your living quarters?"

"I'm staying with a friend for now until I decide where to live," she answered.

Scott looked down at the files on her desk. "I'm surprised that these survived the explosion. How fortunate they were somewhere safe."

"Yes, I keep everything in my apartment and not in the actual bakery."

They were interrupted when Cindy brought in coffee for both of them. Setting down a tray with two cups, creamer and sweeteners, she asked how Angel liked her coffee.

"Oh, I'll fix it," she replied, smiling at the assistant she knew was a favorite of Marcia's. "Thank you."

Cindy nodded and returned her smile as she barely glanced at Scott. Turning, she left his office, leaving his door open.

"So," Scott said, bringing them back to business, "you don't need our assistance for the new shop right now."

"That's right," she agreed. "Although, when all is said and done, I may be investing some of the insurance money if possible. What I'm really concerned about are the discrepancies." She held his gaze but felt the prickle of guilt sliding through her. "I can't believe that Marcia was doing anything wrong or purposefully harmful, but...well, I'm confused."

Nodding, Scott agreed. Taking the file from the desk, he opened it, his eyes scanning the documents. A crease furrowed his brow as he said, "I...well, I'm not sure exactly what some of these numbers or companies are. I'd like to look into this before I give you an answer."

"Of course," she said. Biting her plump lip for a second, she then looked at him with a determined expression. "I'd like to have a copy of everything before I turn these over to you."

"Absolutely," he agreed. "Cindy?" he called out. She appeared at the door. "Will you copy these files for Ms. Cartwright?"

Cindy walked into the room, taking the files while smiling at Angel. "I'll be right back with these," she promised, once more barely sending a glance toward Scott.

As she moved down the hall toward the workroom, Scott sighed heavily. Angel looked back, wanting to ask about their relationship, but stopped herself. *It's none of my business.* Glancing around the office, she saw that Scott had changed very little since taking it over. *Marcia was so efficient he probably discovered it needed no change.*

Cindy walked back into the room setting two sets of files on Scott's desk. "Here you go, Ms. Cartwright. Scott." Turning, she left once more.

"I'll take a look at these," Scott promised, "and will get back to you. Can you give me a couple of days?"

"Sure," Angel smiled. "I'll be busy with the new shop anyway. I needed them so that when I send everything to my accountant for taxes, they'll be correct."

Shaking his hand, she took her duplicate set of files and walked out of his office. Cindy rose from her desk, saying, "I'll show you out."

Placing her hand on the young woman's arm, she asked, "How are you doing? I know there are a lot of changes now and you worked so well with Marcia. I loved her like a sister and knew she appreciated your help."

At that, Cindy's eyes jumped up to Angel's. "Yes, we... well, we just clicked. So many people wondered why I didn't strive higher in my career but, honestly, working for Marcia was a dream job. She was so efficient. So dedicated." Sighing, she looked back toward Scott's office. "I won't deny it's hard, but there's a lot to keep an eye on now."

Arriving at the reception desk, Angel offered her hand to Cindy as they parted. Walking back to her car, she wondered about her words. *A lot to keep an eye on now.*

Unbeknownst to Angel, dark eyes followed her to her pink VW, anger flowing from them. Knowing they missed her with the explosion, they vowed to not make the same mistake again.

Luke worked diligently using the new program his mystery assistant had sent. Smiling, he was making more headway in a few hours than he had in the previous week. As the meta-data analyzed, he moved over to the work-room counter to fix another cup of coffee. Rubbing his chest, he noted the slight pain. Knowing it was time for his physical, he hoped he did not have an ulcer. As he poured a liberal amount of creamer in his cup, he heard the ding of his secure email. He jogged over, quickly scanning his screen.

I see it is helping.

He immediately replied, **Yes, thank you. How can you know what I'm working on?**

I'm just that good. Lol

A joke? This person has a sense of humor? **No doubt about it. Can you tell me where you are?**

You know I can't. Too dangerous. Eyes everywhere. But I will help when I can. Remember, do not take everything at face value. Some things are not what they seem.

Shaking his head, both in gratitude and frustration, he knew whatever this person was involved in, he did not want to risk their life. Imagining a young man, hunkered down in their messy apartment, hacking into Gods-knows-what accounts, Luke finally decided on, **Then I will just say thank you again.**

No reply came, but Luke knew they could still see what he worked on. For the first time, he was not upset someone had hacked him. *If it helps solve these fuckin' murders and keeps Angel safe, then bring it on!*

He glanced over to another computer, seeing results of the analysis coming up. Scanning the side-by-side comparison page between the investments of the three women, he quickly saw an interesting development.

The amounts in the various investments portfolios differed between the women...but the companies did not. Marcia had placed all of their money in exactly the same companies, regardless of what the individual women had requested.

Angel stood inside the space that would soon be the new Angel's Cupcake Heaven. She had been surprised at the number of former customers who left notes of consolation, assuming the damage to the old shop was from a gas explosion, that were also excited about her new shop.

The building owner for the new location, Mr. Jameson, was standing with her, his exuberance almost matching her own.

"Ms. Cartwright, when the previous tenants left and the restaurant closed, I was distraught. Obviously, the rental income loss was felt, but it was more than that. This area of town is being revitalized and the empty space just felt like it did not belong. I'm thrilled that Angel's Cupcake Heaven will be here."

She smiled at the man's enthusiasm before turning to Stan, the kitchen equipment contractor, who was meeting them here.

"I'll have the counters put in tomorrow," Stan assured, "just like we talked about. The ovens and stoves here are all in working order. So is the large, walk-in refrigerator and freezer."

Angel held back on the desire to dance around at the larger space and some of the new location's amenities. The huge refrigerator and freezer were something she did not have in her former shop and would make pre-baking cupcakes for weddings and events easier.

She and Stan walked around the kitchen space as she explained how she wanted things to be and he took notes. Nodding, he assured her that by the end of the next day it would be ready.

Just then, another provider walked in and introduced himself. Mike, of Restaurant Necessities, walked around the shop area with her. She had needed to purchase a sales counter, display cases, tables, chairs, and dishware. Going over the list with him, he also agreed everything could be in place tomorrow.

Mr. Jameson beamed at her. "Oh, my, Ms. Cartwright. It looks like everything is right on schedule."

She shared his smile, her heart feeling lighter than it had in days. "I know I will need to get the walls painted and my business logo on the window, but it'll take place soon enough."

"Well, you have your keys now, so you take care of whatever you need," he replied before taking his leave of her.

Shouts of greetings and laughter sounded from the door and Angel whirled around to see what the commotion was. Miriam, Sabrina, Bethany, Faith, and Felicity with her two children all walked in, carrying paint buckets and supplies.

"Wha..what is this?" she asked, her mouth hanging open.

"Monty wanted to help organize a painting party," Felicity responded. "I overheard him on the phone to these lovely ladies, so I convinced him to let me and the kids in on the surprise!"

"We'll get the walls painted in no time," Sabrina said, her interior-decorating eyes darting around.

Angel opened her mouth, but no words came out, overwhelmed by their generosity. As each woman came over to hug her, she battled back the tears.

"Now, none of that," Miriam admonished. "We need to get to work. We've got pink, purple, and teal paint so you tell us which colors go where."

Swiping at her eyes, she pointed to each wall with instructions and the women got to work. Within a few minutes, drop cloths were on the floor and paint poured into the pans as rollers were readied for their tasks.

"Kids, I'd better not see any paint anywhere except on

the walls," Felicity threatened. "Or I'll tell Miss Angel not to give you any cupcakes on opening day!"

As the group dispersed around the room, another sound came from the door. Turning, she was stunned to see her parents standing there.

"Mom? Dad? I thought you two were still on vacation in Florida?" She rushed into their outstretched arms.

"Well, it seems a nice young man, named Monty, gave us a call," her mom explained. "He thought we needed to know what was going on and asked us to contact your brother."

"What I'd like to know, young lady, is why we had to get a phone call from your new boyfriend, who we did not know about, to find out you're embroiled in the investigation into your friends' deaths, and," he paused for effect, "to find out what happened to your bakery!"

"I didn't want to upset you, dad—"

"Bullshit, Angel! You were injured and we should know about it. Hell girl, he said you were deaf!" he shouted, his bushy eyebrows quivering.

Monty picked that moment to walk into the pandemonium. His niece and nephew were running through the open space. The four friends and his sister were already using paint rollers on the white walls, creating swatches of color. An older version of Angel, silver-blonde hair bobbed at her shoulders, wearing a blue blouse and a multicolored skirt was standing next to a tall man, who appeared to be giving Angel a scolding.

Cam, Bart, Jack, and Jude had followed Monty inside, planning to meet their women, came in behind him at that moment, taking in the scene as well. All four laughed as they caught the smile on Monty's face.

"Damn, bro," Bart laughed. "You sure went from boring to scoring when you met Angel!"

Three hours later, three walls inside the shop were covered in pink, purple, and teal. The back wall was still white, awaiting Angel's muse.

The large group sat on the floor, pizza boxes laying around. Soda and beer bottles littered the area as the occupants finished their impromptu meal. The rumble of conversations was lost as she no longer strained to hear them.

Her parents fit in with her group of new friends and had thanked Monty profusely for contacting them. In fact, her father had taken Monty aside, grilling him about the investigation. Monty answered the questions he could and politely deflected the ones he could not.

Mr. Cartwright had eyed him carefully before sticking out his hand, grasping Monty's. "I can't think of anyone I'd rather have with our Angel than yourself." As he had walked back over to his wife, he muttered, "A lawman. Best damn person our girl could have ended up with!"

Monty had stood for a second, the acceptance washing over him, easing the last remnants of not measuring up to his parent's expectations from his being. Now, sitting on the floor with his arms around Angel, he knew he was right where he was supposed to be.

Angel leaned back against Monty, feeling him nuzzle her left ear. "Happy, baby?"

She nodded, smiling her answer. Tomorrow the furniture and counters would be in place in the shop and the baking equipment installed in the kitchen. One of her former customers had come by earlier and offered to paint her logo on the front plate glass. After she gave him a picture of what the original logo looked like, he handed her his card, assuring her he would have it finished tomorrow also. The only thing was the unique painting in the back, but she would ask the young artist if he was able to take care of that as well.

Looking around the room as the occupants lounged leisurely on the floor, she was filled with a sense of contentment. She knew someone was still out there—someone who wanted her dead and had killed her friends. The thought angered her and, if she were honest, frightened her. But, for the moment, she allowed the comfort of good friends to settle over her with the arms of the man she loved around her.

B ounding out of bed the next morning, Angel rushed into the bathroom, calling over her shoulder, "Monty, you've got to get a move on, honey. You have to drop me off at the new bakery before going to Jack's."

Monty rolled over, propping his head up on his elbow, the sheets tangled around his waist. Her pillow smelled of sugar and vanilla. Actually, her whole apartment used to smell of vanilla. Having become used to floral women's perfume, the sweet scent of a bakery felt like...*home.* Naked, his morning wood wanted nothing more than to have Angel right back in the bed, under him and moaning his name.

"Hurry," her voice came from the bathroom, pleading him onward.

Tossing the sheets to the side, he looked down at his erection. *Down boy. No time this morning.*

Stalking into the bathroom, he noticed hair products, toiletries, and makeup all over his counter. Catching her reflection in the mirror, she glanced around as well.

"I promise I'll put all this away before we leave this morning, sweetie."

Stepping behind her, he settled his chin on the top of her head, his arms wrapped around her body. "Babe, if you think for one minute that this concerns me, then you don't know me well at all. You in my life. Your stuff in my home. That's what makes life worth living. This place was just an apartment until you came."

Whirling around in his arms, she pressed herself up against him, soft breasts to muscular chest. Opening her mouth to speak, she noticed the prominent erection nudging against her stomach. Glancing down, she jerked her eyes back up. "Um...I think—"

"No worries, Cupcake," he laughed. "I know we've got to hurry."

Dropping to her knees, she grinned up at him and his cock twitched eagerly. "There's always time for breakfast."

Before he could think, she took him in her mouth, gliding her lips down his silky cock, fisting him at the same time. *Holy fuck.* Grabbing her hair in his hands, he moved gently as she sucked up and down. As turned on as he was, there was no way he would last very long with her exquisite ministrations. He tugged gently on her hair to indicate he was ready, but she kept going. *Not this time*, he decided.

He pulled her up quickly, her mouth letting go of his dick in surprise and turned her while whipping the t-shirt over her head. Barking, "Hands on the counter," he watched as she acquiesced.

Grinning as she complied, he bent over her from behind and plunged into her ready and waiting pussy. *No panties...easy access!* He continued to thrust, trying not to pound into her harshly, but consumed with the feel of her tight pussy pulling at his aching cock.

With one hand on her ass and the other on her shoulder, he kept his eyes on hers in the mirror. Her full breasts bounced in rhythm to his thrusts and the sight took him over the edge. He watched as her face tightened, moans slipping from her lips. Just as she cried out his name, he thrust several more times, pumping himself deep inside.

Pulling her back in tight to his front, they stood there panting as their legs struggled to hold them up. Finally, he kissed the top of her head. "Sorry, babe. I hope that didn't make you late."

"If it did, I'll gladly be late every day," she laughed. Tidying herself up, she threw all of her makeup into a bag and tossed it under the sink. Winking, she headed into his kitchen, popping the bagels into the toaster, shouting, "Bagels and coffee?"

"Perfect!" he called back. Looking out into the kitchen as she hustled to make breakfast, he lifted his hand to his chest, rubbing gently. The woman he loved was in his house. He hated like hell the reason she was there, but could not deny the desire to keep her with him always. He eyed the living room and chuckled, seeing a few colorful pillows now adorning his sofa. *She must have bought those yesterday.*

As he drove her toward her new shop, he said, "Remember to stay there today. Jack will have security duty over you today."

She turned her head toward him so quickly her blonde, colorful tresses whipped around her face. "Jack? Isn't it unusual for the owner of the business to do menial security?"

Monty shook his head, answering, "Nope. He wants to know everything that's going on. If it comes under his business, then he's going to take every precaution to make sure things go well and that includes security shifts."

They arrived at the new location and she hopped out of his vehicle, seeing the delivery trucks pulling up. "Just in time," she grinned as she unlocked the door. Waving to Monty, she headed inside.

He saw Jack securely in place, parked right in front of him. Jack stepped out of his truck and walked over to Monty.

"I'll be here until you're finished today," he assured.

"I appreciate it, boss."

Jack gave a little glare, indicating he did not need to be thanked for doing a job. "You going to talk to Mitch today?"

"Yeah, he's going to be in the area and we're meeting up in about an hour. After that, I'll check in to see what Luke's got and then I'll be back here." He turned to glance at the shop over his shoulder, "There'll be a lot of activity here today with a lot of people coming and going."

"Don't worry, I'll be watching her until you return," Jack promised.

Jack observed Angel flitting around the space like a hummingbird as the bakery furniture was delivered and set into place. Helen and her other employees arrived, excited to help. The white tables and chairs gleamed against the colorful walls.

The display cases came in next and were installed according to her plans. She paced between the bakery and the kitchen for the installations of the baking equipment. It only took a couple of hours for the large empty space to be transformed into her vision. The young artist worked diligently on the front window, the pink, purple, and teal swirls making the words Angel's Cupcake Heaven. Popping out to check on him, Angel's heart swelled with pride at seeing her dream coming true a second time. Taking out her camera, she clicked a picture and sent it to Monty. Her phone quickly indicated an incoming text. **Love it. Love you. Congratulations.**

Smiling, she darted back inside, ready to continue seeing her shop take shape. Jack made sure to station himself to keep his eyes on the deliveries. He called Chad and asked him to come by, wanting their explosive's expert to check out the kitchen before it would be in use. He warned Angel what he was doing, but hated to see the flash of fear cross her face, marring the delight that had been there.

"We need to make sure that whoever is doing this isn't sneaking in now with all this chaos," he explained.

Angel placed her hand on Jack's arm as she nodded. "I understand. Really, I do," she said, offering him a smile. "And I thank you so much for this."

Before he could respond, the front door slammed open, startling Angel and causing Jack to whirl around, shoving her behind his large body, his gun drawn.

In the doorway stood a large, blond haired man, still in his Army uniform with the signature Green Beret on his head. Seeing Jack's gun pointed at him, he roared, "Who the fuck are you and where the hell is my sister?"

"Patrick!" Angel screamed, hurling herself across the room and into his arms. Her brother picked her up easily, swinging her around.

Jack eased up on his weapon, placing it back in his holster. He noticed Patrick eyeing him over his sister's head.

"You want to introduce me to your guard?" Patrick asked, looking back down at Angel. "I know he's not your new boyfriend since he has a wedding band on his finger. Unless there's something else you need to tell me."

Laughing, she pulled out of Patrick's arms and led him over to Jack. "This is Jack Bryant, owner of Saints Protection & Investigations, the company Monty works for."

Jack stepped forward, his hand already reaching for the young man in his Special Forces uniform. "Pleased to meet you," he said. "I'm retired Special Forces."

Patrick immediately responded, grasping Jack's hand in return. A crash sounded in the kitchen and Angel rushed into the next room, checking to make sure her dishes were not on the floor. Thankfully, it was several metal bowls and Helen was in there, taking care of everything. Turning to the two men, she walked back over smiling.

"You want to tell me why I got a phone call from mom and dad, telling me your building exploded and you didn't call me?" Patrick asked.

"I never know where you are or what you're doing," she complained. "And anyway, I'm fine and we're taking care of everything."

Patrick looked down, frowning. "Sis, for you, unless I'm on a mission, I'm always available. As soon as they called, I caught a flight. I've got to report back tomorrow, but I had to make sure you were fine."

While Angel spent the next couple of hours making sure everything was going smoothly, Chad came to supervise the deliveries and keep watch over her. Patrick and Jack stayed right with her but found time to connect, discovering they knew many of the same people.

"I've only been retired a few years," Jack explained. "My last mission had me leading a multidisciplinary team. We had members from SEALs, FBI, CIA, and of course, SF. I assumed we'd have ego issues, but the team ran smoothly, each member bringing their own skill set. I knew then I wanted to recreate that when I got out."

Patrick was impressed, listening to the former commander. "I respect the work you're doing and I'd be remiss if I didn't tell you that I'm grateful for what you're doing for my sister." He stared over as she walked back into the room again. "She means the world to me."

The young artist came in from the outside, his work finished. Smiling, Angel pulled him toward the back, pointing to the wall and showing him pictures from her phone. The young man assured he could make her dreams come true and left to buy more paint with promises to return the next day. Twirling around, Angel delighted at her new space, eager to begin baking and open for business once again.

Monty sat at the table with Mitch, reviewing the information they had at the time. "It's coming down to CFG and what was going on there. We've got Luke processing the data from them—"

"And I won't ask how you obtained that," Mitch interrupted with a laugh.

Grinning back, Monty simply nodded, before continuing. "Marcia was in charge of the three accounts and if she was doing something illegal and someone found out, they took out Marcia and the others."

As he said the words, something niggled at the back of his mind. Something he had just said, but made no sense. Rubbing his face with his hand, he groaned, causing Mitch to look up.

"What's wrong?"

"There's something I'm missing. It's right in front of

me," he said. "It's as though the solution is staring me in the face, but I can't pull it together."

Mitch nodded sympathetically. "I hear you, man. I've had that feeling in just about every case I've ever worked. It'll come to you."

"I hope so because I'm fuckin' tired of trying to figure out all these puzzle pieces and leaving Angel's ass hanging out in the wind."

An hour later, Monty was back at the compound talking with Luke who, for the first time was smiling. Monty immediately approached him, looking over his shoulder at his computer screen.

"I've set up a data comparison page for the three women using the disaggregate program from my mystery assistant. Look what pops up each time."

Monty scanned down the page, noticing the similarities. "What—"

Before he could get his question out, Luke was already speaking. "With the intel Bart and Cam gave me, I saw each woman's application for investments and they checked different levels of risk. Betty was really conservative. Angel was moderate, and Theresa was more of a risk taker with her money."

"Their portfolios should be completely different," Monty added as Marc came down the stairs and peered at the screen as well.

"If you've found something, hang on," Marc said. "Bart, Cam, and Jude are just arriving. I don't know if Blaise is here or not."

Monty nodded and Marc yelled up the stairs to tell the others to come on down. With a quick call to Jack to let him know what they were working on, they proceeded. Feeling as though a piece of the convoluted puzzle was about to fall into place, each man leaned forward, forearms on the table, riveted to the wall screen as Luke projected his findings.

Reviewing what he had found to the others, he projected a comparison of the tax statements sent to the women and what was actually in their records.

"Son of a bitch," Bart said. "They're different."

"How the fuck can that be?" Marc asked. "Aren't those things computer generated?"

Luke looked over, a mixture of pride and disdain on his face. "Come on, man. You know hacks like me can make anything appear legit."

Marc shot him a grin, then studied the screen.

"Okay, you're gonna have to explain to me in general terms exactly what this means," Cam said. "I rely on my broker to make the decisions for me and then I sit back and hope the money comes in."

"Exactly!" Luke said. "Many people who invest do just that. Now, there are some who follow their investments on an almost daily basis, tracking everything. And I'm not being sexist when I say that these three didn't, but I'd bet the bank that they didn't."

"I know Angel doesn't," Monty said. "She's mentioned how, even with her major in business, she hates the investment and tax side of everything."

"Still not following," Cam said, the numbers on the screen appearing as a mishmash of information.

"The figures themselves don't really mean anything," Luke explained. "Nor do the companies. It's the similarities that make it suspect. Marcia was doing something to these accounts that just wasn't kosher."

"Could she have dummy companies set up and be siphoning money that way? She was wealthy on her own, so the extra money coming in would be more masked," Jude said.

"But why was Marcia killed if she had a great system set up?" Cam pondered.

"No!" Monty suddenly shouted. "Marcia wasn't the broker for these three. Not at first. Remember, the company's policy, that the broker wasn't supposed to have clients that were personal friends first. She took these over from someone else."

Luke pounded on the keyboard, searching for the information needed. The men looked up as the original brokers came up on the screen. "Scott worked with Angel and Betty. Roy Johnston was the broker for Theresa."

"How can that be? Two different brokers had the three women in precisely the same investment companies?" Bart asked. "Unless they were in cahoots with each other."

"Maybe they were and Marcia found out. She took over her friends' accounts to see what was happening," Jude surmised.

The men looked at each other, all thinking what Marc voiced. "And Marcia was killed to silence her."

A collective *fuck* sounded around the table. "We're getting closer," Monty confirmed. "What we need to do now is dig deeper into CFG, focusing on Scott and Roy. I want to know what ties they had with the three women. Jude, dig into their phone and email records. I don't want to question Scott and Roy again until we have a little more to go on. Bart, you talk to Betty's parents again and get more on Bill Bradley. I want to know if he so much as sniffed around her investments or ever met with CFG. Marc, you take Theresa—same thing. Luke, I want you to find out about those particular companies. Are they real? Fronts? Dummy corporations?"

The men eyed each other, the air having changed from one of frustration to the scent of resolution. Finally, a few pieces were sliding into place.

"I'm heading to Angel's place. I'll fill in Jack and Chad and then I'll question Angel about her investment involvement as well."

"Damn, man. That's a downer in the middle of her trying to open the new store," Marc commented.

Monty pierced him with his gaze. "I want her alive to enjoy the new bakery."

Now the room was filled with *Hell yeahs.*

2 8

Pulling up to the new bakery location, Monty saw the intricate window sign with pink, purple, and teal swirls creating the letters in Angel's Cupcake Heaven. Smiling to himself, he headed inside. Struck by the completion of the bakery, his eyes immediately sought Angel, wanting to make sure she was happy. He saw her back with another man's arms wrapped around her. The man moved slightly and Monty could see the Army uniform. Pushing back the unfamiliar jolt of jealousy, he walked toward the trio, assuming he knew the young man's identity.

Angel heard the noise at the door and turned her head toward the sound. "Monty!" she called out, rushing over. He opened his arms and she ran into his embrace. "Isn't it great?" she exuded, throwing her arm around, indicating the colorful bakery. "And you have to see who came!" Grabbing his hand, she pulled him toward the soldier.

"Monty, this is my brother, Patrick, who came home just for the day to see me! Patrick, this is my boyfriend, Monty Lytton."

The two men shook hands, Monty knowing the brother was sizing him up. Patrick's demeanor stayed relaxed and smiling, so Monty assumed he met the brother's approval. The tall, blond soldier with the muscular build had the same blue eyes as Angel, the familial bond easy to see.

"You're only here for one night? Monty asked.

"Yes. Mom called and I was able to take a day of family emergency leave to check on sis."

"Well, I'm sorry you had to burn up a day of leave for me, but I'm so glad to see you," she said, before being called into the kitchen by Chad. Patrick followed her, leaving Monty alone with Jack. Filling him in quickly on their meeting, Jack nodded.

"So if someone else fucked with their investment accounts and Marcia got wind of it, took them over, and discovered something, then she could have been killed. And the other women as well."

"Now, we need to find out who without spooking them into running...or trying to kill again," Monty added, his eyes following Angel in the kitchen. "I was going to question her later, but with her brother here for only a night, I'll wait and do it tomorrow."

"I think they're planning a family dinner tonight, but you could get the info from her after that," Jack stated. "We can meet after we get the new info from the others. Tomorrow afternoon good for you?"

Monty agreed and Jack moved into the kitchen to say goodbye to Patrick and Angel. He noticed Jack taking Patrick to the side and speaking to him for just a moment before Jack kissed Angel's cheek and headed back toward him.

"You offer him a job, boss?" Monty laughed.

"Hell, yeah," Jack answered, grinning. "I told him if he ever got out of the Army and wanted a job to let me know."

"And he said?"

Laughing, Jack answered, "Said he'd keep that in mind." With that, Jack left and Monty headed into the kitchen.

Chad saw Monty and said, "Everything looks good. The ovens and stoves are fine. The gas and electric companies have been out to inspect and I've been here the whole time. Alvarez Security came by and have the place wired already."

"That reminds me," Angel said, turning to look at Monty with her hands on her hips. "Who was this Tony person and who the hell is paying for the system they put in?" she asked, pointing to the cameras in the corners of the kitchen and the security panel by the back door.

"That, my dear," Monty said leaning in to quiet her with a chaste kiss, "is not for you to worry about. Anyway," he added, "they're friends of ours and we do some work for each other. They actually owed us, so we're good."

She sighed, hating the need for such security, but knowing she needed it. "Okay," she smiled, leaning up to kiss his cheek. "I admit I'm glad to have it."

"So am I," Patrick said. Looking directly at Monty, he added, "And if there's any help needed with the cost, let me know."

"No worries," Monty said. "The Saints have her covered."

Lying in bed that night with Angel in his arms, Monty thought back over the evening as sleep eluded him. The slight snores from her let him know that at least she was able to find rest in the midst of the investigation, for which he was grateful.

The evening began with the family dinner. At first, he tried to beg off, but Angel insisted. "It's my family, honey, but we're together now so that makes it your family too," she argued.

In the end, he was happy to have participated. He discovered dinner with the Cartwrights was far different compared to a dinner with his parents. The conversation stayed lively, and it was evident Sylvie and Sam Cartwright were proud of their children. Patrick appeared to relish his home cooked meal and his sister's cupcake dessert. Once more, Monty had to try to eat the moist, delectable treat piled high with Angel's signature colors on the frosting without getting it all over his face. Unsuccessful. But with everyone else at the table emitting groans of delight with the icing on their lips as well, he fit right in.

At the end of the evening, Angel held on tearfully to Patrick as she said goodbye. He would be leaving in the early morning hours to fly back to his duty station. Monty watched as the two of them stood on the porch for several minutes, the long goodbye agony for his woman.

Sam walked up behind him, his typical gruffness tempered. "Sylvie gave me two good children," he said. "Now one of them's found a good man."

Monty turned and looked into Sam's eyes, seeing them shining with emotion. Shaking Sam's hand, he listened as her father continued.

"Keep her safe for us, Monty."

"Yes, sir. I intend to. For as long as she'll have me."

Sam smiled as Sylvie approached them and he pulled his wife in closely. "Then, from what I can see...welcome to the family."

After Monty and Angel were back in his apartment, he

told her they needed to talk.

"Oh, dear. This sounds ominous," she said, looking as he pulled off his tie and loosened the top button of his shirt. "Do I need wine for this conversation?"

Chuckling, he said, "It might not be a bad idea. I'll pour while you go change."

She hurried into the bedroom, deciding after working all day she needed a quick shower. Stepping under the warm water, she quickly washed away the dirt and grime from the day before slipping into comfortable yoga pants and one of Monty's large FBI t-shirts.

He looked up as she walked back into the living room, face and body glowing from the fresh scrub and looking as delectable as one of her cupcakes. Handing her a glass of wine, they settled together on the sofa, facing each other.

"Okay, hit me with it," she tried to joke.

"It seems as though we may be getting closer to solving the case and from where we are now, it definitely appears as though Betty, Marcia, and Theresa's deaths are linked, as well as your attempted murder. And the link is CFG."

Angel took a large sip of the wine, finding swallowing difficult. "You want to know what's crazy? Part of me really wanted Betty's to just be natural causes, Theresa's to just be a stupid accident on icy roads, and mine to be a gas leak. I know none of those things are true, but it was easier for me to think that way."

Reaching out, Monty linked his fingers with hers. "I know, Angel, and I'm sorry."

Taking another sip for fortification, she nodded. "So, what have you got?"

Monty stared at her for a silent moment, taking her emotional pulse. Seeing her steady, he began. "In a nutshell, it appears that somehow, even with Scott and another broker working on the investment accounts with the three of you, they set up something unusual. I won't say illegal until we delve into it more, but definitely your accounts are almost identical and that shouldn't be. We now surmise that perhaps Marcia noticed or since Theresa was killed first, she may have brought something to Marcia's attention. But Marcia took over your accounts, which was actually against company policy of working with clients that you also had a social connection with. If she was digging, then that would explain why she was murdered, and then if Betty had already noticed a problem, she was silenced as well."

"So it wasn't Marcia doing something wrong, but trying to fix things for her friends?"

"We don't know anything for sure yet, but that could be a real possibility."

Angel's eyes grew wide with each statement from Monty. She looked over his shoulder at the nighttime view outside his window for a moment. Licking the wine from her lips, she hastily took another sip. Swallowing hard, she looked back at him. "So in effect, even with my business degree, the fact that I never watched my investments too closely and prefer baking, may be what kept me alive so far."

"I hadn't thought of it in those terms, but yes, I'd say that's a good assumption."

"Fuck," she whispered, setting her now empty wine glass on the coffee table with shaking hands.

"Babe, I need to know in detail what your dealings with CFG looked like. Who you talked to, what you talked about, everything."

She nodded, but her expression was dubious. "There's not much to tell. Marcia had been after me to invest some money I got from my grandparents. I was nervous, but she convinced me to be kinda moderate in my portfolio." She barked out a laugh. "Listen to me. I sound like I fucking know what I'm talking about. Honestly, I don't have a clue how it all works. I wrote Colonial Financial Group a check and they took it and invested it. I got a quarterly statement and usually only glanced at it. I seemed to be making some money so I didn't worry about it too much."

"Who did you deal with?"

"Um, I guess Scott was the only person I dealt with. He was my broker and I only met with him about two times. I would email him if I had a question, but" she blushed, "I think that was only a couple of times."

"Did you know Marcia took over your account about three months ago?"

She cocked her head to the side, a confused expression on her face. "No. Hmmm, I wonder why?"

"Who else did you talk to when you were at CFG?"

"Well, the receptionist when I came into the office. Um...Cindy would take me back to him. I know she was Marcia's right-hand woman and I got the feeling she never liked Scott very much."

"Yeah, well, she's working for him now," Monty commented.

She nodded, already knowing this tidbit of information. "And she hates that. She and Marcia were tight. I always thought that the two of them connected being in a male-dominated business."

"What dealings did you have with Carlton Creston?"

Her brow creased as she considered his question. "Marcia's cousin?" Seeing his nod, she answered, "I think I met him at a Christmas party at Marcia's parent's home. Um...I did see him once when I was at CFG. He was the next appointment after me. At least, he was going in to see Scott when I was coming out."

Interesting, Monty thought, as he closed the space

between his body and Angel's. His arms snaked around her body as he pulled her in tightly. Kissing the top of her head, he held her for a long time, each quietly with their own thoughts.

"Monty?"

"Right here, Cupcake," he murmured against her hair.

"What do you do when you can't solve a case?"

Sucking in a deep breath, Monty pulled her tighter. "This case'll be solved, baby. I promise."

Twisting in his arms, she looked up into his face, seeing sincerity…mixed with anger. Lifting her hand, she cupped his stubbled jaw. Rubbing her thumb over his cheek, she smiled. "When I'm in your arms, I feel the safest."

He bent his head over, pressing his lips against hers. "Then this is where you should stay," he mumbled into her mouth.

Now, hours later, after making love long into the night, he lay awake turning the clues over and over in his mind. *The fuckin' answer is staring me straight in the eye and I can't find the last piece of the goddamn puzzle!*

Early the next morning, Luke stepped into his kitchen, firing up his expensive coffee machine. While it brewed, he moved to his window, overlooking the park beside his property. He loved the little house he found. The side bordered the park, the back was woods, and his closest neighbor was an acre to the side. The house was small, just the right size for him. He knew Bart and Cam had bought larger homes, Monty lived in a nice apartment, Jack built his large cabin, Blaise needed lots of room for his animals, and Marc had a cabin in the woods. Chad rented a small house in a family neighborhood, which always seemed strange to Luke, who preferred solitude. He had never been to Jude's place, but assumed he and Sabrina rented a house as well.

His coffee ready, Luke moved away from his window and the musings of what people's homes say about themselves. Chuckling as he sat down opening his laptop, he sat his large cup on the table and immediately pulled up his latest work.

Late last night he had spent time investigating the companies that were shared by the three women's portfolios. Finding nothing, he finally went to bed and was now ready to resume his work. Within thirty minutes, he hit the jackpot. Corsten Defence Technology Industries. Betty, Theresa, and Angel were all heavily invested in the company...and it did not exist.

How the fuck did this happen? And who the hell is Corsten Defense Technology? Realizing he had found a dummy corporation, he began to dig, once more frustrated with the levels of protection hiding the data.

An incoming email pinged. **I can tell you now see the light.**

Sucking in a breath, he typed, **Yes. Now to peel back the layers.**

Keep at it. You will succeed.

Will we ever meet, Luke typed, knowing the answer, but hopeful all the same. No reply came and he stopped watching, focusing all of his efforts on Corsten Defense Technology. Peel back the layers, one at a time, he told himself. This has to be it—the key to the murders. With a call to Jack and Monty, he continued his work as his fingers flew over the keys.

The email alert came in, distracting him. Opening it, he smiled.

Maybe. One day, we'll meet. Maybe.

29

The Saints were meeting to review Luke's findings and Angel decided to make a visit to Colonial Financial Group. Ever since had Monty told her of the possibility of her investments being tainted by someone at CFG, she had grown more furious.

Walking in, she told the receptionist she needed a moment of Scott's time and she would not take no for an answer. Sitting on the leather sofa in the waiting room, she tossed her hair over her shoulders, righteous indignation flowing through her veins.

A minute later Cindy appeared. "Ms. Cartwright, Mr. Robinson isn't here yet. Is there something I can help you with?"

Angel pondered for a moment before hoisting her purse up on her shoulder. "No, I suppose not. I really need to speak with him, though, so if you can tell him to call me, I would appreciate it."

Cindy moved closer, her eyes darting over to the receptionist filing her nails. "Let's go into the back," she whispered.

Angel, sensing Cindy did not want to speak in front of the receptionist, nodded and followed the other woman down the hall to a conference room.

Shutting the door, Cindy said, "I'm sorry, but I have a feeling that receptionist was hired by Scott, after Marcia died, for her bra size rather than her intellect. I don't trust her at all."

Smiling at the description, Angel relaxed slightly. "Look, Cindy, my accounts don't match up and I brought this to Scott's attention the other day and have heard nothing back. With my friends having died recently and this place being investigated as well, I want him to know that if he cannot explain things to my satisfaction by the end of the week, I'll be pulling my investments out and going with another brokerage firm."

She saw Cindy's face fall and softened her next words. "I'm sorry, Cindy. I really am, but I swear something fishy is going on here and my investments are not play-money for me. This is what runs my business."

"No, no, you're exactly right," Cindy assured her. Sighing deeply, she looked into Angel's eyes and admitted, "I think my days here are numbered also."

"Is Scott getting rid of you?" Angel asked, incredulous. It appeared to her Cindy was invaluable.

"No, not overtly. But I'm miserable with Marcia gone," Cindy said, her voice cracking with emotion. "And I agree that there's something fishy going on. I had hoped to stay long enough to figure it out."

"Was Marcia working on it?"

Cindy's eyes darted back to the door and she lowered her voice. "I don't know. If she was and she suspected something, she didn't confide in me, but...I have my suspicions."

With that, Angel said, "Well, pass on my threat to Scott.

I want to hear from him as soon as possible." Shaking hands with Cindy, she made her way to the front door and out to her car.

Once more, from a window in the building, angry eyes followed her as she departed.

———

That afternoon, Jack and Monty, bolstered by Luke's findings, were escorted into the CFG conference room where they found Scott and Roy waiting for them.

"We moved several appointments around for you, Mr. Lytton," Scott said, frustration on his face. Roy's eyes shifted between the others at the table, allowing Scott to speak for both of them.

"Then we'll make this brief. As of this morning, we have ascertained that Colonial Financial Group has invested clients' money into at least one phony company that we have determined. We have sent our findings to the FBI, who at this moment are looking into your company as a whole." Monty slid a folder in front of the two men sitting in front of him.

Scott reared back, his face expressing complete shock. Monty kept his eyes on him, having agreed with Jack beforehand that he would be watching Roy.

"This...this...there's no way...it..." Scott stammered, his eyes roving over the papers.

"Oh, Jesus," Roy moaned, slumping in his seat. "I knew something was wrong. I just knew it."

Scott shot his eyes over to Roy. "What the fuck are you talking about?"

Roy, deflated, just sat staring at his hands in his lap. "So close. So close to retiring."

"Mr. Johnston, what was wrong?" Monty asked, now

looking between the two men, both appearing equally stunned.

"I've been slacking a bit this past year. Not paying as much attention as I should to my clients. Marcia wasn't giving me any new ones since I planned on retiring and the ones I had were doing okay. I delegated some of the work to the assistants, figuring it would help them get ahead."

"So?" Scott spouted. "That's not unusual. Broker assistants often do that."

"One day Marcia marched in and went straight to my file drawer. She rummaged through it for a moment and then pulled out a file. Theresa Constantine. She promptly told me that she was taking the account over and she would have Cindy go into her account online and switch it over to her."

Rubbing his hand over his face, he continued, "I was pissed at the time. I mean who wouldn't be?" He looked up at the other three. "It was insulting, but that was how Marcia was. If she wanted something, she just took."

"So were you willingly and knowingly placing these women's investments into a phony company?" Monty asked.

"No!" Roy shouted, sitting up straight in his chair. "If there was something wrong, it wasn't my doing." Looking over at Scott, he accused, "What about you? She took the baker's account and that other woman away from you."

Scott looked askance for a moment, then admitted. "It was a lot less dramatic than yours. She just came in one day and said she wanted to look over her friends' account since she hoped to expand the business one day. I gave her the files and about two days later I noticed that my online files for Ms. Cartwright and Ms. Mavery were now missing and she was listed under Marcia's name as one of her clients."

"That didn't piss you off?" Roy asked, anger written on his face. "Or was the fact that you slept with her make it all okay for you? She gets your client and you get the fuc—"

"Shut up!" Scott yelled. "It wasn't like that at all. We slept together one time. That was it. And it never affected our relationship in this office. Not then. Not after. It was a one-time thing, over and forgotten."

Roy huffed, his face still angry as his eyes roved over the papers in front of him. Looking at the company name, he said, "Is it Corsten Defense Technology Industries? I've never heard of them."

Scott leaned over the table, eyeing the copies of the three women's account portfolios. "Huh?" He scanned the information then pulled out his phone, looking the company up on the internet. "They don't exist," he stated.

"Jesus, Scott. How'd you get to be the president after Marcia died? Did you screw your way to the top? Of course it doesn't exist if it's a dummy company," Roy argued.

Throughout the exchange, Monty and Jack eyed the interaction between the two men, with occasional glances between themselves. *These two are too stupid to come up with this plan*, Monty thought and, from the expression on Jack's face, he felt the same.

Pointing to a signature at the bottom of each page, Monty asked, "If neither of you were aware of the company, then why did you sign off on the forms?"

Scott and Roy leaned over the papers once more, examining them, and then both answered almost in unison. "That's not my signature."

"The broker assistant would handle some of the transactions for us. That's common practice. But we were supposed to sign off on everything," Roy said, his pudgy face pale and sweating profusely.

Monty and Jack looked first at each other and then to the two men in front of them. "Then who signed for you?" Monty growled, his fist hitting the table.

Once more the two men spoke in unison, "Cindy."

"We need to speak to her immediately," Monty demanded.

Scott, his complexion pale, responded, "She's not here today. She left earlier saying she was sick."

Angel spent the morning bustling around the kitchen with her staff, arranging the area to her satisfaction. She was able to discern conversations more clearly, but if there was too much background noise, her hearing was still muffled. Her staff quickly became used to speaking directly to her. They made a practice batch of cupcakes and enjoyed them out in the shop. The young artist, hard at work, finished the small mural on the back wall. The painting of an old man from medieval times at a stone oven pulling out a flat wooden paddle with bread loaves on it, now graced the wall. Painted in muted colors, it did not immediately jump out at patrons. Instead, it was evident to those who sat near the back or were curious enough to walk toward the wall to stare at the painting.

He finished in the early afternoon, taking his check and a box of ACH cupcakes away. Helen laughed as he left the bakery. "I swear, I think he's happier with the cupcakes than the money."

A large batch of muffins was next out of the oven and they opened the front door, offering them to the pedestrians walking in, with shouts of, "Grand Opening on Saturday." Many of the homeless persons who had come to her other shop found her new location and she offered them a muffin as well. The shop swirled with customers wanting a free treat.

Marc hustled inside as soon as he saw people entering, cursing under his breath for not knowing she was going to have the shop doors open at all today. He watched, eagle-eyed, assured the customers were in just the shop and her employees were the only ones in and out of the kitchen. As soon as the muffins were all gone, Angel and her staff headed back into the kitchen to begin their cleanup as Marc checked to make sure the front door was locked, after visually sweeping the entire bakery, before taking his position across the street once more.

Looking around in satisfaction, Angel smiled as she dismissed her staff for the day. "Okay, guys, we'll spend tomorrow baking and get things into the refrigerator to be ready for the soft opening the following day. And then, of course, next Saturday will be the grand opening of our new location!"

Helen and the others cheered as they offered hugs and congratulations. Angel walked to the back door, letting them out. Moving around the kitchen, she trailed her fingers along the gleaming stainless steel appliances and counters. Yesterday the smell was paint, cleansers, and even the cardboard boxes containing supplies. Today, the smell of chocolate, vanilla, and lemon filled the air.

She walked into the shop, noting the spotless display case. *And tomorrow it'll be filled with cupcakes.* She continued her perusal as she wandered around the white tables, covered in pink tablecloths and glass tabletops. *Beautiful!* She smiled, remembering her promise to Felicity's children that the first party hosted in the new ACH would be with their friends in honor of the help they had given.

Stopping at the back wall, she stared at the new mural. Her hand lifted to the figure, her fingers splayed over the design. The artist captured the calm expression on the face and Angel heaved a deep sigh. *Marcia, Betty, Theresa...I did it. No,* she thought, remembering the encouragement of the other sisters whenever she talked about her dream. *We did it.*

She checked the lock on the front door and, looking across the street, she saw Marc in his SUV and she gave a little wave to him. She knew he would stay until Monty came to pick her up later.

Walking back toward the kitchen, she came to an abrupt halt. Standing in the kitchen doorway...was Cindy. And in her hand...a gun.

Monty and Jack rushed out of Colonial Financial Group, jumping into Jack's SUV. Calling Marc, he was assured Angel was safely inside the bakery and the doors were locked. Marc told him he was heading around to the alley to recheck the back.

Then, calling Luke, he bit out, "Find out everything you can about Cindy Bartley. She's behind the discrepancies and probably the dummy corporation. We're heading to her house now."

With Luke working his magic, the two raced toward Cindy's apartment. Arriving at the modest brick building, they moved along the outdoor walkway until they came to her door. When she did not answer their knocks, Monty picked the lock while Jack kept watch. Within thirty seconds, they stepped through the door.

Monty looked around the living space as soon as they entered. Neat, clean, with nothing out of place. The magazines on the coffee table were stacked and angled perfectly.

Pictures on the mantle and end tables were all of Cindy and Marcia or Marcia by herself. All of them.

Jack moved to the right, down the hall to the one bedroom. Returning a minute later, he reported, "She's not here, but then, I swear it looks like this place is a mausoleum it's so neat."

Monty turned and looked at Jack. *Neat. The workroom at CFG. The offices at CFG.* Stalking into the kitchen, he threw open the cabinets. *Every can, every box...stacked perfectly. It was her all along!*

Whirling around, he said his thoughts aloud. "It was Cindy, not Marcia. Cindy made sure Marcia's housekeepers kept things pristine. She was in Marcia's house, keeping the house, including the kitchen cabinets, this orderly."

Monty rushed past Jack as they ran from the apartment, calling Marc. "Get inside the bakery! Our suspect, Cindy Bartley, may be inside somehow. ETA is five minutes," Monty barked, disconnecting.

Jack ran behind him, calling Luke, ordering him to get hold of Mitch and then the other Saints.

Arriving, Monty noticed the front door locked and lights off inside the bakery. Marc ran from around the corner, his weapon drawn. "Goddamn back door is locked and I can't get Angel to answer."

"Fuck!" Monty swore, his mind rushing around, not focusing.

Pulling out his phone, Jack called Tony Alvarez's Security Agency and had them pull up the live feed from the cameras inside. "Got it," he said, disconnecting a minute later. Turning to the group, he confirmed, "Two women in the kitchen. One with a gun."

The sound of squealing tires on the street was followed by the pounding footsteps of the Saints. Running over, they surrounded Monty, both in support of him and to be briefed. Before they could begin, Mitch arrived with a contingency of police as well as FBI.

"What's upstairs?" Monty asked, thinking of her old shop with the apartment above the kitchen with stairs leading down.

"No access," Marc said, with the building's owner on the phone.

"If they've moved into the kitchen, we've got to get into the front door," Monty said, forcing his mind to clear of all but the rescue. *Successful rescue.*

30

"I loved her. Don't you see...she was my world," Cindy stated as though those words would explain everything.

Angel wanted to look up into the face of the distraught woman in front of her, but the gun pointing at her stole her focus. Forcing her mind to concentrate on what Cindy was saying, she said, "Marcia liked you very much."

Cindy barked an angry noise, the gun waving as she said, "Liked? Jesus, liked? I. Loved. Her. Do you hear what I'm saying? I loved her." A tear slipped down her cheek and she used her free hand to swipe at it. "But no, it was always about her sisters. The goddamn, fucking sisters."

"The sorority sisters?" Angel asked, her gaze jumping up to Cindy's face. "What...wh—"

"I met her when she hired me, straight out of college. I wanted to be a broker but the only job they had was broker's assistant. I took it—it would pay the bills and she said she would train me. I worked with her every day." Cindy's voice shook with emotion, the gun waving in the process. "I fell in love with her. But she only saw me as a friend."

Angel watched the distraught young woman, her eyes darting between the tears and the weapon. Her insides quivered with fear as her mind rushed with what to do. Her eyes landed on the security camera in the corner. *Keep her talking. Keep her talking.*

"We occasionally had lunch together, but that was all. No, no," Cindy moaned. "For Marcia, her world was getting to the top, her precious sisters, and the men she would sleep with. She never looked at me like that."

"So...did you work with the accounts?" Angel asked hesitantly. "Was that you?"

The sad expression slid from Cindy's face as one more maniacal moved in. "No one knows how much power I wielded in the office," she admitted. "All she talked about was the sisters. I couldn't do anything about all of you, but there were three of you with accounts. I could become part of the group that way."

Shaking her head slowly, Angel stood still, her mind unable to process what Cindy said fast enough to try to reason with her. Still standing just inside the kitchen, her eyes darted around to see if she could arm herself. Her purse was on the counter to her right and she knew her gun was inside. *It's too far away.* Cindy's gun hand wavered, the fatigue of holding it steady taking over. *I've got to keep her talking.*

"Are you the one who messed up my investment statement?"

A snort came from Cindy as she jerked the gun up. "Messed up? Jesus, you are stupid aren't you? You give money to the broker and then sit back and don't even know where it's gone. I set up a company name and took part of the money to go into that company. But it actually went to me. All me."

"Why?" Angel asked. "I don't understand how that would affect you and Marcia."

"I was only going to do it for a couple of years—just long enough to make me rich enough for her. I might not be one of her precious sorority sisters but, with money, I could be on her level. Then I'd be in her rich, my-daddy-is-a-Senator world."

"Money didn't matter to Marcia," Angel cried, sliding a step closer to her purse. "She liked you as you were. Wasn't that enough?"

Dragging her free hand through her hair, her face contorted. "You don't understand. I wanted her. I wanted her to love me the way I loved her."

Licking her lips, Angel stared at the agonized young woman in front of her. "I...I don't know what to say, Cindy."

Swiping another tear, Cindy continued on her rant as though eager to talk now that she had a captive listener. "But she didn't want me. God, do you know how many men she slept with? I would follow her as she went to bars, meet some swinging-dick and head to a hotel. Over and over and over. She would fuck anyone with looks, but never once paid that kind of attention to me." She looked over at Angel and implored, "Haven't you ever wanted someone so badly that you'd do anything to get them to notice you?"

Until Monty had walked into her life, Angel would have said no to Cindy's question but, loving him the way she did, she knew what it felt like to want to be with someone...*but not that desperately!* Wisely keeping quiet, she slid one more step closer to her purse.

"My plan was so good. Get some money, then I could

easily fix the accounts and no one would be the wiser. I'd be on Marcia's social level and planned on attending the same parties and family gatherings she attended."

Angel's mind focused on getting to the gun in her purse, but as she heard Cindy's plan she realized the women was completely bonkers. *Marcia was never about money. Marcia was about laughter, fun, old friends, good times... Cindy was never going to be able to buy her way into Marcia's love.* She watched as Cindy's gun arm moved downward, growing tired. *Keep her talking.* "So what happened?"

"That stupid teacher, Theresa, went to Marcia and questioned her account. She noticed something. Marcia must have looked at it and she took it over from that idiot Roy." Her eyes lifted back to Angel's and she implored, "Don't you see? I had to get rid of Theresa. A dead person's account would just be closed out. I...I could have fixed it and no one would be the wiser."

At that, Angel's eyes grew wide. "You? You killed Theresa?"

Laughing, Cindy said, "Do you know how easy it was? It only took me one week to learn her routine. Come home from school, park in the garage and wait for her mechanic to come home to her. God, she was such a loser...and that greasemonkey she was with? And she got to be a close friend of Marcia and yet I wasn't? How does that happen?" Swiping at the sweat on her forehead, she shook her head as though remembering every detail. "It was simple. Sneak into the garage, barely cut the brake line so that the fluid would seep out slowly." Laughing, she added, "The snow and ice were a bonus. I hadn't planned on that. The next day, I went in and took out the dummy company from her portfolio and no one was the wiser."

"But Marcia? Betty?"

The smile slid from Cindy's face. "I knew I had to do the same with Betty before Marcia got wise. I knew she had a heart condition from hearing Marcia talk about it a couple of years ago when Betty stayed in the hospital." Giving a little shrug, she admitted, "It was easy to break in and add some drugs to her pills. They were sitting right in the medicine cabinet. I had to hurry, though, so I didn't tamper with them all, just some. So I never knew when she might die."

Angel's knees buckled at the premeditated deaths of two of her friends. *How does someone even think of these things? It's crazy, but she made it work.* Gripping the counter with her knuckles to hold her up, she felt the adrenaline quivers begin to move over her body. *Hold it together. Hold it together.* Sliding one more half step, she was almost to her purse.

"But Marcia? Cindy, you said you loved her."

At this, Cindy's face fell, her chin quivering. "I did. I loved her so much. After Theresa died and I set things up for Betty to die, I thought I was good. We'd go to lunch. We'd gossip and laugh about the men in the office. But she kept digging into the accounts. She told me that when she found out what had happened, she would fire Roy and then she decided to take back your account as well. Because that was against company policy, I thought I'd be safe, but she really investigated." Waving the gun around, she shouted, "All she cared about was you all...not me! I was nothing more than just a lunch buddy!"

"I'm sure that's not true, Cindy," Angel said, her hands behind her now, reaching her purse.

"I followed her the night she was supposed to meet up with you. I planned on dropping into the bar casually and then joining the two of you for drinks. I was going to befriend you also and...and...be one of the gang."

"But I wasn't there," Angel prompted, her fingers feeling the cold metal in her purse.

"No. And just when I realized you weren't coming and was going to make my move for Marcia and me to have an evening together, she picks up some guy at the bar. Jesus, he wore a wig, but Marcia's eyes lit up the way they always did when she knew a fuck was coming." Several more tears slid down her face. "I was right there...right in front of her, but she never looked at me like that." Taking a breath, she lifted the gun a little higher as though remembering it was in her hand. "I followed them to that stupid motel. I stood outside the door, listening to the grunts and moans. I got sick. I actually got sick."

"You killed Marcia?" Angel asked, Cindy's twisted story not making any sense. *Why would she kill someone she loved?*

"I followed her out to her car. I got inside and surprised her. I held my gun on her and told her to drive. We went... I don't know...somewhere. Down some road. I made her get out and I didn't mean to kill her. I didn't. I just wanted to make sure she understood how tired I was of watching her with men all the time. And you sisters."

"But you couldn't make her love you at the point of a gun, could you?"

Cindy shook her head slowly. "No. When she realized I'd killed Theresa, she lunged toward me. I fired." She looked up, eyes now flowing with tears, her body ready to crumble and said, "I didn't mean to. I didn't mean to. I killed the one person in the world that I loved."

Cam, the best at breaking and entering, worked quietly on the front door. His large body squatted in an awkward position, trying to stay out of the line of sight in case

Cindy came back into the shop from the kitchen. Bart, also skilled in getting into locked places, worked on the office window, facing the alley, but was more hesitant since the two women were in the kitchen, close to the office.

Cam, the first to be successful, slid the door open noiselessly. Mitch, as FBI, was in charge of the investigation, but nodded to the Saints as Monty slipped inside the shop, followed by Mitch, Marc, and Jack. The others at the back alley were alerted that those men were now inside.

Hearing Cindy confess to killing Marcia, Mitch crept around the empty display counter, creeping forward inch by inch. Monty, needing a better visual, moved stealthily toward the back wall of the shop in the dark, allowing him to see through the door leading to the kitchen. Jack and Marc spread out in the room. Using radio signals through their earpieces, they each knew the position of the others.

Once Bart opened the window, he stepped back, allowing a much smaller FBI agent to crawl inside, but guarded the back door. The door from the office into the kitchen was closed, halting the FBI agent's progress.

Monty, listening to Cindy, knew she was nearing the end of her story—unfortunately, the time when the suspect decides what needs to be done next. And that is often when they kill again. *I can't get a fucking shot from this angle. He slid forward another few feet.*

"My other bakery," Angel said. "You tried to kill me too."

Cindy's glazed eyes moved back to Angel, her despondency being replaced with renewed anger. "Yes! It was all for nothing. The money I took from you three. The risk of killing Theresa and then Betty died. And...oh God, my Marcia. Work is fucking killing me. I'm now under Scott, one of the biggest idiots in the industry." She sniffed and wiped her nose with her sleeve. "He never would have figured anything out...never know there was a problem. At least, I could make the changes to your portfolio and then quit. Get another job and no one would be the wiser."

Her eyes held Angel's for a moment. "But you found the problem and sent an email to Scott. I had to get rid of you too."

"Didn't you think that the authorities were putting it all together? Both the fact that the victims were all connected with the sorority and CFG? How did you think you would get away with it?" Angel's voice rose with each word till she was screaming in rage. "And now? You're going to shoot me in my bakery?"

"It'll be easily explained," Cindy said. "You had all those tramps in here earlier. I shoot you and head down the street, slipping my gun into the pocket of one of them. The police will think one of those bums came back to get money or something and shot you." Monty, listening from the other room as he moved into position, his sights on Cindy, cringed. *Baby, keep calm. Speak softly...don't piss the crazy off!* He knew Cindy was close to losing it and he only had one good shot to take her down.

Just as he moved into position, a broom in the back corner of the room fell over, landing with a loud *Whack*, startling everyone. Cindy jumped, whirled and pointed the gun through the door of the shop, as Mitch shouted, "Halt! FBI! Put your weapon down!"

Angel heard the shout and jerked her gun up, firing at Cindy's arm just as Cindy fired toward the back wall of the dark shop. Screaming in pain, Cindy dropped her gun and fell to the floor, holding her bloody right arm.

Screaming for Monty, Angel ran past Cindy into the darkened shop. Seeing Monty stalking toward her from the back, she launched her body into his. He caught her in mid-air, clutching her tightly. One hand holding the back of her head to his shoulder and the other around her middle, pressed to his chest. Their hearts pounded, a disjointed staccato as both bodies shook in unison. Jack moved behind them, gently taking the gun from her hand. Monty shot him a grateful look as he continued to hold her.

Too many things happened at once for Angel to process, as Monty moved forward to set her on top of one of the tables. Pulling back, he peered into her eyes, seeing a mixture of emotions. The ringing in her ear intensified, making all other sounds muffled. She brought her hand up to her ear, a grimace on her face.

"Baby, can you hear me?"

She nodded, mumbling "Yeah. I put cotton in it this morning." Taking deep breaths, she looked around, seeing the bakery filling with men. Agents with FBI emblazoned across the back of their jackets. The Saints. Rescue workers were already on site and working on Cindy. "She killed them all and I…I shot her," Angel said, the adrenaline still pumping through her veins.

"Good thing too, baby. I didn't have a clear shot of her at first and she could have easily hit me."

At that, Angel's gaze hit Monty's, held for a second and then she surged forward. Latching onto his lips, she kissed him. A tangle of teeth, tongues, and lips, the kiss became their reason for breathing. For being.

Slowly pulling apart, he glanced down at her kiss swollen lips before gradually moving his gaze over her face, memorizing every inch. Holding her face in his palms, he leaned back in until his lips were a whisper away from hers. "I love you, Angel. The idea of losing you…fuck…"

Her eyes slid from his ravaged face, over his shoulder, to the back of the store, now bright with all of the lights. Bart, Cam, Jack, and Marc circled nearby. A bullet hole was in the middle of the mural, where Cindy's missed shot landed. She smiled tentatively as her chin quivered.

Monty glanced to the wall where Angel was looking. "You saved me, baby."

"No," she said, pointing to the mural. "He did."

The men looked over at the painting. Seeing the medieval man serving loafs of bread from the stone oven. Monty looked back at Angel, her face serene as she pulled out the charm necklace from underneath her shirt. Nodding her head to the back wall, she said, "Your namesake, Monty. I've worn him around my neck ever since my brother gave this to me and I had him painted on my bakery wall."

He looked at her, his expression confused. "My...my namesake?"

Smiling, she said, "I knew you were the man for me the first time you told me your name. Montgomery Honor Lytton." Glancing around at the other Saints before looking at the face on the mural, then deep into Monty's eyes, "He's St. Honoratus. The patron Saint of bakers."

3 1

SEVERAL DAYS LATER

The Saints gathered around the table with Mitch on video-conference, finalizing the case records.

"With Angel's witness statements and Cindy's confession, the case will proceed to the grand jury. I want to thank you for all your help," Mitch said. "I know you've reported to the Senator, as have I, and he's grateful for us solving his daughter's and the other women's murders."

Jack nodded and threw out, "Glad we have you to work with, but if you ever decide to call it quits, you know where we are. There'll be a place for you at Saints any time you want."

Mitch laughed, saying, "I'll keep that in mind."

Ending the video, the Saints finished their reports as quickly as possible, wanting to head upstairs.

Chad's phone buzzed and he excused himself, walking to the side of the room to take the call. "Oh, fuck," he swore softly. "Yeah…yeah…I'll leave as soon as I can. Funeral is the day after tomorrow? Got it. I'm sorry, honey."

Chad disconnected and turned, seeing the concerned

faces of the other Saints. "Jack, I'm gonna need some time off."

"You know that's no problem," Jack replied. "Family?"

"No...well, yes and no. Not my real family, but that call informed me that my former ATF partner was just killed on the job, trying to detonate a bomb."

Collective *'fucks'* and *'so sorrys'* were sounded around the room. Chad scrubbed his hand over his face. "That was his wife who called. Jesus, this is going to be agony."

Marc stood and walked over to place his hand on Chad's shoulder. "You need company, bro?"

Smiling, Chad shook his head. "No, no. I'll be fine. But I want to stay for a couple of days to be with his family and wife. I was real close to them...at one time."

With hugs and handshakes, Chad left the conference room. The others left their reports on the table as Jack said, "Let's go upstairs and unwind. Nothing here that can't be done later."

The Saints smiled at Jack, each knowing their tough boss knew when to work...and when to take care of each other. They made their way upstairs where the women were waiting.

Bethany was just saying, "It's so hard to believe the lengths some people will go to in the name of love." She smiled at Jack as he approached her, linking his fingers with hers.

"Oh, I think love has been the reason...or excuse...for many things," Faith added. Bart walked around and pulled his fiancé against his front, kissing the top of her head.

Miriam stood up from the sofa, allowing Cam to sit, and then settled back in his lap, smiling as she nestled in closely, his large hand on her baby bump. He pretended to groan at her added weight, but his grin was a testament to his true feelings.

Jude and Sabrina were already sharing a chair as the others piled onto the sofas, chairs, and even cushions, in front of the fire.

Each remembered to speak clearly so Angel could hear what they were saying. Monty kept his mouth close to her left ear in case he needed to repeat what someone said.

"As angry as I was," Angel said, "I'm mostly filled with the most unbelievable sense of sadness for Cindy and the futile way she was living her life. Yes, we sorority sisters were close, but we only got together about once a month. We all had other friends...other people in our lives. But Cindy couldn't accept that."

"Don't you think that was because she was in love with Marcia and jealous of everyone else?" Bethany asked.

"I don't know. The sexual relationship she wanted made her angry that Marcia was only into men. The obsessive relationship she required had no room for former friends."

"What will happen to her?" Sabrina asked, looking over at Jack.

"She'll be indicted and go to trial. She'll also have a psychiatric evaluation beforehand."

"Well, I need to bring out my thanks for everyone's help," Angel said, moving over to the kitchen counter where white boxes tied with pink, purple, and teal ribbon were placed. The men jumped up immediately, heading over to peer down into the boxes. Vanilla and chocolate cupcakes topped with huge swirls of vanilla bean frosting, Angel's signature colors mixed into each one. The Saints dove into the moist treats, no one minding if the colorful frosting covered their lips as they devoured them all.

Angel looked over at Monty, shoving the last bite into his mouth. Laughing, she walked over, wrapping her arms around his middle. Moving in closer while standing on her tip-toes, she kissed-licked the extra frosting off of his lips. "Was it good?" she murmured.

His eyes flared in lust as he discreetly patted her ass. "It was great, but you're the best cupcake of them all."

Four Years Later

Angel waddled in from the kitchen, the platter of cupcakes in her arms. Monty looked over at his wife and hustled to take the tray from her. "Babe, you should have called out for me," he gently chastised.

"I carry trays every day, you know," she said, rolling her eyes at him. Her blonde hair still had the signature color stripes but was now trimmed to just below her shoulders.

He placed the colorful cupcakes onto the table, watching the children scream and clap in delight. Felicity moved among the group, assisting with the children. Her three were in attendance, as well as several of the Saints' children. Monty's father tried to get the children to stay still while he snapped pictures, while Angel's father simply let his IPad video do all the work.

"Angel, I simply can't get the top off the ice cream," Lois said. "And like I was saying earlier, I don't know why you insist on making so many muffins to give away. If you had a better eye for your profit margin—"

"Mom," Monty interrupted, as Felicity and Angel shared a knowing grin. "Angel runs her business exactly the way she wants to."

"I know," Lois agreed, "I was just making a suggestion. Now where's the birthday girl?"

Monty and Angel's three-year-old daughter giggled as her two grandmothers fawned over her. Soon mouths were all covered in pink, purple, and teal icing, including most of the adults'. Angel moved toward the back to press her aching back against the back wall. At eight months pregnant, she was feeling the effects of being on her feet all day. Helen would once again take over when she gave birth, this time to a son.

Monty walked over to her, kissing the top of her head as he lowered his hands to massage her lower back. His eyes roved past her shoulder to the mural on the wall, the bullet hole still visible if someone knew where to look. Angel had refused to have it patched, insisting St. Honoratus had saved them both.

He confessed, "It used to bother me that I didn't have a Saint's name when the others I work with do. Not that it mattered to the job, but...well, I have to admit that finding out my name meant something, besides just my grandfather, means a lot to me." Gazing back into her eyes, he saw her staring at him, smiling. "What are you thinking, Cupcake?" he asked, his lips a whisper away from hers.

Kissing him softly, she pressed her body close to his, until their son kicked. Monty's laughter was drowned by the children's shouting, but Angel leaned in closer to whisper in his ear.

"When Patrick gave me the Saint Honoratus medal on the opening of my first bakery, he said it would give me protection. But it really sent you to me. You're my very own Saint...and love."

Ready for Chad's story? Click here!
Sacrifice Love

Don't miss any news about new releases! Sign up for my
Newsletter

ALSO BY MARYANN JORDAN

Don't miss other Maryann Jordan books!

Lots more Baytown stories to enjoy and more to come!

Baytown Boys (small town, military romantic suspense)

Coming Home

Just One More Chance

Clues of the Heart

Finding Peace

Picking Up the Pieces

Sunset Flames

Waiting for Sunrise

Hear My Heart

Guarding Your Heart

Sweet Rose

Our Time

Count On Me

Shielding You

To Love Someone

Sea Glass Hearts

For all of Miss Ethel's boys:

Heroes at Heart (Military Romance)

Zander

Rafe

Cael

Jaxon

Jayden

Asher

Zeke

Cas

Lighthouse Security Investigations

Mace

Rank

Walker

Drew

Blake

Tate

Levi

Clay

Cobb

Hope City (romantic suspense series co-developed

with Kris Michaels

Brock book 1

Sean book 2

Carter book 3

Brody book 4

Kyle book 5

Ryker book 6

Rory book 7

Killian book 8

Torin book 9

Saints Protection & Investigations

(an elite group, assigned to the cases no one else wants…or can solve)

Serial Love

Healing Love

Revealing Love

Seeing Love

Honor Love

Sacrifice Love

Protecting Love

Remember Love

Discover Love

Surviving Love

Celebrating Love

Searching Love

Follow the exciting spin-off series:

Alvarez Security (military romantic suspense)

Gabe

Tony

Vinny

Jobe

SEALs

Thin Ice (Sleeper SEAL)

SEAL Together (Silver SEAL)

Undercover Groom (Hot SEAL)

Also for a Hope City Crossover Novel / Hot SEAL...

A Forever Dad by Maryann Jordan

Letters From Home (military romance)

Class of Love

Freedom of Love

Bond of Love

The Love's Series (detectives)

Love's Taming

Love's Tempting

Love's Trusting

The Fairfield Series (small town detectives)

Emma's Home

Laurie's Time

Carol's Image

Fireworks Over Fairfield

Please take the time to leave a review of this book. Feel free to contact me, especially if you enjoyed my book. I love to hear from readers!

Facebook

Email

Website

ABOUT THE AUTHOR

I am an avid reader of romance novels, often joking that I cut my teeth on the historical romances. I have been reading and reviewing for years. In 2013, I finally gave into the characters in my head, screaming for their story to be told. From these musings, my first novel, Emma's Home, The Fairfield Series was born.

I was a high school counselor having worked in education for thirty years. I live in Virginia, having also lived in four states and two foreign countries. I have been married to a wonderfully patient man for thirty-five years. When writing, my dog or one of my four cats can generally be found in the same room if not on my lap.

Please take the time to leave a review of this book. Feel free to contact me, especially if you enjoyed my book. I love to hear from readers!

Facebook
Email
Website

f